Indecent
Werewolf
Exposure

Werewolves, Vampires and Demons, Oh My

Eve Langlais

New York Times and USA Today Bestselling author

EVELANGLAIS.COM

Copyright © November 2013, Eve Langlais
2nd edition © February 2017, Eve Langlais
Cover Art by Yocla Designs © February 2017
Edited by Devin Govaere
Copy Edited by Amanda L. Pederick
Line Edits Brieanna Roberston
Produced in Canada

Published by Eve Langlais
1606 Main Street, PO Box 151
Stittsville, Ontario, Canada, K2S1A0
http://www.EveLanglais.com

ISBN-13: 978 1988 328 63 8

Foreword

Please take note that this story was originally titled Two's a Couple, Three's The Law. Over time, I grew to hate the title of this book, hated it so bad, lol, so I renamed it and had a new cover designed to better convey the humor inside.

But Indecent Werewolf Exposure is not just funny, it's steamy too.

Expect a dirty and erotic romance. You will sweat, squirm and Oooh in shock. There is sex, lots of it, but there's also a mystery, a fascinating new paranormal world, and lots of fun.

Ready to go see what a naughty werewolf has been up to?

~Eve

Warning: This story contains adult subject matter, polyamorous situations and language that is not suitable for all audiences. Reader discretion is advised.

More Eve Langlais Books:

- Crazy
- Freakn' Shifters
- A Lion's Pride
- Dragon Point
- Bitten Point
- Kodiak Point
- Princess of Hell
- Welcome To Hell
- Alien Abduction
- Alien Mate
- Hell's Son
- Furry United Coalition

Chapter One

What is it about me that draws the craziest cases and clients? Did I have an invisible tattoo on my forehead that said, *Bring it?*

A prime example—and I meant prime, as in one hundred percent, hunky male sprinkled with way too much sexy and too much clothes—sat across from me.

"Let me get this straight, you've been charged with—" I peered down at the werewolf's file, not because I couldn't remember the charges, but because I couldn't hold his stare while reciting the ridiculous claims. "Digging holes in your neighbor's yard. Howling after eleven, and peeing on her roses." I raised my gaze and had it snagged by my client's chocolate-colored eyes.

I should mention that when I said chocolate, I didn't mean the cheap stuff you could purchase at the local 7-Eleven stuffed with peanuts and caramel. I was talking about sinful, melt-in-your-mouth, quality mocha that could almost replace an orgasm it tasted so damned good.

Although, given Mr. Cavanaugh's stellar good looks, rockin' bod, and general fuckable vibe, I imagined sex with him might prove even more enjoyable than the best chocolate available on the market. Not that I intended to find out in person. Good lawyers didn't screw their clients—until they'd won their case at least and gotten paid. Contrary to popular belief, we did have *some* morals.

A shame because were I a girl of looser moral fiber I would have totally thrown myself on that desk, and screamed, "Take me."

Disturbed at the direction of my thoughts, I mentally kicked my mind out of the gutter. "Are any of these claims true?"

"Yup," he replied in a rough voice that tickled over every single one of my nerve endings, plus a few I didn't realize I owned.

Damn, I so needed to get laid if just a masculine rumble could get my panties wet. Mental note to self—hit the store for some C batteries on my way home.

B.O.B. and I were going on a date tonight.

Even though much of my blood had flooded my girl regions, I frowned at my client's single syllable reply. "Yes to which charge?"

"All of them."

Like I'd said, the office always seemed to give me the craziest cases. Then again, I enjoyed the challenge. It kept me from getting bored with mundane petty theft crimes.

I leaned back in my creaky chair—creaky because it was old and not because I needed to hit the gym more. Okay, so maybe I did need to hit the gym more, I didn't need the furniture taunting me about it.

Keep it up and I will replace you with a new ergomatic model.

I fixed Mr. Cavanaugh with a stare while

tapping my ballpoint pen on my scarred metal desk—a government-issue relic from the eighties back before melamine took over the office world. "Are you admitting, Mr. Cavanaugh—"

"Call me Pete."

Call me yours. Ahem. "That you did all the things you're charged with?"

"Yes, I did." A smug smile creased his face and his sex appeal went up another notch, as did my state of arousal. I shifted in my seat, crossing my legs under the desk. "I also peed on her petunias, but I see she's not complaining about that, probably on account they've never looked healthier."

With a claim like that, I dared anyone not to imagine a grown man whipping his penis out and using it as a hose. Oddly enough, it didn't detract from his overall sexiness.

"And you want to fight these charges instead of pleading guilty to a misdemeanor and paying the fine?"

"I do."

I could see the court docket headline now, the state versus Mr. Cavanaugh in the case of Indecent Werewolf Exposure. I really should write a book about my experiences.

Or for once maybe I could have a normal day, one that didn't involve dealing a guy who turned hairy on the full moon.

Twirling my pen, I tilted my gaze up to my perforated, suspended-tile ceiling and counted to ten. One–*Why the fuck did I become a lawyer?* Two—*Who did I piss off in a previous life to get stuck with this crap?* Three—*Where is a strong cup of coffee when I need one?* - Four—*Why can't I stop wondering if he did those things while man or wolf?*

He broke my moment of silence at Seven—*I think I'll have Chinese for lunch*—with a clearing of his throat. "Is there a problem?"

My annoyed glance snapped back in his direction. "You're wasting my time."

"How?"

"You're guilty."

"Yes. But she doesn't know that for sure. No cameras." He smiled. "She is assuming it's me."

"Because it is you."

"She has no proof."

"You just admitted it." I couldn't help the exasperation in my tone.

"Ah, but isn't our conversation protected by that client/lawyer privilege thing we hear about all the time on TV?"

"Yes. Nothing you say while with me can be used against you," I replied through gritted teeth.

Damn television. People with a little bit of knowledge were so much more irritating to deal with. Ah, for the days of ignorance when clients just did as their lawyers told them to. While on a nostalgic track, why not rewind further to a time when hunky men didn't pee on flowers and require flea collars.

Ever since werewolves came out of the doghouse, the world hadn't been the same—and the stock prices on companies offering shotguns and silver multiplied overnight.

He leaned forward in his seat, his earnest puppy brown eyes capturing mine. "As far as the world is concerned, I'm innocent unless she can prove me guilty. Isn't it your job to make sure that doesn't happen?" He grinned at me, an engaging tilt of his lips that tugged at my inner mischievous child.

I sent it to sit in the corner and scowled. "Mr. Cavanaugh—"

"Pete."

"I'm all for defending the innocent, but your neighbor's complaints are valid. To go to court is a waste of my time and yours, not to mention taxpayer money." Of which I paid too much on a meager salary as far as I was concerned. "Do us all a favor and do the right thing. Plead guilty. Pay the fine. Then buy some candy and flowers, put on your nicest shirt, go over to her place, smile, and apologize." I almost told him to put his dick to better use than fertilizer where his neighbor was concerned but held my tongue. He didn't need sexual harassment charges tacked on to his current case file. "Promise her you'll never do it again and, from here on out, keep your peeing to your side of the property line and refrain from howling after hours."

For those that wondered, I actually managed to say that all with a straight face. Get a few drinks into me later, though, and I'd probably wet my pants retelling it. Client confidentiality only went so far. The actual incident report was public knowledge, and given the giggles I'd get out of it, it had already made the top of my "Stupid-Shit-Of-The-Week" list to be shared with my closest, drunkest friends.

My advice didn't receive a warm reception. The smile on his lips disappeared, and damn it all if he didn't pout, which should have made him appear less desirable. Lower lip jutting, eyes flashing darkly, totally disgruntled, the perfect picture of a man not getting his way. So why did I want to gnaw on his mouth until his unrepentant grin reappeared?

"Apologize? Never. She's a witch."

Imagining myself straddling him as I licked my way down his neck to a surely superb set of pecs, it took me a moment to register his words. I must have misunderstood. Surely he'd said bitch, not witch. "Name calling won't help."

"Just saying it like it is. The woman is a witch."

Forget cleaning my ears. I'd heard him right the first time. "A witch? As in a cackling, cauldron bubbling, incantation-reciting witch?"

He nodded. "With a cat. I hate cats. Especially this one." An honest-to-goodness growl rumbled from him.

A shiver went down my spine—and tickled my pussy. Stupid hot werewolf. "And what has her cat done to earn your ire other than the fact it's feline?"

"Damned thing keeps sitting in my window scaring my lovebirds."

Once again, he said something completely oddball, ruining my fantasy of the ways I could make him growl…in pleasure. "You have lovebirds?" I sounded like a parrot.

"I do. Why are you looking at me so strangely?"

Could I help it if this conversation was making me cross-eyed? "You're a werewolf." Or so his license claimed. Ever since the Great Coming Out in early two thousand, anyone with a canine—or other—pedigree was forced to have themselves registered, or they couldn't claim the newly instituted tax breaks. Apparently, the werewolf population believed flea remedies, vaccinations for ticks, and other usual canine supplies should count as medical deductions. Registering also meant they could seek protections under rapidly developed, and still evolving, laws.

"We prefer the term Lycan. And what does me sprouting fur and howling at the moon have to do with my choice in pets?"

"Werewolves don't own lovebirds." I don't know why I believed that, but I did. Surely it was printed somewhere in the werewolf handbook of rules they all followed—available at all good bookstores for the low price of only $9.99. Thou shalt not own cute, tiny avian creatures. Or fluster human lawyers who finished top of their class and took a job as a public defender for the government. Little did I know, my choice would involve too many cases of alcoholic misdemeanors and hot tempers to trump common sense. So much for defending the innocent against evil.

"Listen, honey, whoever is giving you info on my kind needs to get their facts updated. I'd be more than happy to meet with you and give you a rundown on what Lycans are really about. We love animals. Except for cats. Stupid things think they're so high and mighty." Again, he rumbled, and for a moment, I couldn't help imagining the vibration on a certain body part. *Oh yum.* "As for my lovebirds, I've owned Rocky and Periwinkle since before that old witch moved in and I do not appreciate her cat coming over and terrifying them."

Yanking my mind from the gutter, I tried to focus on the conversation. "So you've been intentionally antagonizing your neighbor because her feline is sitting in your window staring at your birds?"

"In a nutshell, yes."

Insane? Definitely. Still hot? Sadly, yes. "But the cat hasn't actually done anything to them."

"No, however, you can see the evil intent in its eyes." He said it with a straight face.

My forehead hit the desk as I moaned, "Why me? Why?" Why did I always end up with the freaks? An office full of legal aides, government paid for and supposedly on a rotation, yet I ended up with more than my fair share of the whack jobs. *And, even more cruel, why did he have to be so bloody hot?*

"Is that a rhetorical question?"

"Of course it is," I grumbled. "Actually, on second thought, no it isn't. Why do I keep getting these cases? Why can't I ever get a nice normal break-and-enter charge? Or an attempted murder?"

"Would it help if I told you it was because you're good?"

I lifted my head enough to peek at him through the hair that flopped over my eyes. "Says who?"

He shrugged, which meant one massive shoulder lifted, a fascinating motion that sent a ripple effect across his whole impressive upper torso. "Says everyone who's ever dealt with you. Apparently, you're not only good at what you do, but you're fair. And you treat Lycans with respect."

"Because you're people too." According to the Supreme Court Judgment of Simpson Versus Fido.

"Not everyone acts like we are. Do you know how many times I've had to punch some idiot out because he tossed something and told me to fetch?"

"Violence isn't the answer."

"In some cases, it's the only way to make people truly listen. Or at least mind their manners."

"You can't hit your neighbor."

"I wasn't planning to, but I'm also not paying a fine when she started this little vendetta. Listen, I know this isn't the most glory-filled of cases, but I am not letting the witch win. I need your help."

"Help to what? You've admitted you're guilty and no judge in the country is going to care if the supposed witch next door has a cat that likes to sit in your window scaring your little birdies."

"So what do you suggest I do? And forget apologizing. It's not fucking happening."

"I already told you what to do. If the cat is really bothering you, then get a dog." Too late I realized how ludicrous that sounded. But then again, so was this entire meeting.

I expected some kind of outburst. Indignation at the very least. Instead, I got booming laughter.

Mr. Cavanaugh shuddered with it. Apparently, he was the type of man who, when amused, let his whole body in on the fun because his massive frame shook with energetic chuckles. Despite myself, my lips twitched into a smile.

"I like you, Ms. Bailey. I can see why you're so popular. You aren't afraid to tell it like it is. I appreciate that in a woman."

"If you appreciate me so much, then do what I'm saying. Don't drag this out."

He slapped his knee. "You know what. I'll pay the darned fine and leave the sorceress alone because I like you. But I draw the line at getting a dog."

"I thought you loved pets."

"I do, but dogs shed, and I hate vacuuming." He spilled out of his seat, signaling the end to our meeting.

"You know, you could inform animal control about the stray cat roaming your neighborhood," I offered.

Rising from my chair, I was reminded, even in my heels, of Mr. Cavanaugh's impressive stature. There weren't many men who towered over me. At six feet, plus another two inches in heels, I never slouched or downplayed my size. In spite of my height, I still had to tilt my head to meet his gaze. He thrust out his hand and enveloped mine in his large grip. I couldn't see his feet, but if they matched the rest of him…

The roughness of his fingers grated pleasantly along my skin as he shook my hand. Tingles shot through me and let me know, in no uncertain terms, that I'd gone too long without taking care of my needs. Way too long, apparently, if I gauged it by the dampness of my crotch. *I'd better stock up on batteries before going home because I don't think a cold shower is going to cut it.*

I only hoped the rumors of werewolves' super ability to smell were exaggerated. I'd hate to think he could tell with a sniff how attractive I found him. Judging by the sensual grin and stroke of his thumb across my palm, though, I feared I might have just discovered the answer.

Slowly, he released my hand, a sensual glide that brought a vivid image to mind of how that same hand would feel stroking across my body. I tucked my over-imaginative appendage behind my back before it decided to place Mr. Cavanaugh's hand in a more interesting spot to test my hypothesis.

"Now that you've solved my case, I don't suppose we could meet for dinner?"

Having fielded this question numerous times, my answer emerged by rote. "I don't date clients."

"Are you sure? What if I promise to behave from now on?"

The noticeable bulge in his pants and the naughty gleam in his eyes stated in pretty vivid detail the unlikelihood of that happening. At least the attraction went two ways. What a shame about his mental state. Not only did I not date clients, I also tried to stay away from whack jobs.

What grown man actually thought he lived beside a sorceress? Scientists had disproved many times over the existence of magic. The only witches around were posers, women who mixed up herbs and vile concoctions claiming they were magical. There weren't any real laws against it, unless they accidentally poisoned someone.

Not that Mr. Cavanaugh seemed to care that his neighbor practiced witchcraft; his issue centered more on her roaming cat. Why did it not surprise me that wolves didn't like cute little kitties?

I terminated the meeting. "It was nice to meet you, Mr. Cavanaugh."

"Liar. I can see it wasn't, but I'm sure glad I met you," he drawled, adding in a naughty wink. "We'll be seeing each other again real soon, Ms. Bailey."

"Why? Are you intending to get in more trouble?"

"Yes. As a matter of fact I am."

Somehow, I didn't think he meant the legal kind. And, horny as I currently found myself, I kind of looked forward to it.

Chapter Two

The rest of my day involved more mundane cases—petty theft, shoplifting, a spousal altercation between a pair of husbands over whose turn it was for marital rights with the wife, a new legal problem since the introduction of polygamous marriage.

The world had changed vastly since I first came into it just over twenty-six years ago. Now, no longer was marriage defined as a union between one man and woman. As the world's population dwindled and the realization emerged that men outnumbered women five to one, laws changed, as did society. Women were now encouraged to take on more than one lover at a time. Threesomes, foursomes, and moresomes flourished. Or crashed. Jealousy kept the courts hopping, and business boomed for lawyers.

Love triangles, squares, and pentagons weren't the only thing that had emerged since my birth, though. The realization that humans came in more flavors than we realized was still something everyone worked at adjusting to.

I still remembered the cheap thrill of my first werewolf movie. Of course, the sexy on-screen version of a werewolf didn't come anything close to the reality. Truth was, werewolves, or Lycans as they kept reminding us, didn't actually turn into overgrown dogs. Don't get me wrong, they sprouted fur, growled, howled and sported great big claws and teeth, but they did so while retaining their human shape. Less werewolf and more wolfman, in other words. Disconcerting didn't come close to describing it when the first one was discovered.

One had to wonder, though, if the conspiracy theorists had a valid point when they argued that the little girl in foster care—featured on *The View*, who at the age of five with her blonde pigtails, big blue eyes, and adorable smile—wasn't a setup. Who would have ever expected the cute little darling of being anything other than she appeared, a poor abandoned waif in need of a loving family?

The television crew of *The View* and its hosts certainly didn't, but when that little girl transformed on live TV into a growling blonde hairball, frightened by the bright lights and loud noises, no one could deny her existence.

She became an instant media sensation. Scientists and doctors from all over the world wanted a piece of her. The government itched to get its hands on her. Everyone demanded an ounce of blood and a chance to examine the anomaly. Some true freaks even put in grotesque requests to dissect her.

Things could have turned out badly for the little girl with no one to advocate for her rights. The Lycans, hidden amongst us for centuries, could have left her to the mercy of those who wanted to treat her like an alien. To their credit, they didn't.

Werewolves came out of the closet, so to speak, and into the light. The media spotlight. One man, John Benedict, came forward on behalf of the Lycan packs. A well-spoken, handsome man in his late fifties, he met with the media and admitted that, yes, werewolves did exist, and had, for as long as they could remember, lived amongst us and none of us ever knew. Well, the rag magazines claimed to have known all along, but then again, they still screamed Elvis lived, so no one paid them much mind.

But it wasn't just werewolves. Dryads stepped forth from the redwoods and the Amazon wilds, begging we stop cutting their trees. Merpeople also rose from the sea, tired of getting caught in oil spills and fishing nets. Fairies flitted to the halls of justice and filed injunctions against the use of bug zappers.

Ever heard the sound of millions of jaws hitting the floor at once? Yeah, realizing a whole mystical subculture existed rocked the planet on its axis.

From that moment on, everything changed. Laws changed. The world shifted. And humans, or at least those without the twisted DNA gene that made them go fuzzy or fish-tailed, had to learn to live with it. So humans did what we did best. We started committees.

Groups formed for the ethical treatment of Lycans, dryads, and merpeople. Others formed to exterminate them. Religions were born, some for, some against. Fairies tied up the courts as they sued the makers of the bug zappers and sticky fly strips. And life went on.

As for poor Mary Sue, the little girl who started it all? She got adopted by a nice werewolf family and the doctors got their hands on some grown adults instead, who under the watchful media eye, let the population at large know that, hey, we're just like you, only hairier.

As if anyone totally believed that. Oh, and those who invested in Gillette and Nair? They made a bloody killing when the stocks soared.

As for me, I'd dealt with a fair number of "special folk" since my ascension to the lofty position of public defender and resident of government cubicle number five. For some reason, the newly emerging species always seemed to end up in the chair across from my desk.

I found them to be just like anyone else, if more demanding. Lycans, by far, got into more trouble than the other new races discovered. It seemed they couldn't help causing havoc. Indecent exposure being their most common crime.

They kept me busy even if I secretly mourned the fact none of them was as hot as the romances I surreptitiously read on my tablet. Or, at least I'd never met a truly hunky werewolf until today.

Mr. Cavanaugh was the first Lycan I'd met who fit exactly my perfect image of a werewolf. He was totally how I'd pictured them when I went through my paranormal romance phase where I devoured books about them like crack candy.

But lusting after a wolfman didn't mean I would break my no-screwing-clients-or-crazy-people rule. Mr. Cavanaugh would have to eat dinner with—or from between the legs of—someone else. Some other lucky woman would have to enjoy his boyish grin. His callused, yet electric touch. His big, muscled body…

The tip of my pen snapped and ink leaked all over my desk. Lovely.

At exactly five o'clock, I called it a day. The government didn't pay me by the hour, so they never got a minute more of my time. Altruism was for those with trust funds. I'd long ago lost my innocence when it came to my job.

When I'd taken the job of public defender, I'd had big dreams of coming to the rescue of battered women, falsely accused victims, and getting mired in environmental cases a la Erin Brockovich, that would get my name in the news as I argued to victory.

Reality sucked, as did my paycheck.

Exiting my closet of an office, without even a window to let me know the weather outside, I ran into Brenda, or more like she bowled me over as she sprang out of nowhere to verbally assault me.

"Chloe! You lucky fucking bitch. Me and the rest of the girls are so jealous."

"Why?" Had I won the lottery and not noticed? Was that hottie Channing Tatum here looking for me?

"Why, she asks?" Brenda rolled her eyes. "Because you got to spend time with Mr. Hotness."

She could only be referring to one person. "You mean the werewolf?"

"As if you had any other clients today who could even come close to that title. Yes, I mean the werewolf. You are the envy of the office."

"I don't see why. His case was pretty freaking dumb. Not to mention, I think he's not all there." I twirled my finger alongside my head in the universal sign of craziness.

"But the man is so fucking hot. Please tell me he asked you out."

Yes, he had, but if Brenda found out I'd turned him down, I'd never hear the end of it. I lied. "No."

"Did he at least act inappropriately?"

"Not really." Liar, liar, pants on fire.

"With a face and body like that, I'll be he growled at you." Brenda shivered.

I threw her a bone. "A bit, but only because he was talking about his neighbor's cat."

"Oh." She seemed so downcast I strove to find something to please her perverted, one-track mind.

"He did promise to not behave, though, and see me again soon."

Her mouth rounded and her eyes opened wide. "Oh. I wonder what that means."

My dirty mind hoped it meant him, me, and five minutes alone—all I'd need considering the state he'd left me in. But, more than likely, he'd do something to piss his witchy neighbor off even worse and he'd end up back in my cubicle on more charges, meaning no nookie for me with the hairy hunk.

How depressing. Finally, I'd met a guy who got my motor running and he ended up not even a contender for a one-night stand. Was it too much to ask that I meet a nice, normal man who made my pulse race just a little? Not for anything permanent. A boyfriend wasn't on my list of things I needed or wanted, but a fuck buddy? That would totally work and save me on batteries.

"Are you done for the day? I think it's time for a liquid dinner." I mimed tipping one back.

Brenda's nod was so energetic I feared she might have whiplash.

Best friends since elementary school and now coworkers, Brenda and I had a weekly tradition of hitting a martini bar located only a few blocks away every Friday after work. Getting tipsy on brightly-colored drinks served in fancy glasses didn't make our jobs any better, but I personally enjoyed the ritual.

Given that the male population outnumbered the women—scientists theorizing the reason had to do with a lack of a great world war in the last half century to properly decimate male numbers—we usually drank for free.

We also got offers to get laid, eaten, screwed, and even proposals of marriage from perfect strangers. One time, an eager fellow had even produced a ring. I politely declined. Despite his healthy bottom line—which he showed me on his IRS return over drinks—I just couldn't imagine staring down at the bald head on his five-foot-five body for the rest of my life.

But back to TGIF. Brenda and I, along with some other girls in the office, tended to head over to the hopping joint with its muted, flattering lights, retro eighties interior and spinning strobe disco ball—known to cause seizures in the unwary.

Guys in suits tripped over themselves in their attempts to get noticed. Flattering, but at the same time, overwhelming. The number of offers we received to have our every need satisfied—said with a salacious wink or leer—proved too many to count, but flattering to the ego.

You'd think with all the male attention we received, the problem I was suffering with my girl parts—AKA an urgent need for erotic attention—

wouldn't even exist or would be easy to resolve. However, while I enjoyed a healthy round of sweaty hardcore sex, once I got past the whole orgasm and itch scratched part, I couldn't stand the hopeful "Call me." Or how they expected repeat performances.

See, the thing was, once they gave me what I needed—their cocks—I lost interest in the men. Not on purpose. I mean, I tried to connect with them outside the bedroom. Engage them in conversation, see if we had hobbies or even television shows in common. It didn't work. None of them stirred anything in me other than a general sense of relief when we parted ways and traded the oft used, "I'll call you." It didn't help, I guess, that I didn't want a permanent man in my life. I'd come to the conclusion a while back that boyfriends just required too much maintenance.

As Brenda had told me, on more than one occasion when I tried to explain my lack of interest in a relationship, I was comparable to a black widow. Using and discarding men with no care for their feelings.

Cry me a river. What about my feelings? Why did I have to settle down with someone who didn't inspire that can't-live-without-you spark? Why couldn't I hold out for Mr. Right? I was still young. Still having fun. I had a career—of sorts. A decent life—with free drinks. A nice condo—which I'd own in twenty-nine years and three months. Why did I need to rush? Why did I need a steady boyfriend? Well, other than for the obvious.

Which led me to ask, whatever happened to no-strings sex? Why couldn't I just enjoy a hot and sweaty, wall-banging fuck? The kind where I could say thank you as I tucked my skirt down and went back for another drink with my bestie.

For some reason, a certain werewolf I'd just met came to mind. *I'll bet he could pin me like a bug to a wall and pound me until I found religion and screamed, oh my God.*

Sure, his eyes promised decadence. His lips promised pleasure. But would he be like all the rest and think he owned me if I gave in to his allure?

And even more important, would he shed all over my three-hundred-thread-count, Egyptian cotton sheets?

So what if I got them on sale? I'd never slept better and the thought of having to keep a lint brush on my nightstand just to have great sex really didn't appeal.

Sometimes even I wondered where I got my warped ideas from.

Entering the bar, with Brenda chattering a mile a minute—the only speed my BFF knew when it came to speech—the noise of the TGIF crowd hit and rocked me as if battered by a wave.

Packed with bodies, my favorite bar was hopping tonight. People looking to escape the mind-dulling, yawn-inducing doldrums of a week spent cooped in offices. With the weekend here, many felt a need to throw off the shackles of boredom and remember what it felt to be alive.

I was one of those people. Bring on the booze and the booty shaking.

Wading through the throng, I endured a good number of pinches and gropes to my full bottom. I had a weakness for cream-filled donuts in the morning, which I ate as a dessert to my pair of toasted cream cheese bagels. Sue me for having a healthy appetite. I knew a good lawyer who'd argue my case to enjoy copious amounts of food and screw the health nuts who said otherwise.

Some women might take offense at the touching of their person without express permission. I saw it as a compliment. Worship me for I was awesome.

And thirsty.

In dire need of an alcoholic beverage, we inched our way to the bar. Despite her petite stature—five-foot-five when wearing her highest tottering heels—Brenda could always find a spot. She also knew how to make one if needed.

Cute as a button with curly blonde hair, a pert nose, and a sassy smile, her sweet "Excuse me," "Pardon me," and, "Hello handsome" never failed to garner attention, and just like that Moses guy, she parted the testosterone sea. The few times when that didn't work, a jab to the ribs, a subtle hit to the groin, or a stomp on the toes did the job.

Brenda might appear adorable and benign on the outside, but piss her off and she turned into a vicious wolverine—a verbal one, not a real one— who could tear into a person and leave them sobbing for their mommy.

Gawd, I loved her. Best friends forever. We'd even sworn on it with blood and ice cream.

Reaching our objective, a barstool magically vacated—probably because my BFF shoved the guy off when he least expected it—and Brenda popped her butt onto it while I leaned my hip against the polished granite countertop.

While Brenda thanked the fellow who'd given

up his seat, whether he liked it or not, I ignored the ardent gazes checking me out to order an Ocean Breeze martini. Not too sweet, a shocking bright turquoise, and oh so yummy, it was my drink of choice when we came here. I also wasn't averse to blowjobs, the alcoholic shot variety, not the kind with hairy balls and a creamy finish.

With a promise to dance with him later, Brenda turned from the stool donator and ordered something bigger than my puny girly drink. A monstrous-sized beverage with high alcohol content, an umbrella, and a trio of cherries.

Brenda might lack height, but the girl could drink and do things with a cherry stem that made more than one man fall at her feet fervently promising everlasting love. She usually settled for jewelry.

The bartender slid us our concoctions and said, "Courtesy of the gentlemen."

"Which one?" I asked idly as I took a sip.

"All of them," replied Liam.

And, no, it wasn't strange I knew our bartender's first name. When you visited a place often enough, even your local bar, after a while, you got to know someone, not to mention Liam and his life partner, Dave, had come to our rescue more than once when a gentleman needed a little extra persuasion in understanding the word "No."

"All of them?" I wrinkled my nose. That was more than usual. "We just got here."

"Yeah, well, we started charging the guys a cover to enter. Fifty bucks a head."

I almost spit out my mouthful of tropical paradise. That would have been a waste of a great drink. I swallowed before I replied. "Fifty dollars? That seems pretty steep."

"Only if you're cheap. We were getting too crowded. Fire marshal gave us a citation. So, in order to weed out the undesirables and cheapskates, we imposed a cover charge. You'll be glad to know that these new proceeds mean ladies drink for free at all times."

Really? I brightened. "I like that part."

As Dave slid by with a tray loaded with empty glasses, he added, "I thought you might. We've also noticed since we put the new door charge in effect that we're having to deal less with guys thinking a girl owes him because he bought her a drink. And it keeps the riffraff out."

"I think you should raise the rate," I muttered as my gaze caught the arrival of a certain guy in a suit.

Say hello to my nemesis. Anthony Vanderson. District prosecuting attorney and pain in my ample ass since he'd transferred to our district six months ago.

Gorgeous and always impeccably attired, Anthony never appeared in public without every hair in its proper place and his tie perfectly straight.

I'd had to contend with the stone-faced, eloquently spoken bastard more than once in a courtroom. We'd never technically interacted outside of work, but he'd dismantled enough of my cases that even though he was super hot, I disliked him on general principle.

The fact he could bring a quiver to my treacherous lower parts irritated me even more than the fact I'd yet to win a legal battle against him.

Figures he'd show up. Way to ruin my night.

"Ooh, do you see who I see?" Brenda poked me in the arm. "It's that hunk from the DA's office." Brenda eyeballed my enemy.

"I saw him. The guy's a jerk."

"I didn't know you'd finally met him."

"I haven't."

"Then maybe you shouldn't judge him."

"Any man who looks that pretty and wears suits that are ironed is too high maintenance for me," I stated. Who the hell ironed shit? Hang it in the shower and steam it like everybody else.

I listened with half an ear as Brenda extolled his virtues—tall, about an inch or so more than me, chiseled features, short-cropped, blondish hair, pale skin as if he didn't see much sun, probably because he spent it all in his office plotting ways to make me look stupid in front of a judge.

"—wonder what he's doing here? I don't think I've seen him in this bar before."

"Maybe he's slumming." Because the one thing everyone knew for sure about the wonder boy of the DA's office was that Anthony Vanderson was loaded, as in, lived in a gated mansion, drove the nicest car, and wore thousand dollar suits loaded. It made me hate him even more.

I'll bet he doesn't have to work in a tiny cubicle at a desk with one leg propped on a notepad and using a dinosaur of a computer still running Window's Vista. I ignored the fact I'd chosen to work in a public office. When it came to reasons to dislike the panty-wetting DA, any reason, rational or not, would do.

"Are you still peeved he won that last case?"

Yes! And the case before that. And the one

before that. Poor loser? Bet your last fucking dime I was. I could hold an epic grudge.

Given the number of horseshoes he must have shoved up his ass, I had to wonder how his buttocks managed to look so trim in his perfectly cut slacks. Yeah, I'd looked. What else could I do but sit and glumly stare at his excellent glutes as he took my defense and expertly unraveled it before a riveted judge and jury?

"Are you calling me a sore loser?"

"Yes." Brenda never spared my feelings.

"Am not. Even if I won, I'd still dislike him."

"Oh, please. We both know you think he's hot."

"A little. Doesn't mean I'd do him."

"Chloe is a liar," Brenda sang.

She was right. I totally would do him, but I wasn't about to admit that. Last time I had told my BFF about how I'd like to get intimately acquainted with the UPS guy's abs, she'd arranged a blind date and I spent the whole dinner removing his hand from my upper thigh—as he told me how bad things were with his girlfriend. "You're a witch."

"Better than a bitch."

"Hag."

"Slut."

We burst into laughter, not taking offense at our name-calling, a habit of ours we'd never outgrown.

"Cheers!" She clinked her glass against mine. "I wonder why he's here. I pictured him more of a boys' club kind of guy. You know, one of those dark, wood-paneled places with stodgy old men and big club chairs."

"You watch too many movies," I retorted. But I knew what she meant. Anthony came from old money, the kind that arrived with a silver spoon and a servant to hold it. Guys like him didn't belong in sweaty, middle class bars with an aroma of desperation.

"Ooh," Brenda exhaled. "He's looking this way."

"Don't make eye contact." First rule of a singles bar. Never meet their gaze unless you wanted them to hit on you.

"Too late. He's heading in our direction."

Of course he was. Any man who came here was looking for one thing and one thing only.

If a hook-up was what Mr. DA wanted, then Brenda could have him. I, despite the expectant jiggle of my girly parts, would never sleep with the enemy, no matter how good-looking. My morals wouldn't allow it, which made me wonder if perhaps I needed fewer of those.

This was the second hunk today I'd stricken off my doable list. Perhaps I needed to rethink some of my rules. After all, shouldn't I prefer real dick to plastic?

"Don't turn around now, but he's almost right behind you," Brenda whispered in a shout.

I rolled my eyes. Thank goodness Vanderson didn't have a werewolf gene, or he might have heard her less-than-subtle warning, but I did appreciate it and kept my gaze on the gleaming array of bottles lined up behind the bar.

A body brushed up against my back and a shiver went through me.

Please don't be him. Please don't be him. Not for

the first time, I wished Liam would invest in a mirror for the wall behind the bar.

A hand flattened itself against my lower back as a hard body, sporting an aftershave that tickled my nose pleasantly, wedged itself against my left hip. "Excuse me," murmured a low voice that I would have recognized anywhere. My girly parts certainly knew who it belonged to and quivered.

Damn. It seemed my plea for him to go away had gone unanswered. Despite myself, warmth flooded my senses as my less-than-discerning libido enjoyed the closeness of another body.

"Would you listen to that, they're playing my song," Brenda shouted as she abandoned me.

The traitor.

Trapped by Anthony's masculine frame, I couldn't follow and instead found myself peering sideways at the jerk who never let me win in court.

Bright blue eyes met my gaze. "Ms. Bailey, what an unexpected, yet pleasant, surprise."

Funny, he didn't appear surprised.

"Mr. Vanderson." I inclined my head in acknowledgement.

The right corner of his mouth tugged upward. Damn, the man oozed gorgeous. I wanted to look away, my eyes however preferred to remain locked on him.

"No need to be so formal. We have, after all, met before." Way to remind me. "Since we're not in the courtroom, please call me Anthony."

Pretend we were friends? Over my dead, horny body. Never in a million years. No way. Hell would freeze over first.

"Hello, Anthony." I purred. What could I

say? My mouth had a mind of its own and, right now, it liked the fact that he stood so close, close enough that it would only take a little effort to see if his mouth tasted as minty as his breath smelled.

"I do hope there are no hard feelings over last week's case."

Hard feelings? Yes. And as for the three extra pounds around my waist from the gallon of ice cream I ate? Also his fault. "Of course not. Win some. Lose some." Please don't tell me that tittering giggle came from me. If I could have slapped myself without appearing mentally unstable, I would have.

"Glad to hear it."

"What are you doing here? I mean, I don't think I've ever seen you here before."

Great. Now I sounded like a drunken lush who spent enough time in a bar to know all the patrons. Sometimes, the truth hurt.

"A coworker suggested I try this place out. Apparently, they make the best Earl Grey martinis in town."

I held up my mostly empty glass and tilted it, draining the contents for liquid courage. "I don't know about the Earl Greys, but Liam here sure knows how to dish these up."

"Let me get you another."

"No need," I hastened to say, realizing too late how it sounded.

Anthony held up two fingers and pointed to my empty glass. A moment later, Liam slid two fresh beverages our way, both a bright blue. Looked like Mr. DA would have to wait to taste his Earl.

Not that he seemed to mind. He slid a twenty at Liam, waved away the change—show off—and lifted the flared glass with long fingers, the nails perfectly rounded and clean. No calluses on him.

Wonder what those smooth fingers would feel like on a certain sensitive body part?

Shudder. My poor panties. I might have to wring them dry.

He tilted the martini in my direction. "To finally meeting outside a courtroom." Anthony chimed his glass off mine.

"Ditto," I mumbled before gulping back half the contents. I couldn't have said why a languorous heat spread through my limbs.

Perhaps I was still horny from my meeting earlier with werewolf Pete? I mean, the dude totally rocked my libido.

Yet, I'd controlled myself.

So why this sudden fierce arousal for Anthony? It wasn't as if he did anything overtly sexual, just leaned against me. What choice did he have? The place overflowed.

Yet, a simple brush of our bodies shouldn't ignite my senses.

Was it the alcohol? I didn't think I'd drunk enough.

Unconsciously—or not—I caught myself shifting, almost rubbing myself against the guy.

Someone get a spray bottle. I was acting like a pussy in heat, and he didn't help things.

The hand on my back no longer lightly touched but firmly pressed, his thumb stroking me, branding me through the thin silk blouse I wore.

I should have moved away, or made some attempt to ignore him. A smart girl would have joined Brenda—my traitor of a friend who'd ditched me. She currently gyrated with a few guys in suits and loosened ties, her jiggly little body doing some kind of techno bop on the barely existing dance floor. It looked fun, especially since I enjoyed dancing.

However, I didn't move.

Neither did Anthony.

"I have a confession to make." His lips practically brushed my lobe as he leaned over to whisper in my ear.

A shiver went through me.

"Are you going to tell me you've made a deal with the devil, which is why I can never win a case against you?" I blurted the strange accusation, my martini courage giving my wayward tongue free rein.

A normal man might have taken offense, but not Mr. Hot Shot DA. He threw his head back and laughed. Had I mentioned he possessed the most incredible laugh?

"Not quite, but I might need a deal with the devil if you keep up your good defensive work. You certainly keep me on my toes."

"Glad to know I'm giving you some exercise." My wry reply didn't daunt him in the least.

His lips brushed my ear lobe again. "I enjoy the challenge, which is why I'm glad we finally get to meet outside of work."

"You are?" I couldn't help but turn my head, which brought our faces incredibly close.

He possessed the most incredible skin. Smooth, unblemished, and his lips…they moved.

"You sound surprised," he said.

"Probably because I am. We are, after all, working on opposite sides."

"But it doesn't mean we can't be *friends*."

Oh my freaking gawd. I recognized that inflection. He was hitting on me. "I don't know how appropriate that would be."

"There are no laws against it. I checked."

He'd done what?

The grin curling his lips short-circuited my brain for a second. The man blinded me with his good looks and his charm.

"No laws maybe, but I have my own personal rule, which states no fraternizing with coworkers."

"And yet didn't I see you here with one of the legal secretaries?"

"That's different. We've known each other since kindergarten." And I didn't want Brenda to put a dick into my pussy.

"So long as we're not sharing information on a case, or actively arguing a case, I don't see why we can't explore certain *opportunities*."

The guy just wouldn't give up. Flattering. Disconcerting. And annoying because, despite my dislike of him, I couldn't help enjoying his flirting. Just like I couldn't stop wondering if his lips would feel as soft as they looked.

Is he a giver or a taker? A part of me was tempted to find out.

But the smarter part of me knew better than to play his game.

"Listen, Mr. Vanderson—"

"Anthony."

What was it with guys insisting I use their first names today?

"While your attention is flattering, I just don't think this is appropriate." Taboo, my body agreed. So taboo. Naughty even. Very naughty. Could I blame the drinks on my rising temperature?

A body jostled mine from the other side and the hand on my back went full circle to steady me. Anthony drew me in to his hard chest, pressing me flush against a torso that I instantly noticed was really happy to see me. Up went my gaze to meet the brilliant blue one of my nemesis—a man who claimed he wanted to get to know me better.

Maybe I should let him. Wasn't there an expression about getting to know thy enemy? And what better way than naked?

"Crowded place," he observed, making no move to let me go or allow any space between us.

"No more than usual."

"What do you say we adjourn somewhere quieter? Maybe grab some *dinner*."

Actual food? Or did the inflection imply something else, something I'd just said no to?

A smart defense attorney would have rejected his offer, however I'd already proven myself stupid when it came to Anthony.

Mesmerized by his gaze—my body melting like butter in his grasp—I found myself nodding.

With his arm around my waist, he managed to guide us with more ease than expected from the bar.

Outside, the cool night air brushed over my fevered skin. It brought back some of my sanity and I pulled away from him, determined to put some distance between us, to tell him I'd changed my mind.

What was I thinking agreeing to go to dinner with the enemy? I hated Anthony, I mean Mr. High and Mighty DA Vanderson. I—

Before I could say anything, he spun me in

his arms and his lips came down hard on mine.

Holy shit. Talk about instant, flaming heat.

Good intentions? Kiss them goodbye.

Reasons to walk away? Burned to a crisp under the expert caress of a man who knew his way around a woman's lips.

He left no part of my mouth unexplored, sucking my upper and lower lip, one at a time, massaging them, tasting them.

He didn't suckle alone. I gave as good as I got, tangling my tongue with his, groaning when his teeth grazed me. The man could freaking kiss.

We stood on the sidewalk, in plain view, without a care for who might be watching, embracing passionately. Hungrily.

I clung to him, my fingers laced at the back of his head while his arms hugged me tight, his hands cold brands over the silk that impeded his way to my bare skin.

A strident whistle with a catcalled, "Fuck yeah, buddy. Do her!" brought me back a semblance of rationality.

What the hell am I doing?

I drew back, lips swollen, breathing uneven and legs wobbly. For a moment, I could have sworn Anthony's eyes flashed with blue fire, but he blinked and the odd light disappeared.

Am I drunk? I didn't feel drunk. Aroused, wet, and hungry for kisses, yes. Yet, I seemed in perfect control of myself, if I ignored the fact I wanted the man before me to fuck me.

Now.

Screw our public location or my dislike of him. Need consumed me. A need he could take care of.

I licked my swollen lips. "We shouldn't be doing this," I whispered, my voice not quite as steady as I would have liked.

For a moment, he didn't reply, just stared. When he did finally speak, his low tone slid over me, a sensual tickle of sound that I swore actually touched me between the legs. I quivered.

"Come with me. My car isn't far. Just a few blocks."

A part of me urged me to say yes. I wanted to go with him and steam up the windows of his luxury sedan. Leave ass prints on his surely leather seats. But why resort to a quick, uncomfortable coupling when I knew of a bed nearby?

I did the unthinkable.

"My place is closer." I later blamed this poor decision on my pussy, which mutinied and took over my body, a total limb assault on a quest for sex.

At my words, I could have sworn I saw, once again, a blue flare in his eyes. Probably just the glint of the neon lights flashing around us.

A smart man, he didn't say much after my invitation, else I probably would have had time to change my mind.

His fingers laced with mine and even though I'd not told him which building I lived in, off we strode, just another couple, hurrying to get home so we could screw like wild animals.

No denying, I wanted to feel him inside me.

Something about my behavior should have rung warning bells. I didn't take coworkers home. Especially ones I abhorred. I also never left the bar without telling Brenda, my wing-woman. Then again,

I'd also never experienced such an ardent need for a man before.

I barely registered the walk to my place. I floated, my body on fire and aching. My breasts heavy and tender. My pussy soaking and so ready for his cock I thought I would die if we didn't get there fast.

It seemed I wasn't the only eager one. We'd no sooner entered my elevator and pressed the button for the seventh floor than he pinned me to the wall, his tongue thrusting into my mouth, his body flush against mine. The hardness of his arousal ground against me, titillating evidence of his attraction for me. Did I forget to mention its sizable nature?

We made out in the elevator like frantic teenagers, groping and kissing with wild abandon.

The cab dinged and the doors slid open. Another ten seconds and I would have probably had my thighs wrapped around his waist. Stupid modern elevator. If I'd not feared getting caught, I would have slapped the close button and given in to my fantasy.

Down the hall we glided to my apartment. I fumbled with my key. His cool hand covered mine and guided the stupid metal thing home. With a click, we were in and the door had barely slammed shut before buttons went flying.

Normally, I embarked upon sex with a practical nature. Have a few drinks. Neck a little. Find a bed or a car. Get undressed then do the bump and grind until my little O came along.

Yeah. Apparently, I'd been missing out.

What flared between Anthony and I didn't

want to wait. It didn't care that my hundred dollar blouse—bought on a clearance rack for a discounted $19.95—got torn from my body with a ripping sound that just titillated me further.

My eager fingers gripped his shirt, which probably cost more than I made in a week, and tore it open, the satisfying ping of buttons feeding some unholy savage inside me.

In record time, we stood naked amongst the rags of our clothes and, dear gawd, he lifted me. Me! The six-foot-tall Amazon whom universities had courted, begging to play on their basketball team.

He hoisted me as if I were light as a feather, slamming my back against the wall, not hard enough to hurt, but firm enough to show he meant business.

Incredibly hot. As if my wet pussy needed any more encouragement.

He kept his mouth latched to mine as he pushed his body between my thighs and I wrapped my legs around his waist and eagerly pulled him to me. And missed his damned cock.

Swollen and hard, it rubbed across my wet pussy, not where I wanted it.

Inside me.

I groaned against his lips.

"Looking for something?" he teased, the gyration of his hips seesawing his shaft against my sensitized flesh.

"Keep doing that and I won't," I gasped, digging my fingers into the muscles of his shoulders. It seemed Mr. DA hid a nicely toned physique inside those designer suits. Pale in color didn't mean he neglected his body. Not that I'd had time to admire it much before he'd pinned me to the wall—a fantasy come to life.

"We can't have that now, can we?" he murmured. Pulling back, he thrust his dick home, and by home, I meant he drove it into me. A powerful stroke. A deep penetration. Oh, how he stretched me nicely.

Back went my head as I savored the way he filled me. I'd gone without a real man much too long, which made his slow in-and-out movement that much more maddening. I didn't want a languorous ride to the top. I wanted him to fuck me.

I urged him on. "Faster. Give it to me. Don't hold back."

Not all men could handle a woman giving them directions during sex; some whined it distracted them. Some got performance anxiety.

Not Anthony. I asked for more and he gave it to me. My gawd, did he give it to me. Held up by his hands and the wall, such a novel position, he pistoned me, his cock pounding my willing pussy, striking my sweet spot with each and every stroke.

I fucking loved it.

Wanton and wild in his grasp, I showed him my pleasure by clawing at his back, his shoulders, anything I could get my sharp fingernails on. My breathing turned harsh, the sounds coming from me a cross between a moan and a high-pitched scream. He buried his face in the hollow where my neck meets my shoulder and he sucked the tender flesh there, just another sensation to add to the pile already driving me wild.

My body tensed and coiled and the muscles in my channel gripped him tight, forming a suction he had to fight against with each stroke, pushing and shoving.

It was freaking fantastic. It also tipped me over the edge.

I came first with a scream that I hoped the neighbors didn't mistake for a cry of help. Not that I could have stopped it. The orgasm sweeping through me demanded acclaim.

Anthony proved more restrained. With his mouth still buried in my skin, he thrust a few more times before his body pulsed. Instead of yelling, he pinched the skin of my neck as he bit down, not that I cared in that moment, not with my own climax still rendering me limp as a rag doll.

I don't know how long we stood there, him sucking on the sore spot he'd bitten, me panting, trying to regain my breath, our bodies intimately joined.

Then it hit me.

Shit. "You forgot to use a condom!"

And I couldn't believe I'd gotten so caught up I didn't remember. Pregnancy didn't worry me. I took my pill religiously. But, who knew what icky germs my seducer carried?

He gave a final lick to my neck before lifting his head to stare at me. "I'm clean."

"Says you."

"Says my last medical check-up."

"And how long ago was that? Also, how many women have you slept with since?" I showed no quarter.

I'll admit, I didn't say it nicely. STDs were a fact of life and I couldn't believe I'd gotten so caught up in the moment I'd forgotten to keep myself safe.

"I was declared medically sound not even

three months ago and I haven't slept with anyone in over five months since I broke up with my girlfriend. What about you? Should I be concerned?"

Of course he'd flip it around and try to make me feel guilty. Never mind he was justified in questioning me back. As a woman, I held tight to my right to irrationality, especially since I didn't understand how things had gotten so out of control in the first place.

Tone indignant, I answered, "On the pill and clean as a whistle." An expression I didn't get. I mean, whistles were things you blew in and covered with spit, which meant bacteria. Wouldn't a better saying involve soap?

"No lovers or boyfriends I need to worry about either?" He arched a brow as he put me through the inquisition.

I scowled. "I do not sleep around." Which given I still had my legs wrapped around his waist might seem kind of hard to believe. "I don't usually do things like this."

"Like what?" he asked, his lips curved in a slight mockery of a smile.

"Take guys home and screw them without even a first date." When flustered, I resorted to bold language, and lies.

I did believe in one-night stands, so long as a thick layer of latex was involved and I could sneak out before they woke up.

He laughed. "I feel honored."

"You should."

"Is there any way I can thank you?"

Good thing he didn't use the naughty grin he tossed me when we battled in court. I would have probably declared my clients guilty myself just before I tackled Anthony to the ground to have my wicked way.

"What were you thinking?"

"How big is your shower?" Anthony cocked a brow at me and threw me a slow, sexy grin that made me immediately horny. He let my body down slowly, a sensual glide of skin on skin that sent a shiver through me. As he turned and walked to my bathroom, I licked my lips at the view of his taut buttocks. Yuuuummmy.

My body thrummed with anticipation as I followed and I crossed my fingers, praying to whichever sex god was listening that my shower and tub were big enough to fuck in. With our almost matching heights, the pair of us took up a lot of space. Sex in the tight confines of my shower could prove challenging. But I was still willing to try.

Anthony already had the water streaming and stood under the spray when I entered. I took a moment to admire the view through the glass door, thanking the fact I'd opted against the frosted version.

Good grief, he was so sexy, even more so with water glistening over his toned flesh. I swear he did it on purpose to tease me, especially when he grabbed the soap and lathered himself, his hand closing around his semi-erect cock, sliding back and forth in a manner that seemed more pleasurable than cleansing.

My mouth watered. I knew what I wanted for a snack. In I stepped, my hands using his chest to steady myself, a cheap excuse to touch him. His lips quirked in amusement.

"Your shower isn't as big as expected."

"Big enough for what I have planned." I slid my hands down from his pecs, palm flat, fingers spread, feeling the heat of his skin and his rapidly thudding heart. His nipples puckered, begging for a nibble. I leaned forward so I could bite one lightly. He sucked in a breath and it was my turn to smile wickedly. I played with his chest, alternating between sucking his little nubs and rubbing my cheek against his slick skin. I might have teased him for a while, but something kept poking me in the belly, something hard and demanding.

Apparently, his cock wanted some attention too. I was more than happy to comply. I dropped to my knees and brought myself eye level with his shaft. Despite our recent coupling, there was nothing semi or soft about it now. I reached out a hand to stroke it lightly and it jerked in response. I peeked up and saw Anthony gazing down at me, his blue eyes seeming alight from within.

My lips curved into a wanton smile as I touched him again. This time, I wrapped my hands tight around his length. Back went his head, a hitching sigh leaving him. Pleased at his response, I pumped his rigid cock, back and forth. The thickness and length of it tempted me. Out flicked my tongue to lave the head, already swollen and blushing with color. Fingers tangled in my hair as Anthony shuddered under my ministrations. Gawd, I loved how he responded and how he groaned, a long low rumble and then a bark of pleasure as I finally took him into my mouth.

The fingers in my hair tightened, a little tug of pain that excited me. Deeper I took him into the warm recess of my mouth as my hand reached up to fondle his heavy sac. I fucked him with my mouth, taking him in and out, the slick length of him grazing my teeth. With his fingers still entwined in my hair, he aided me, thrusting his hips in time to my oral cadence.

In the past, I'd sucked guys; it was kind of expected, but frankly boring for me. Those guys weren't Anthony. For the first time, I realized that the pleasure of the act could go two ways. With him, I didn't do it because I had to. I did it because I wanted to. Needed to taste him. Needed him to lose his mind like he had made me lose mine. And oh, he did not disappoint. The guttural sounds he uttered, the way his cock jerked and pulsed in my mouth... Damn did it excite me.

Using my free hand, I stroked myself, my pussy wet not just from the shower but from arousal. I would have happily sucked him to completion and probably come on my hand, but he abruptly pulled his cock from my mouth with a wet pop.

"I wasn't done," I protested.

"Good, because neither was I," was his reply. He yanked me upright then turned me so I faced away. A hand in the middle of my back pushed me over so that I presented my buttocks to him. Understanding his plan, I braced my hands on the shower wall just in time for his first deep thrust.

I just about expired of pleasure on the spot. Thankfully, I didn't because the best was yet to come.

Despite my tight shower, he managed to fuck me, his throbbing cock driving hard and deep, each stroke leaving me panting and climbing a peak toward ecstasy.

"Harder," I begged. Then, "Faster." Each time he complied, and soon I couldn't speak, so ragged was my breath. But I had enough air to scream when my orgasm finally hit.

"Dear fucking gawd!" Not that there was anything holy about the carnal bliss roaring through my pussy. Whatever mighty power he'd used to sate me, it left me boneless and happy, enough that I let him carry me, cradled in his arms, my body dripping wet onto my fine Egyptian sheets. But I didn't really care, not when my body hummed so happily. And later, my usually sacrosanct sheets got a workout too.

Chapter Three

Waking up the next morning, alone, my first thought was what an oddly erotic dream. *And involving Anthony of all people.*

Then I caught the lingering scent of cologne, took note of my sticky skin and pleasantly sore pussy, and bolted upright in bed with a shrieked, "Oh fuck me, I didn't."

Yet I had. I'd screwed my nemesis. And not just screwed. I'd indulged in amazing, pulse-pounding, sweaty, hardcore sex, the kind I'd read about but never experienced—until now. On the wall, in my shower, in my bed.

Three times we'd done it!

It was a freaking record for me. Usually I managed a one or two-hit wonder. The man must have had some magic in his dick; he certainly did in his tongue, because he'd not even had to work me too long to get me to orgasm so many times. Yay for me.

Reality slapped me and she wasn't gentle about it.

Did the most amazing sexual experience of my life have to be with *him*? I hated him. Loathed him and everything he stood for. Or did I?

I analyzed my feelings in regards to

Anthony—forget relegating him back to Mr. Vanderson status. I'd seen his penis. It seemed kind of dumb to pretend a distance that no longer existed.

Back to the hating thing? Okay, so maybe he wasn't the total asshat I'd painted him to be. Yet, at the same time, I couldn't state that I liked him. In spite of his prowess when it came to playing my body, the burning annoyance that he constantly bested me in court still existed. My general dislike of his arrogant airs and his luck in front of a judge hadn't diminished. The only thing that changed—other than knowing what his dick looked like and could do—was now I not only resented his luck in the courtroom, I wanted to ride him like a cowgirl, maybe hit him with a riding crop and yell, "Giddy up!"

What is wrong with me?

If I believed in magic, I'd swear he put a spell on me.

Or drugged me!

No way. A man with his appearance wouldn't have to resort to chemicals to get a woman to fuck him. Or would he? Was that how he got his kicks?

Springing from bed, I dashed to the bathroom and checked myself out in the mirror.

Yikes. Hello, morning-after hair. It stuck up all over the place. I resembled the poster child for why conditioner existed. Good thing Anthony hadn't stuck around. I'd have given him ample evidence for a case to never see me again. However, my hair wasn't what needed examination. Leaning in, I peered at myself.

My eyes appeared clear. Not even a touch bloodshot. My head felt fine, even when I shook it and swung it around like a groupie at a head-banging concert.

No blank spots seemed to exist in my memories. I remembered every decadent moment of last night. As for my body…it hummed happily. A little sore between the thighs from our enthusiastic coupling, but the good kind. Other than the tenderness, the only sign of the previous evening's aberration was a red mark on my neck where Mr. DA got a little enthusiastic with his sucking.

"The jerk gave me a hickey." This, even more than the sex with my nemesis, irritated me.

Now I could just imagine what some people would think at this point. Half would call me a sex-crazed slut. But those who knew me, who knew how I abhorred Anthony and liked to remain in control, would call the whole thing suspicious. Totally out of character. He must have slipped me something. What, though? Or the better question, when?

I racked my brain, replaying the previous evening's chain of events. No matter how many times I ran them by, even in slow motion, I just couldn't see a moment when he'd had a chance to slip me something.

I'd drunk my first cocktail before his arrival. And, while I'd chugged half my second, which he'd ordered for me, I'd had my eyes on it from the moment Liam made it until it hit my lips. Unless rich boy could move faster than light, I couldn't blame drugs.

Damn it. One look into his mesmerizing blue eyes and I had succumbed. It appeared I had only myself to blame for my slutty actions.

That wouldn't do.

I chose to blame Anthony. Somehow, someway, this was his fault. Him and his good looks, sexy suits, and…and…whatever else he possessed that had rendered me so horny—and given me the most intense orgasms of my life.

At least he'd had the good sense to leave before I woke. I don't know what I would have done had I opened my eyes to see his face on the pillow alongside mine.

Screamed possibly.

Slapped him.

Or looped my leg over his and drawn him in for a good morning tussle.

Yes, I still disliked the man on principle; however, all I had to do was picture his pale body poised over mine, his hips thrusting, his gaze intent, and my nipples hardened while my pussy gave a happy shudder.

Damn him for giving me great sex, and worse, for making me crave more.

At least I wouldn't have to face him anytime soon. I didn't have any court cases scheduled next week or the week after against him. Thank freaking gawd. It would give me time to brace myself for when I eventually needed to come up against him in a courtroom.

Or was seduction part of his master plan? Get me in the sack and fuck me silly so that the next time he had to deal with me in front of the judge, I'd remember him naked. Flustered, I'd throw my case and give him victory. A great theory except for the fact that I never won!

Enough of the Saturday morning regrets. I couldn't change last night. I could just bury it deep in my subconscious and hope I never had to face him again. *I might have to move.* I wondered if Alaska needed any lawyers.

Flopping back onto my bed, I buried my face in my pillow, looking to catch a few more hours of sleep. The shrill ring of my phone messed with my plan. Scrambling through my clothes—the shredded remains, which made me sob—I located my hidden purse. I dug my pink bedazzled smartphone out and answered it.

"Oh my god." Brenda's squeal just about deafened me.

"Good morning to you too."

"I can't believe you took Mr. Hottie home."

"That makes two of us," I mumbled as I made my way to the kitchen in search of some caffeine. Forget sleep. Brenda would demand details.

"So how was it?"

"Isn't the better question, why did I do it? I hate the guy."

"Love. Hate. Who cares how you feel about him? DA Vanderson is HOT!"

She didn't know the half of it. In a suit, he was delicious. Naked...shudder. I couldn't believe my body still had the ability to get horny after last night's debauchery.

"Sorry I didn't warn you I was leaving with him. Events kind of moved suddenly."

"Not too suddenly, I hope. Nothing worse than a man who comes before the main event, if you know what I mean."

Subtlety wasn't her strong suit. "I do know."

"And?"

"And what?"

"How was he?" Brenda practically yelled the question in her eagerness to know every single detail of my sex life. Ha. How funny to think I kind of had one. Usually, it was the other way around.

"How was he?" I paused before I gave her a tidbit I knew she'd enjoy. "Hot and hung."

"Hung as in a horse or a mule?"

I'd never understood the difference, or the comparison. I mean, comparing a man's junk to an animal? Who the hell came up with that? Despite the inanity of the query, I replied, "Elephant."

As Brenda waxed on eloquently—using language her mother would have washed her mouth out with soap for—about the equipment she never saw but envied me test driving, I brewed myself some instant coffee, lamenting the fact that I couldn't yet afford one of those awesome Keurig machines. Fabulous instant coffee makers were for the lawyers not working as a government drone. Not me, in other words. With my paycheck, I got stuck with hot water poured over some Folgers' crystals.

As I sipped the bitter concoction, which I preferred black, I couldn't help thinking of Anthony. Did he also drink coffee? Actually, a man like him probably enjoyed something fancier. I bet he had an espresso machine in his mansion. With a butler to serve it.

I hated him with a passion.

Wished he was here asking me to shower with him again.

I wondered if I needed a lobotomy.

Phone tucked against my ear, I waited until Brenda ran out of breath—ha, like that would ever happen—and managed the occasional "Uh huh" in edgewise.

"So are we still getting together this afternoon for that marathon thing?" she gushed, finally finishing a sentence and pausing for a reply.

I'd just about forgotten about the marathon for cancer research. Not that I intended to run. Long-legged didn't mean athletic. But I had told my mom I'd show up and cheer her on, along with my dads, who'd signed up to do the five-mile jog.

My stepfather had lost his first wife to the nasty disease, so we did what we could in honor of her memory. "Of course. I'm going," I replied. "You?"

"You betcha. I've got my foam finger out and my travel mug ready."

"Special coffee or iced tea?"

"I was thinking of having one of each, you know, in case the race runs a bit longer than expected."

"You are a lush, Brenda Parker."

"Lush and curvy, you jealous giant."

"Pipsqueak."

"Titan."

"Munchkin."

"Prosecution dick lover."

I exhaled. "Oooh, that was low."

"Not as low as you went on him last night," she said with a snicker.

How did she guess? Speaking of which, I couldn't help remembering my worship at the altar of his magical dick. I couldn't believe he'd pulled me away instead of letting me finish him off. Maybe next time, I'd tie him down so I could get the job done.

No! There would be no next time. Ever. Not

happening.

Now, if only I believed myself.

A hot shower managed to erase the scent of my shame—but not the memory of pleasure. I dressed in comfortable clothes, athletic gear comprised of black yoga pants, a T-shirt with an Angry Bird saying something rude, and running shoes. The picture of an athlete—who exercised with a TV remote.

Hungry and in need of calories to replace the ones I'd burned the night before, I treated myself to a greasy breakfast at a diner around the corner from the subway. I devoured the Hungry Man; three eggs, two slices of bacon, two sausages—the edible not manly kind—three pieces of toast, and home fries washed down with a cup of horrible coffee and orange juice. For dessert, and the ride uptown, I brought along an apple Danish. Some people fasted and stretched before a marathon. Apparently, after a sexual one, I needed to eat.

I met up with Brenda at the volunteer table where I managed to avoid answering questions as we hurried to get our station ready. Lucky me, I snagged the spiked ice tea she brought along while Brenda sipped her thermos full of coffee, generously flavored with Bailey's.

Our volunteer position involved manning a water station at the halfway point of the course, which put us out in the middle of nowhere. Bored out of our skulls, my BFF slightly hung over and wearing giant shades, we waited for the first runners to reach us.

I'd already given Brenda as many salacious details as I dared about my sexual encounter with Anthony. In return, I'd gotten way too much information about the threesome Brenda got into— or that got into her more accurately—with a pair of bailiffs, who, while short in the penile department, made up for it in enthusiasm and endurance.

"But sweaty," Brenda exclaimed. "I mean, these guys should have worn those headbands you used to see back in the eighties for exercise, you know the fabric ones that soak up moisture."

For some reason, that brought to mind an image of a pair of Mr. Cleans with white terry cloth headbands. Not a sexy thought. "Sorry, but no man should ever wear a headband."

"Skiers do."

"And few can carry it off. I'm also sure they take them off before sex."

Had I mentioned that many of our conversations seemed to center around the almighty O? As single gals, with no dependents—not even a cat or a budgie—we tried to avoid the depressing topic of work and never spoke about politics or religion—unless we were exclaiming over the newest laws pertaining to threesomes and moresomes.

Brenda already knew everything about my family, seeing as how she'd practically grown up in my house. What did that leave? Shopping, food, and sex.

The first we couldn't afford often. The second, we'd indulge once the race was done. As for the third, while I did go through dry spells, Brenda didn't and she loved to discuss her love life—in living detail.

What a novelty that, for once, I actually had some dirty deeds to share too. I swear Brenda almost shed a tear she was so proud.

A wave of runners came into sight, fit and toned freaks—whom I envied with a passion. Not for the first time in my life, I wished I possessed the kind of drive and enthusiasm they did when it came to staying in shape.

Sadly, my idea of working out involved doing the vacuuming and laundry. By the time I got around to doing either, it was a total workout and left me with a pearly sheen of exertion. That sounded more attractive than the reality. In other words, dressed in my cast-off rags, I sweated like a sumo wrestler as I tackled the accumulated dirt, stunk like a pig as I washed the grubby bathroom, and wore a layer of dust atop it all once finished with my Swiffer. How Cinderella pulled off the sexy-servant-girl shtick, I'd yet to figure out. *Must have been the glass slippers.*

Handing out the water cups as the paragons of fitness jogged in place to keep their blood flowing, I didn't pay much attention, tossing out generics to sound supportive. "Good job," "You're halfway there," "Keep up the good work."

Look at me, doing my part for charity, the encouraging cheerleader with a pasted smile on my face.

Head ducked as I grabbed another cup, I thrust out the paper cone at the shadow that fell over me, sloshing water over my hand in the process. "Oops. Sorry. Let me get you another."

"Take your time. Or, even better, spill the next one a little higher. I'm always up for a wet T-shirt contest."

No way. I recognized that rumble even if I'd only heard it once before. Up flew my gaze to meet the amused one of a certain Pete Cavanaugh. And, oh boy, forget putting a headband on this big boy. Sweat looked good on him. Real good. *But it would look even better on me.*

Down, girl.

Towering over me, wearing a black sleeveless shirt and athletic shorts that stopped mid-thigh—oh my, what muscled thighs he owned—my werewolf nutjob sucked the breath from me and tickled my pussy with just an amused tilt of his lips.

Despite my more than satisfying sex the night before, my body responded. My nipples poked the tip of my shirt, my sex sent out a moist SOS, and a herd of butterflies took up residence in my lower anatomy.

"You." It emerged sounding accusatory.

His brow lifted. "Yes. Me."

"You're running in the marathon?"

The wide grin did nothing to quell the winged visitors doing somersaults in my tummy. "I'd say that was obvious."

Fighting the heat that threatened to rise in my cheeks took effort. It would have helped if I could stop sounding like a freaking idiot. But something about this man—just like a certain DA—flustered the hell out of me.

I tried a different tactic and went on the offensive, calling forth my sarcastic, cynical side to the rescue. "I'm surprised you aren't leading the pack."

"Why?"

"You seem like a guy who stays fit. Or am I

wrong? Is your girlfriend not taking you out for regular walks?" Me, fishing for info? Never!

A grin showed he didn't take offense at my jab, and he satisfied my curiosity. "No girlfriend. For the moment. What about you? Is your special friend running today?"

"My special friend prefers to stay in my nightstand drawer." Too late. I said it out loud. Blushed beet red too as I slapped a hand over my mouth.

My obvious embarrassment did not stop him from laughing, and Brenda, instead of saving me from myself, practically fell to the ground in stitches.

Just how much "truth juice" did my special coffee contain?

"If you were my girlfriend, I'd let you take me for a walk, and while I wouldn't let you store me in a drawer, I'd definitely engage you in some strenuous activities that would keep me in top shape."

I'll just bet he would. Hot, sticky, panting activities.

I gulped. "Dream on. I prefer guys who don't sweat so much." Spoken a faint voice as he mopped his damp brow by lifting the hem of his shirt.

Good grief, I couldn't help but stare. Did he have the world's most perfect abs? If I'd not seen another perfect set the previous night, I would have said yes. As it was, he tied for first.

The shirt came back down, hiding his perfection, and thankfully before I did something stupid, such as ask if I could test their firmness by bouncing a roll of quarters off them.

Okay, I didn't have quarters, but hey, I could sacrifice a little dignity and bounce myself. What could I say? My scientific side really wanted to know if they were as hard as they looked.

"If you're making out with a guy and you're both not getting hot and bothered, then they're not doing it right."

A naughty smile shouldn't make a girl cream herself. Apparently, I didn't get the memo. I clenched my thighs tight.

"You never did answer why you're so far behind the other runners," Brenda interjected, finally coming to my rescue.

"I started late," he replied with a shrug that sent mounds of muscles rolling.

I watched, utterly mesmerized by the motion. Brenda also noted it, or so I surmised because a terse runner had to ask her twice if she was going to give her some water or what. Brenda muttered something about whiny women ruining her fun as she thrust the cup at her.

"For a guy who started late, you're not doing so bad, I guess."

"I had to sprint for a while to catch up."

"Sprint? Son, if that's what you call a sprint, I'd hate to see you in a full-out run."

Cue the big groan. Figured my parents would show up while I ogled the hunk in front of me.

"Mom, Dads. You made it. How are you guys holding up?" I asked, reaching for some more water cups, glad for an excuse to focus away from Tall, Dark and I-want-to-fuck.

Perhaps I could fight my treacherous body by keeping my attention on something slightly more rational like my three parents.

I eyed my family. Mother appeared flushed,

but happy, her cheeks holding a rosy tint, although she panted a little bit. My two dads, on the other hand, seemed fine. They went for daily jogs farther than this, so to them, this marathon thing was a breeze.

"Beautiful day for a run," Mother gushed in between gulps of water.

"Indeed it is," my werewolf client replied.

"Shouldn't you be off chasing a cat?" I muttered.

"Don't you mean pussy?" he murmured back as he leaned forward to toss his empty cup into the pail by my feet.

I gaped at him and the jerk winked.

Thankfully, he'd said it low enough that I didn't think my parents heard, but they must have sensed the undercurrent between us because my first father said, "I get the impression that you've met our daughter before."

"As a matter of fact, I have. She helped me out with a minor legal matter."

"Nothing too serious, I hope?" dad number two inquired.

What was this, the sweaty-guy inquisition?

"Nope. Turns out her advice was just the thing I needed."

"It was?" Color me surprised. I didn't hear that one too often. Usually my clients did the opposite and went back out to commit the same offenses that had landed their asses in front of me in the first place.

Wearing a smug smile, Pete said, "Animal control came right out and took care of the issue before suppertime."

Oh dear. "You didn't?"

"I most certainly did. The menacing feline critter is behind bars. Rocky and Periwinkle send their thanks."

"Pets of yours, I assume?" my mother asked.

"Lovebirds."

"Beautiful creatures. They make the most delightful music."

"Yes they do. I'd show you a video of them chirping a duet, but I left my cell phone locked in my car."

"What a shame. I would have enjoyed seeing it. I work at the local zoo. Marketing department."

"I love the zoo," Pete exclaimed.

What was this, charm my mother day? I scowled as my mother beamed up at Pete.

"Find me after the race, and I'll play it for you." Pete flashed his hundred-watt grin.

Mother wasn't the only one taken in by it. I could see my dads relaxing instead of forming a daddy wall between the male interloper and their little girl.

Did no one grasp his despicable plan to seduce me? Would no one save me from his incredible charm—and rock hard body?

"You know what. I have a better idea. Why don't you join us for dinner tonight? You already know Chloe. You can show us the video then."

And there it was. Out of the blue, but not unexpected. My mother the matchmaker making an appearance. I should have known she'd try something like this.

I tried to halt the will-you-date-my-daughter train before it got chugging. "No. He can't. He's probably busy."

"Actually, I don't have any plans and would be delighted to join you for dinner. I'll bring my phone so I can show off my birds." Oh the stupid, stupid man. Did he not see a ploy by a mother desperate to see her daughter settle down? Apparently not, because he took the pen Brenda scrounged from her bottomless purse and inked my parents' address on his arm. I could only watch in more or less stunned silence.

"I should probably get going if I'm going to sprint past the leaders. I'll see you tonight." With a grin, off jogged Pete Cavanaugh, his long-legged stride eating up the ground.

Only now did I regain the power of speech. "What were you thinking?"

My mother blinked innocently. "Whatever do you mean? He seems like such a nice boy. Handsome too."

"But he's a werewolf." I'm not sure why I felt a need to blurt that out. On the surface, he appeared nice enough, if one ignored the fact he liked to pee in public.

"A werewolf, really?"

Shit. Trust my mother to find that tidbit fascinating rather than detracting. "Yes. And he claims to live next door to a witch."

Uh-oh, wrong tactic. One of my dads perked up. "You don't say? I've long said they must exist."

At that point, I gave up. One way or another, Pete, with the ultra sexy abs, was coming over for dinner. As was Brenda, to meet a certain man mother gushed was perfect for her. Oh, and I had to go too. Oh, yay.

This Saturday was sinking faster than the cookies I made a few weeks ago and then pitched from the public marina dock. The only thing missing was a certain DA to make my life hellishly complete. Thankfully, Brenda's purse came with more Bailey's. It tasted a lot better without all that coffee diluting it.

Chapter Four

When the last straggling runners huffed and puffed their way past our checkpoint, Brenda and I packed up our crap and headed back to her monster truck. Before you picture an SUV with all-wheel drive, let me interject that the only thing small about my friend was her stature. As if to make up for her lack of inches, the rest of her went above and beyond normal. Such as her vehicle of choice.

Big, blue, with flames along the side, her Dodge turbo diesel truck with twenty-two inch wheels didn't just rumble when you started its three hundred and fifty-nine cubic inch engine, it *growled*.

Perched behind its leather-wrapped steering wheel, her feet barely hitting the pedals, Brenda should have appeared absurd and might have, if not for the maniacal gleam in her eyes, the evil sneer on her lips, and the quick to react middle finger when another driver dared to get in her way.

Getting a ride with her always provided a great reminder to never let your medical or life insurance lapse.

As she drove us back to the city and my place—cutting people off and making aspersions on their origins when they dared glare in her direction—I complained for like the zillionth time that day. "I can't believe they invited him for supper."

"Hey, aren't you the one always bitching dinner at your folks' is so boring?"

"Did I complain? Turns out boring is good. Nothing better than a cheesy lasagna with garlic bread to make a Saturday night perfect."

"Add in some hot abs made for dripping chocolate sauce over—"

"Or caramel with whipped cream," I interjected with a hint of drool.

"—and I'd say you've got a new tradition I'd kill for."

"But he's a werewolf. A crazy one who believes in witches."

"So what?"

"What do you mean, so what?"

"Why does his belief in sorcery make him crazy? What if he's right? I mean, think of it. Years ago, everyone thought Lycans didn't exist. Then poof. Turns out they're real. Ditto for those tree-hugging wenches, mermaids, and fairies. What else have we thought was fantasy that actually exists? Who's to say witches and other things from storybooks don't exist too?"

"Next thing I know you'll try and convince me vampires are roaming the earth," I tittered, but damn it all if I didn't picture Anthony and his alabaster skin when I said it.

As if the district attorney was a vampire. I'd seen the guy outside the courthouse in daylight. He didn't ignite into a ball of fire—nope, his power over fire seemed to extend only to lighting my libido.

"Hey, you want to pretend you know everything, that's your business. Me, I have an open mind."

"And bedroom door," I muttered cattily.

"Jealous? Awesome. Not my fault I have a better sex life than you."

"My sex life is fine, thank you, or have you forgotten who I got it on with last night?"

"Ooh, one night. Fuck Mr. Werewolf after dinner tonight, and maybe I'll be impressed."

"You like him so much, you make a play for him," I offered, and immediately wanted to take back the words.

I did not want Brenda sinking her perfectly manicured nails into my wolf. Yes, mine. It seemed my attraction to him had jealousy issues. I might not want him, but I wanted him enough not to share him. How confusing.

"I am not taking your man."

"He's not mine," I answered automatically.

She snorted. "Says the girl who practically leapt over the table to rip the shirt off him and lick the sweat from his impeccable body. You might be able to fool yourself, but you can't fool me. You want the wolf."

"Do not."

"Do too. I don't know why you keep denying it."

"Because I just had sex with one guy I dislike. How can I want sex with another?"

"Because you're horny."

"But I shouldn't be."

"Thinks you. Maybe your body is trying to tell you something."

"Like what?"

"That you've been an uptight lawyer for too

long, and it's time you loosened up, spread your legs, and indulged in a little me-time for once."

"You want me to turn into a slut?"

"Slut sounds so harsh. I prefer to think of it more as enjoying a harmonized body with a splash of selfish well-being." Brenda made it sound eloquent.

Reality was sex could get sticky. "Oh, it involves a splash of something all right, usually jizz that is a pain to get out of my hair and sheets."

Brenda snorted. "You make it sound gross."

"No, it's called being practical. What I want to know is why is everyone so obsessed with settling me down? You don't have a full-time boyfriend and I don't see anyone bugging you."

"Because I'm at least trying to find Mr. Right. And, in some cases, right times two."

"Boyfriends are so much work, though," I whined.

"Most things are, but at least you'd have a man to provide you with steady sex."

"I don't mind the sex part. It's the whole do you love me, let's make babies, and hey, can you wash my clothes and make dinner part I despise."

"So marry a rich old guy who already has kids, can afford to hire a maid, and just wants you for your body."

"Again, I am not a prostitute."

"I think you're looking at this all wrong. Instead of viewing it with negative eyes, how about focusing a bit on the positive?"

"Such as?"

"Well, for one, you could do the naughty without a condom once you both get your clean bill of health certificates."

I didn't mention my booboo with Anthony. I didn't need a lecture on the dangers of AIDS and STDs, which Brenda took very seriously.

"My vibrator is clean."

She ignored my comparison. "You'd have someone to watch TV with after a day's work."

"You mean someone to put on hockey or football."

"Not all guys force you to watch sports. Some do enjoy the same shows as you do."

Okay, so maybe, for just one moment, I wondered what Pete and Anthony thought of *Survivor*, the new *Bates Motel*, and *Game of Thrones*. "As if a real man would watch *The Carrie Diaries*."

"No one should watch *The Carrie Diaries*. Other positives…" Brenda swerved around someone daring to do the speed limit, and I grabbed my oh-shit handle. "Maybe you could find a guy who cooks so you wouldn't have to eat so much takeout or frozen dinners."

"Hey, I happen to like those." I especially liked that the cardboard containers could go straight to the trash, leaving me a clean sink.

"They're not healthy for you."

"Say he does cook, would he do dishes too?"

"If not, there's always dishwashers or paper plates."

"I'd have to share my bed, closet, and give him some space in the bathroom. Not to mention, what if he leaves the seat up and I go to pee in the middle of the night and fall in the toilet?"

"Then I'll visit you in jail once you kill him. Would you stop looking for flaws? Admit it. It might be nice."

"I don't know. Seems like an awful lot of commitment."

"So you tell them upfront you're not looking for a full-time thing, or even a permanent one, at this stage in your life. Just companionship."

"Can't I just have them over for sex?"

"Since when is that all you think of?" Brenda stopped at a red light—to my surprise—and eyed me. "I mean, what is up with you? Used to be you didn't mind having a little testosterone in your life. Did Roger, the guy whose dick you should have let me rip off, hurt you that bad? He was a douchebag. A total asshat. A loser."

"I know." He was also a big fat cheater and emotional black hole. Just thinking of him made me want ice cream. A whole tub of it. But I couldn't deny I'd gotten a lot of my negative attitude toward men after our breakup. Messy didn't come close to describing it. "Maybe I'm having a midlife crisis."

"You're too young for a midlife crisis."

"Then why do I hate the idea of dating while, at the same time, getting horny over every man I meet?"

"You are not wetting your panties with every man, just the really good-looking ones."

"So I'm a selective slut."

"Hey, at least you have good taste."

"Let's say I decide to try out your crazy plan and *date*." Yeah, I said it with disgust. So sue me. "Which guy do I choose?"

"Which one do you like better?"

"I don't know. Neither?"

"Liar."

"Fine. I think they're both hot."

"Super hot and yet only one is meeting your parents."

"So you think I should take the werewolf for a test drive? What about Anthony?"

"What about him? I thought the plan was to never see him naked again."

"It is." Sob. Such a shame, especially since he looked so good naked, and even better, his nakedness did wonders for me.

"Then what's stopping you from getting sweaty and wild with the wolf? Feel him out on being a between-the-sheets friend?"

Or against the wall. Or in the shower. So many places I wanted to feel him out in. "Nothing. I guess."

"Maybe once you let your hormones have their way, you'll go back to just being your regular bitchy self."

A girl could hope. But, somehow, I just knew it wouldn't be so simple.

Chapter Five

Selecting something to wear for a casual dinner at my parents' took more effort than it should have. Clothes went flying as I tried on outfit after outfit.

Too fancy.

Too slutty.

Too tight.

Not tight enough.

Pants or skirt? Easy access or not? Should the bra clasp be in the front or back? Skip the bra entirely?

The prospect of seeing Pete again and, more appalling, actually planning to have sex with him later to see if I could get this ungodly attraction out of my system, turned me into a frazzled mess. So when the knock came at the door, I was less than polite when I threw open the door with a barked, "What?"

The large bouquet of flowers initially covered the visitor. Once I finished sneezing, allergies being one of the delightful genetic traits my DNA gifted me, I managed through itchy, red eyes to see a perturbed Anthony peering at me.

"I guess a sorry for triggering an allergen attack is in order," he sheepishly said.

For some reason, I found this outrageously

amusing. I snickered, in between achoos, as I scrounged in my medicine cabinet for a remedy. A chug of good ol' Benadryl and I mellowed enough that I didn't sound as bitchy when I emerged from my bathroom and said to poor Anthony, who still stood in the hall outside my apartment, "What are you doing here?"

"I'd planned to surprise you with flowers and then ask you to dinner. Having failed at the first, I'm hopeful I can still convince you of the second."

Ring. Ring. Hello? Is this Hell? I hear you've frozen over. Seriously, his offer surprised me that much.

"You're asking me on a date?"

He nodded. Even more amazing, he seemed uncertain of himself. Mr. High and Mighty in the Courtroom shifted from foot to foot as he did something so mundane as ask me out for a bite. Was it any wonder I gaped at him, unable to answer?

"You seem surprised."

"Because I am."

"After Friday night, I thought…" He shrugged.

"Thought what?" I genuinely wanted to know because, given he'd left without a goodbye or a word, I'd thought what happened was an aberration. A one-time thing we would never repeat or speak about.

Ever.

Before I could find out what he thought, pigs took flight. Really they did. Or the earth stopped rotating. Or I was stuck in some kind of *Matrix* world where someone messed with reality because who happened to show up to make the moment even more fucked up?

Take one guess.

"Who's he?"

That's what Pete wanted to know. Me, I wanted to know who the heck had given him my address. *Mom!* I also wanted to know, why me?

Anthony whirled to face the werewolf, superfast, enough that I blinked and it was done. Like wow. His rapid speed didn't compare, though, to the building storm as he and Pete faced off. I could almost touch the testosterone suddenly filling the room.

Ding. Ding. Round one. Was it wrong of me to wish they wore fewer clothes and that the sprinkler in the hall would shower them with baby oil?

"Do you know this *man?*" Anthony put an inflection on the word that imbued it with a disgust that eloquently related his thoughts.

"Kind of. He's a client." Nothing like having the guy I'd recently screwed meeting the guy I planned to screw. Did anyone know of a better word than "awkward" sung in a high pitch?

"Was a client," Pete corrected. "Now I'm her escort for the evening."

"You are?" I don't know who sounded more surprised, me or Anthony, who echoed my words.

"I ran into your parents after the race and chitchatted for a bit. They mentioned your fondness for wine and since I don't drink often, I offered to drive you to dinner at their place so you could have a few glasses."

"You're taking him to dinner with your parents?" Anthony whirled back and fixed me with an accusing, icy blue stare.

Why did I feel as if I'd done something

wrong? Anthony acted as if he had a right to be jealous. Last I'd heard, a one-night stand didn't give a guy the right to assume anything. Apparently, Anthony thought otherwise.

I would have set him straight on that score, but then I caught Pete's smug smile.

"Not my idea. My mom and dads invited him, against my advice." Ha, that wiped the grin off Pete's face.

"I see."

Judging by Anthony's tight expression, he did, and didn't like it. Later, I'd claim the devil made me do it. And he didn't even have to bribe me with cookies. "Why don't you join us? My mom always makes too much food."

Their matching "What?" was too comical for words, but I didn't enjoy it for long because before I could think of a way to extricate myself, I found myself sandwiched between the pair of them, in a pickup of all things, on my way to my parents' in a simmering, angry silence, which I clung to more tenaciously than a bulldog with a bone.

The vehicle we were crammed in wasn't my first choice. I would have preferred the dark sedan Anthony arrived in, but having the chauffeur in his liveried suit, watching my two unwanted suitors bicker on the sidewalk over who should get to take me, proved too much. I didn't need an audience to my humiliation.

Since my parents invited him first, I told Pete I'd go with him. Anthony, not wanting to miss out, dismissed his driver and we smooshed ourselves into Pete's truck.

It was the longest fifteen-minute drive of my

life. The most titillating too. Big man to the right of me. Even bigger to the left, here I was, stuck in the middle of the ultimate male sandwich.

I could just imagine Brenda busting a gut when she saw us. Although, I'd place money on her exploding in jealousy.

My plan to have both guys stomp off in a fit having failed, I didn't know what to do with the two men—Brenda would have said just do both of them. Nor could I understand their stubborn insistence on pursuing me.

Sure, I was cute, if a touch too tall, but I wasn't the type of girl guys fought over. Yet, here I had two dominant men, each determined to get in my pants. Which, really titillated me more than it should have.

Faced with a rival for my body—because it certainly wasn't because I'd shown them any affection—I wasn't quite sure how to act or what to think. I did know that, unless I clearly favored one or the other, the rivalry would continue.

Despite my intention, or what I wanted, I'd become a prize. The rope in a tug of war. The treasure in a battle between two men.

Fucking Karma and her jokes.

And sue me if a teeny, tiny part of me didn't enjoy it. I mean, hello, two guys were fighting over me. Show me a woman who'd never fantasized about it, and I'd prove her a liar.

When we pulled up to my parents' place, I noted Brenda had already arrived, her monster truck parked at the curb just behind a smart car. Oh god, I hoped her blind date for the evening was the owner. Brenda did such a good job of mocking the eco friendly.

Before Pete could make it around the truck to the passenger side, Anthony had already helped me out, making a show of sliding me down his body. I enjoyed the friction, but his grin of triumph to the wolf? That got him a shot to the gut.

However, I didn't appreciate Pete's smirk when he saw me punishing Anthony. A stroke over Anthony's injured area and an "oops" by me wiped the smile.

With a flounce—a girly move I didn't know I was capable of— I left them on the curb as I went up the walkway to my parents' house.

The three-bedroom bungalow sat on the outskirts of the city. The brick façade and gingerbread trim never failed to make me nostalgic as I recalled growing up here.

An only child, not for lack of my parents trying, I'd enjoyed a normal childhood. Loved by my mom and two dads, I did well in school, had enough friends, didn't get into trouble.

You'd think having grown up in such a well-adjusted environment I'd have turned out less of a bitch. But the opposite happened. Having lived the cookie-cutter dream, I think a part of me yearned for something more. Something less comfortable and more exciting.

And dating a werewolf would fit the bill. My snide subconscious couldn't help pointing that out. But I couldn't help but wonder if that was my ignorance speaking.

Lycans claimed they were like everyone else, just hairier. I guess I'd find out if the evening went as planned, which seemed less and less likely, given

Anthony seemed determined to dog Pete's every step.

Hmm. Come to think of it, wasn't my current dilemma a form of the excitement I claimed to want? Did it get any more wild and chaotic than this? Pitting a rich DA against a werewolf certainly wasn't safe, or sane.

No matter how the evening ended, I did know that I remained far from ready to settle down in the 'burbs with a picket fence. I'd possibly never be. And why was I even thinking about this right now?

Just because I'd brought two men with me to meet my folks didn't mean I was ready to walk down the aisle and pick out china patterns.

The direction of my thoughts made me hope my dads had restocked the liquor cabinet. I needed wine, preferably served via an inserted IV.

Bracing myself for the upcoming disaster of an evening, I entered my childhood home with a male hand on my upper and lower back. Not my idea. The vying men caught up to me before I could get inside and sit down.

My mom's eyes widened in surprise when she saw I'd arrived with not one but two guys. I thought she'd expire on the spot in glee.

"Chloe. So glad you could make it. You too, Pete. And who is this other handsome gentleman?" If my mother batted her lashes any harder, she'd take flight.

"Mom, this is Anthony Vanderson. He's a, um—" *lover, nemesis, pain in the ass* "—friend of mine, who happened to show up. I invited him to come along. I hope you don't mind."

"Mind? Of course not. The more the merrier."

Maybe in her world. In mine, the pit I sank in seemed to get deeper and deeper. Problem was, I didn't really mind the pit.

Discomfited or not, I didn't fail to note how nice it felt to end up squished between two perfect male bods. How even the slightest touch from either made my skin shiver or my temperature rise.

I also couldn't stop myself from recalling some of the threesome stories I'd heard over the years. Not that I could picture either of these alpha males ever agreeing to something of the sort. But my dirty mind... Damn, I almost blushed at the kinky ideas it spewed forth.

The usual me totally wanted to decry the situation, but a girly part of me, the womanly part, couldn't deny a certain enjoyment that a pair of men vied for my affection. Or my body. I still wasn't sure what they were after.

I hoped for the latter. Unlike my mother, I truly didn't think I could handle two lovers in my life, government laws or not. One male was hard enough to balance. Two? Never. I'd rather pay the extra taxes.

Seated on a loveseat meant for two, I ended up thigh to thigh with my dueling beaus, not that they said anything or did anything to show they hated each other. If I hadn't seen them face off at my place and threatened them if they actually resorted to fists, I would have thought them friends.

They laughed and conversed with Brenda, as well as her fellow for the night—who was driving the smart car because he lost a bet. Usually, he raced around town in a gas guzzling Durango. He seemed a decent sort, if on the short side, and I could already tell Brenda would give him a test run.

As for my dates for the evening, they were annoyingly awesome. They engaged my parents in witty conversation on a variety of topics.

I discovered Pete worked as a landscaper and that Anthony enjoyed sketching in his spare time. Odd, I'd pictured him more as the model rather than the artist.

Despite Pete's crazy assertion about his neighbor and the fact he probably chased cars, he proved quite agreeable and funny, while Anthony possessed a rapier wit and intelligence, which actually complemented Pete's more down-to-earth mannerisms. In other words, despite their disparity and their inherent dominant natures, they balanced each other.

They also made it that much harder for me to decide which I liked more. I couldn't rely on attraction to break the tie; I lusted after them both. Of course, Anthony already had an advantage in that I knew what a fabulous lover he was in the bedroom. Pete, for all his innuendos and good looks, had yet to prove himself. Who would win the battle of the almighty O?

I needed to bang my head off the wall a few times to smack some sense into myself. Here I sat contemplating taking one man to bed so I could compare him to another. Time to get myself a membership to the Sluts 'R Us club.

When dinner ended, I escaped to the kitchen with Brenda and my mom. Under the guise of doing dishes, which involved us stacking them in the dishwasher and the sink since usually my dads took care of it, I snacked on homemade cookies and tried to make sense of my dilemma. Brenda didn't provide much help, not with envy staggering her.

"You brought both of them? What happened to choosing one?"

"Why would she do that?" my mother queried. "I say keep them both."

My mother, ever practical.

"Not happening. Heck, I don't even want one. They just won't go away."

"Sure they aren't, just like you're hating every minute of it," my mother drawled.

"Exactly what are you implying, Mother?" I asked haughtily.

"Me? Nothing."

Brenda snickered as my mother adopted an innocent look.

It didn't fool me for one second. "Drop the act. Spit it out, Mom."

"Oh please, Chloe. Anyone can see you're attracted to them both."

Damn it. Was it that obvious? "So? Doesn't mean I intend to do something about it."

"Says the girl who brought both to dinner at her mom's."

I glared at Brenda. "I thought you were supposed to be on my side."

"I am. And your side thinks you should go for it and keep them both."

"I am not getting into a threesome." No matter what my body thought or the decadent things my mind could conjure.

"Oh, really?"

"Yes really."

"You know, most people choosing to embark on a polygamous path in life stick to good friends to make the transition easier," said my mother in her sagest tone. "It's how I ended up with your second father."

"Do I have to get it tattooed to my forehead? I am not sleeping with them. Either of them." Because more and more, I was convinced they weren't worth the aggravation, despite the orgasms.

"Sure you aren't." Brenda rolled her eyes.

"I'm serious. I'm not."

"I really wish you wouldn't lie like that. I already know you've slept with at least one."

"Mom!"

"What? Are you going to lie and say you didn't?"

And risk her grabbing me by the ear, dragging me down the hall, and washing my mouth out with soap for sullying it with anything less than the truth?

"Okay, I slept with one. And only once."

Mother took on a pensive expression. "I'll bet it was Anthony."

Brenda confirmed her guess. "Wow, you are good, Mrs. Bailey."

"How did you know?" Did someone take out an ad in the paper saying I fucked the DA?

"Body language, dear. You don't shy from his touch, whereas, with Pete, you jump a little each time he goes near you."

Huh. I'd not realized I did that. Mom should have become a lawyer with her sharp attention to detail.

"So I slept with Anthony. Big deal. It's not

happening again."

"What about Pete?" my mother asked.

"What about him?"

"Are you going to sleep with him tonight?"

"Mother!" I practically shouted. "This is not appropriate conversation," I hissed.

"Oh don't act like such a prude. Nothing wrong with test-driving the merchandise. It's not like you're committed to just one, and we all know the law encourages you to take on at least two. Granted, those two might take a little adjusting, given they are such polar opposites," she mused.

Not that different. They were both overbearing, arrogant, testosterone-laden hunks I wanted to have wild monkey sex with. To think less than forty-eight hours ago I'd been lamenting the dry spell in my love life.

Judging by the crotch of my panties, I'd gone from drought to monsoon season. I just hoped I could weather the damned storm.

And still remain single.

I tuned back into the conversation to realize my mother and BFF had gone from predicting I'd sleep with Pete to even more outrageous areas.

"Can you imagine the babies they'd make?" My mother stared dreamily off into space. "Those blue eyes on Anthony with Pete's dark hair."

I managed a choked, "Mom!"

"What? I'm just saying they've got some damned good-looking genes. And I didn't mean right away. After all, I would hope you'd get married like me and your fathers did. Of course, we didn't get to do it legally until much later because of the uptight conservatives in power. But, in our hearts, we were committed."

Marriage? Something of my panic must have shown because Brenda physically restrained me before I could bolt for the back door.

"Calm, Chloe. Your mother is getting a little ahead of herself. Why don't we backtrack a bit, like to the part where you brought both because, really, for a girl who claims she doesn't want any men, you've got an awfully odd way of showing it."

"It just kind of happened. First Anthony showed up with flowers and while I was recovering from a sneezing fit, Pete showed up. Funny how he knew where I lived." I paused to glare at my mother, who averted her gaze, scrubbing at a nonexistent spot on the counter. "One thing led to another and next thing I knew, they were toe-to-toe, about to throw punches. I panicked and I invited Anthony to join us. Then before I could change my mind, I was sandwiched between them—"

"Ooh my favorite position," Brenda gushed.

"I agree," seconded my mother.

Interrupted, I adopted my sternest look. I'd long ago gotten over my gag reflex for when they said shocking things. "You guys are impossible. And, Mom, for future reference, that was too much information."

"How did I ever raise such a repressed daughter?"

"Just because I like my fun in single digits doesn't make me repressed. Once upon a time, the majority of the population felt the same way. Or have you forgotten our history?"

"Just doing my part for my country." Mother beamed.

"Um, Mom, you do know that I'm aware you were involved in a threesome before the laws came into effect?"

"What can I say? I'm a trendsetter."

Can anyone say messed-up childhood? When other kids went to school and lamented their single-parent homes, I confused the hell out of my teachers trying to explain the fact that I had an extra father.

Despite my lack of religious belief, I'm ashamed to say, I did use the Mormon religion as my defense when teachers or classmates pried too closely. When the polygamous laws came into effect, my sigh of relief at no longer having to make up excuses for my odd lifestyle could probably be heard around the world.

"Okay, so if you're not planning to keep them both, then who are you keeping? Is this some kind of test?" Brenda ate the last cookie before I could nab it. Thankfully, Mother had fudge cooling in the fridge so I didn't have to wrestle her for it.

"I guess. I hadn't really thought that far ahead. What do you think? Which one do you like better?" Because, honestly, if I had to choose right at that very moment, I probably would have a brain aneurism.

"Well, Pete's got that down-to-earth thing going for him," Brenda noted.

"But he also looks like he's an outdoor lover, which we all know doesn't agree with Chloe."

Mother and my BFF stared at me. It put me on the defensive. "Hey, it's not my fault I'm allergic to nature." More like nature hated me. Between sneezing and hives, I tended to gravitate to indoor activities.

"Anthony, on the other hand, seems more like the cerebral type and they do have the law thing in common."

"But they work together and he's the kind of guy who likes to have his clothes ironed." Brenda knew my dislike of all things related to laundry. "He'd probably insist on folding clothes."

Perhaps he did, but he also didn't mind having them torn off. However, I didn't share that tidbit. I still wondered how he'd made it back to his car without getting arrested for indecent exposure, given what we'd done to his poor suit.

"You act like I'm a slob. I iron my clothes. Kind of."

"Hanging them in the shower so you can steam them while you bathe is not ironing," Brenda pointed out.

"Shoving them in a drawer or closet out of sight also doesn't count as folding. It's barely even putting away," mother added.

"So what you're getting at is neither is right for me." I didn't know if I should sigh in relief or pout because they'd eliminated them both as prospects.

"No. See what I mean about always assuming the worst?" Brenda spoke to my mom, and I frowned.

"Have you been talking about me?"

"Of course we have, dear. Don't ask stupid questions."

"Well, keep it up and let me know what you come up with because the coffee's ready, the dads have tortured the men long enough, and if we don't get this fudge out there, I won't be responsible for the empty plate." It took a little shuffling, but I managed to hide the dent I'd made in the pile of chocolatey goodness.

We rejoined the guys to find them all getting along superbly well, even my two dates. They both stood and smiled at my entrance. Talk about a double whammy. Side by side, one slightly taller and wider than the other, they tempted me. Drew me. Made all thoughts of choosing melt into obscurity.

I wanted them both.

So, of course, being stubborn, I decided then and there I'd rather have neither.

Any man, or men, who could so frazzle me should earn a spot far, far away from me.

Later.

For the moment, I got sucked into the loveseat vortex between them where my hormones went crazy, probably from the excess chocolate and where I didn't protest when they each placed a possessive hand on my thighs. Slapping them would just fuel the amusement already happening at my expense.

The wine kept flowing, easing me, the conversation kept going, and I enjoyed myself.

A buzz against my hip saw my lawyer escort excusing himself for a moment as he took a call. Pete took advantage of the moment and slid his arm around the top of my shoulders, hugging me to his side. Fuzzy with wine, I allowed it. It did feel nice, even if it was kind of possessive.

Anthony reappeared in the doorway and signaled me. I slid out from Pete's grasp and went to see him.

"What's up? You look annoyed."

"Because I am. I have to leave."

"Work?"

"Of a sorts."

I shouldn't care if he had to leave, but a part of me did wilt in disappointment. I pretended nonchalance. "No biggie."

"To you maybe." Anthony shot a dark glare at Pete, and I realized that this evening was a façade.

Despite him and Pete acting as if they didn't mind sharing my attention, they did. Say what you would, jealousy was hot, and I was not immune to the flattery of it.

"I had fun." I blamed the alcohol for admitting it aloud.

"So did I."

"Even though my dads grilled you?"

"Because they did. It's obvious they love you very much. Your family is great."

"Yeah they are. I'm sure yours is too."

"I have no family."

"I'm so sorry."

He appeared startled. "Why?"

"Because it must have sucked losing your parents."

He shrugged. "It happened so long ago I don't even recall them. You can't miss something you never truly had." His phone buzzed again in his hand, insistently. He sighed. "I really hate that I have to leave. This wasn't how I'd planned the evening."

"I don't think this is what anyone planned for their evening," I added with a wry smile.

It earned me a chuckle. I saw Anthony to the door, his reluctance at leaving evident, if inexplicable. I'd made him spend the evening with my parents, crazy BFF, and a guy who made no bones about the fact he wanted in my pants. Anthony should have been looking for an excuse to escape hours ago.

"I wish I didn't have to go." Lo and behold, he sounded sincere.

"Hey, duty calls and all that." The joys of being a lawyer. Crime never slept, or behaved. Good thing, or I'd be out of a job.

"I want to see you again."

I played dumb. "I'm sure something will come up in front of a judge."

"Not for work. Before that. I want to take you on a date. A real one with just you and me."

"Why?" Couldn't we just skip to the sex and ignore all the other mumbo jumbo?

"Isn't it obvious?"

"Not really."

"I like you, Chloe Bailey. Probably more than I should."

As proclamations went, it was cute, even if he said it almost apologetically. But I didn't have time to ponder his meaning. He brushed his lips over mine.

Mmm, instant flames licked between my thighs. My mouth parted, my tongue found his, my fingers clutched his suited shoulders—

His groin buzzed against my hip.

"Damn phone," he muttered against my mouth.

"You should go." Before I had my way with him on the front step.

"I'll call you."

I should have said no; after all, I still didn't like Anthony. Insert loud buzzing noise and a sign flashing False.

Despite his dominance over me in the workplace, I could no longer say with deep conviction that I hated him. Damn it. I think I even liked him. Or at least enjoyed how he made my body feel.

Bzzzt! There went the false sign flashing again. Okay, okay, I also liked him on a social level, something the evening had just proved. The jury, however, remained hung on the whole, should I date him or not. Not to mention there was still a hulking werewolf in the living room behind me, looking to stake a claim on my pussy, something he clearly hadn't forgotten.

"I don't suppose I can ask you to take a cab home?" Anthony asked, his tone hopeful.

I arched a brow. "Do you really think that's going to happen?"

He chuckled. "Probably not. And, just so you know, despite the dog who insists on slobbering all over you, I will be calling you."

He would? Hey, wait a second. Did he just give me permission to sleep with Pete?

Before I could ask or blast him for his temerity in thinking he had a say, after another hard kiss, he left.

A sleek black sedan sat at the end of my parents' driveway, and Anthony paused to stare at me before sliding into the back. Figured he'd have a chauffeur to pick him up.

I watched the taillights speed off into the night, unsure of my feelings toward him. Unsure of what I wanted from him—other than more great sex.

"Hey, Chloe, are you going to come back in anytime soon?" Brenda shouted.

Which reminded me, I still had another six-foot dilemma to deal with.

When did my life get so complicated?

Chapter Six

When it came time for Pete to drive me home, despite the glasses of wine I'd imbibed, I remained much too aware of him. And by aware, I meant my whole body hummed with anticipation.

He didn't say much, but the hand on my leg, the one with the thumb stroking me, effectively let me know he wouldn't content himself with just a good night kiss. Honestly? I didn't think a good night kiss would cut it either.

He pulled into a parking lot across the street from my building and paid the attendant manning the booth. I couldn't help but notice he paid for more than just an hour.

I gulped.

Where was my assertive bitchy side? My sense of indignation at his presumption? I'm sure feminists everywhere would want to slap me silly for not standing up to him and demanding to know who he thought he was, assuming he'd get invited up. How dare he think I'd just fall into his arms and let him have his wicked way?

To them I said, fuck off.

I am a modern woman. A horny one. A lucky woman in the presence of a virile male who'd made no bones about the fact he wanted me.

How much did he want me, how far would he go? I didn't know or care. Would he call me in the morning or the next day? Again, I didn't give a damn.

The only thing I needed to know in that moment was how quickly we could make it to the elevator so I could maul him and get the naked party started. Seriously, after the appetizer of an evening, which I'd spent in a heightened state of awareness, I just wanted some relief.

As for Anthony? Yeah, I preferred not to dwell on my other suitor. Besides, I'd never agreed to anything exclusive. Just dinner. Besides, didn't he kind of give me carte blanch?

Exiting Pete's truck, I shivered as I stood on the pavement, the cool night air prickling my bare arms. I'd forgotten a sweater in my earlier haste to escape my apartment. I didn't lament my lack of exterior wear for long. Pete's warm arm encircled me as he guided me to the main entrance of my condo. I snuggled into him, enjoying his spicy scent comprised of cologne and man. Or, in this case, wolfman.

Too late it occurred to me to wonder if I needed to worry about him losing control of his furry self and me getting hurt. Would he turn into an animal in the heat of the moment? Guess I'd soon find out.

To my surprise, he didn't put any moves on me, even when we got into the elevator and the doors slid shut. Was I mistaken about his intentions? Perhaps he intended to take things slow. To escort me to my door then lope away on his merry way to chase rabbits under the stars.

I braced myself for a chaste kiss, or a hot one

that would leave me in need of a cold shower. As I yanked my keys from pocket, he took them from my damp, shaking hands, unlocking and opening the door for me, ushering me into my own home then shutting the portal behind us.

Before I could ask him if he wanted a drink, Pete yanked me into his arms, and his lips came crashing down hard against mine.

Sweet fucking heaven.

The sudden onslaught left me reeling, in a good way. I clung to his wide shoulders, letting him take possession of my mouth; his passion unleashed a powerful force. When he finally let me up for air, he growled.

"Finally. I've been wanting to do that all night."

Licking my swollen lips, I peered at him through heavily lidded eyes. "Then why did you wait so long?"

A boyish grin tilted his lips and my heart hammered in my chest. "Because I knew once I started, I wouldn't be able to stop."

"Says the man talking instead of kissing." My gift for sarcasm wasn't completely lost. I'd begun to worry.

"I'm not taking you in the hall. You deserve better for our first time."

Ooh, was this a dig on Anthony? Wait a second, had he guessed or somehow figured out— using his special werewolf sense of smell—that the hall was where I'd screwed the DA? I'd ask later. No use in ruining the mood.

Linking his callused fingers with mine, he led me to my bedroom, which I allowed. Truthfully, I enjoyed the dominance he insisted on showing. Tough on the outside didn't mean I didn't like someone else to take control when it came to sex. Too often my lovers assumed my height and attitude meant I took on an assertive tone in the bedroom. The change in roles, with first Anthony and now Pete, turned me on.

Once in my room, girly pink heaven replete with a fuchsia comforter trimmed in black stripes, a shocking bright shag rug and a chair shaped like a woman's high heel, I expected him to turn into an animal and tear my clothes from me.

Wrong again.

He lay down in the center of my bed as if he owned it and laced his fingers under his head. Regarding me with half-open eyes, eyes that somehow seemed to glow with a golden light, in a gruff tone, he ordered, "Strip."

"Excuse me?"

"I said strip. Show me that sexy body of yours. Do it slow."

"Just like that?" Under his avid stare? With the lights on and no music playing?

"Strip."

"And what will you be doing?"

"Watching of course." He grinned, his teeth flashing white. "And thinking about all the dirty things I am going to do. I've fantasized about this moment. Imagined you, naked and wet for me. If you only knew the things I want to do."

I couldn't hide the shudder that went through me at his decadent words. "Such as?"

"Strip and I'll tell you."

Out of my comfort zone, and yet oddly

turned on by his demand, I let my trembling fingers undo the loops of the first button on my blouse then the second.

"That's it, baby. Show me those perky tits of yours."

"Is perky another word for small?" I laughed, high-pitched in order to hide my embarrassment. I didn't have major boob action going. Good bras made it seem like I owned a C, but, in truth, I barely filled a B cup.

"You are the perfect size. A handful for me to grab and squeeze. Can you imagine my hands cupping you as my mouth devours your perfect nipples?"

My breathing hitched as my fingers continued to unbutton. "Who says I have perfect nipples?"

"I do. And I'm going to enjoy sucking on them until they are tight buds." My shirt split apart, revealing the roundness of my stomach and the edges of my bra. "Take it off."

I let the silk slide from my shoulders, revealing my black lace bra. I couldn't hold his intent stare and dropped my gaze, only to have it snagged on the massive bulge pushing at the front of his pants. Good grief. How big was he?

"Take off your bra. Show me your breasts."

Feeling at a disadvantage, I countered. "Isn't it your turn to take something off?"

He chuckled, the sexy sound tickling me. Goose bumps rose on my skin. "Fair enough."

Off came his shirt. My turn to stare and drool. Holy shit, the man was built like a god, a thick, body-building one. Tanned with bulging muscles, his chest had dark curly hair, which started up high between his pecs then narrowed down in a vee until it hit his waist and disappeared into his pants.

A quiver down south sent warm wetness to soak my already moist panties.

"Your turn," he growled.

My fingers fumbled at the clasp to my bra. It took me several tries before I managed to unhook it. I let it fall away and stood, shoulders back, my confidence returning under his ardent appraisal. Despite what I felt were shortcomings, how could I not feel beautiful when his words and his body's reactions said otherwise?

"Damn, baby. I want to fuck you so bad right now."

A small shudder went through me at his ardent words. "So why don't you?"

"Because you're not done stripping yet."

Was that all it would take for him to soothe the ache between my thighs?

I removed my pants quickly until I stood in only my panties. His breathing turned harsh. Panting. In that moment, I felt all-powerful. Sexy and sensual. Desirable.

I hooked my thumbs onto the elastic waist of my undies. I shimmied them down, glad I'd at least recently trimmed my girl parts, pretty certain at this point that he wouldn't care. My panties made it to the swell of my hips before he sprang from the bed.

I shrieked in surprise. He swallowed the sound with his lips. His callused fingers roamed my bare skin, heightening my arousal, making my need unbearable. Their journey already started, my undies finished their downward slide to pool around my feet, and I kicked them away while my hands wedged between our bodies to work at the closure of his jeans.

"Don't," he panted. "I want you too bad. Let me take care of you first."

"Um, what do you think I'm doing?"

"You'll get that after. I want a taste."

He no sooner mentioned it than I found myself on my back on the bed, my legs up over his shoulders, his face between my thighs.

Sweet freaking heaven. He went after my pussy with erotic intent, his moist tongue lapping me from my clit to the end of my cleft. Long wet strokes that had me writhing on my sheets, my fingers clawing and grasping as I tried to buck under the intense pleasure.

He didn't relent. He held me pinned, his tongue flicking my swollen nub until I screamed for mercy. Had I not come so many times the night before, I would have exploded then and there, but my body managed to hold on. Until he thrust two fingers into my quivering channel.

"Oh my fucking gawd." Yeah, I might have screamed it. How could I not when my orgasm crashed over me with unexpected power? I keened as he continued to bathe my clit with his mouth as his fingers pumped me, drawing out my climax.

I saw spots and I lacked the breath to speak. I could only draw ragged breaths. He relented, and I struggled to regain my senses, my body a shuddering mass of jelly. Something hard poked at my sex. I managed to open my eyes and oh my, what a sight.

Holding himself up on those muscled arms, Pete loomed over me, his eyes blazing with golden fire, his skin sheened in a light sweat, his dark hair flopping sexily over his forehead. The nudge between my thighs grew more insistent and I raised my hips, taking the tip of him in me. With a growl, he thrust.

I found enough breath to scream. Not in pain. I mean, yes, his thickness stretched me. Yes, I still throbbed from my orgasm, but damn it all, with him seated inside me, greedy wench that I was, I wanted more.

"Fuck me."

He growled again and, for a moment, his expression seemed more beast than man. It should have frightened me, but being a horny bitch, it turned me on. A quiver went through my pussy, and I knew he felt it by the way his head went back.

"Fuck me," I demanded again.

"Demanding wench," he grunted through a clenched jaw.

"Horny one," I gasped as he withdrew then slammed back in.

"I should be giving the orders," he grumbled, thrusting in and out.

"You were taking too long. Now shut up and give it to me!" I yelled as he began to piston me, his hard body slamming into mine, driving deep. I clung to him and enjoyed the ride. What else could I do with so many pounds of raw sexual energy between my thighs?

Pete pumped me, his thick cock stretching me nicely, decadently. His lips caught mine in a torrid embrace, our teeth clashing as our panting breaths mingled, the wildness of our coupling rendering us frantic.

My desire coiled tight, a spring ready to pop. My muscles clenched, tighter and tighter, until he fought my suctioning flesh, each stroke out making me cry, each thrust in making me scream. When I finally crested, I might have shattered glass, so loudly did I exclaim my enjoyment to the world. The muscles of my pussy milked him and with a primal howl, Pete joined me in orgasmic bliss.

Then squashed me flat as his mighty body collapsed upon mine in a heaving, sweaty mess.

Chapter Seven

"Get off," I squeaked. Shoving at the giant male squashing me, Pete regained enough of his wits—not many due to the lack of blood to his brain—to roll off me.

"Sorry," he mumbled.

My reply? A giggle. I'd never had a man collapse atop me before so obviously spent and sexually sated. I almost beat my chest caveman style, but I had more class than that. I smirked instead.

As I lay there panting and recovering, for the second time in as many days, a horrifying realization struck me. I'd done it again. "You forgot to put on a condom!"

"I'm clean. Lycans don't carry STDs."

"But you can make babies," I snapped. Never mind my birth control, it annoyed me to realize that he'd frazzled me enough to make me forget. Again.

"Speaking of which, how many would you like?"

Good thing I was lying down already, else I might have fallen.

Please tell me he's joking.

I propped myself up to peek at him and caught the big grin on his face. Mini heart attack averted, I frowned. "That was not funny."

"Sorry. I guess you didn't know my kind can tell when a woman is on the pill. Your scent is different."

Disturbing and reassuring at the same time. "Has anyone ever told you that the whole smell thing is freaky? I mean, now you've got me paranoid about stinking."

"We don't perceive odors the same way humans do. To us, they are a unique mark of a person."

"Or a sign they haven't bathed."

He laughed. "Think of your scent as a fingerprint. Bathed or not, perfumed, sweaty, it doesn't matter. Everyone's scent is different. Some, I'll admit, are more appealing than others. Like yours, for instance."

"I smell good?"

"Better than good. From the first moment I got a whiff, I've wanted to taste you."

"So I'm the equivalent of a freshly baked cookie to you?"

"Yummier."

As compliments went, I could live with it. "Since you're on the topic, what else should I know about Lycans? You won't bite me, will you, and mark me as your bitch?"

"No," he said with a snort. "Nor will you turn into a wolf or catch a disease or anything else the crazy media has mistakenly mentioned over the years. Lycans are born, not made."

"Good to know. And other than the whole furry thing and smelling, what other special powers do you have?"

"We recuperate quickly." He rolled until he

caged my body, his upper arms holding him over me, the hard head of his prick poking.

Lucky for me, it turned out, when it came to sex with the right guy, I could go again too.

The warm sunlight bathing my face woke me and I stretched under my sheets, my muscles pleasantly sore. Again.

Fuck!

In vivid detail, I remembered the events of the night before. The passion. The wild sex. The out-of-this-world orgasms. And with a werewolf of all things.

What the hell was happening to me? First Anthony. Then Pete. Who would I screw next? An itty-bitty fairy? The mailman?

Forget Godzilla destroying the city. *Here comes Chloe on an uncontrollable nympho rampage. Put in your earplugs, tie down the breakables because my screaming orgasms are a force to be reckoned with.* Also very addictive.

I finally understood why some people craved sex so much. With the right person, or people, it was freaking amazing. I mean, don't get me wrong, I'd climaxed before. I had plenty of experience, but the sex with Anthony and Pete... It blew those experiences away.

We were talking the hurricane of orgasms instead of a gentle spring shower. Just thinking about the things they did to my body and how I'd responded, a wild woman with no inhibitions.

Surely that wasn't a twinge of lust. Surely my pussy didn't need more attention? Greedy thing. I would have slapped it if I didn't think it would enjoy it so much.

Despite all the sex, I wanted more. I might have even begged for it had I woken beside my newest lover. Fuck me. My second lover in two days. *I am such a slut.*

At least I didn't have to face my newest furry embarrassment. Like Anthony, Pete seemed to have vanished in the night. Whether or not he'd return, like a dog with a stick, remained to be seen.

I'd certainly never expected Mr. Hotshot DA to come back for seconds. Given that unexpected twist, I no longer wanted to wager the same on Pete, although, I could probably safely bet that Anthony wouldn't come sniffing around anymore now that Pete staked his claim.

But only if Anthony finds out.

What was I thinking? I didn't want one man in my life, let alone two. However, I couldn't deny I'd never felt more sexually satisfied. And, hey, the law did say women should do their part to keep the male population content. Of course, they meant by marrying them and popping out babies. I didn't intend to go that far, but at least by fucking them, I was practicing the whole procreation bit. Some could even say I studied *hard.*

Damn, I'd have to remember to tell that to Brenda later when she bugged me. I bet she'd find that outrageously funny. I know I did.

Enough of that. Time to greet the day. Or late morning at least, judging by the light flooding my room. I flung the sheets back, the air of my room kissing my naked body and raising bumps on my skin.

"Well, good morning to me," a husky voice

said.

Yeah, I screamed like a little girl. Or a woman who just about pissed herself as Pete's voice rumbled from the doorway to my room.

It appeared as if I'd erred in thinking he'd left because there he leaned against the doorjamb, a pair of steaming mugs in hand, wearing only a pair of boxers. Low-hanging, thigh-hugging, erection-clinging boxers. I was pretty sure the shudder that went through my pussy was a mini orgasm. No man should ever look that hot in the morning.

"What are you doing?" I blurted out.

"Other than admiring the view? Bringing you coffee. I wasn't sure how you liked it, though, so it's black. Do you want me to add some cream and sugar?"

I already had enough cream pooling between my thighs, thank you very much. As for sugar, my mouth watered for something a little more tart and *meaty*. I really needed to do something about the nympho thing I had going on. It just wasn't natural for me to lust like a bitch in heat. Great, now I couldn't help but picture myself on my hands and knees getting it from Pete as he howled.

First thing Monday, I needed to make an appointment with my doctor for a lobotomy. Or at least hit the pharmacy for some of that cream that numbed gums, anything to deaden the tingles down below. "Black is fine."

I held out my hand and curled my fingers around the heated ceramic, ducking my head as I took a sip instead of meeting his amused gaze. I tried to lounge casually, acting as if posing naked on my bed was a daily occurrence. It wasn't, but yanking up the covers now, after he'd already seen all my goods—as well as licked them—seemed kind of moot.

"So what do you want to do today?" Pete asked.

Do? As in together? I choked on the strong java, spewing dark liquid over my white Egyptian sheets. Fuck. Fuck. Fuck. Where would I find another set of them on sale? Because bleach was not something I used, ever, not since the incident. We'd leave it at it had taken me several paychecks to replace my wardrobe.

"It's Sunday. I, um, usually have brunch with Brenda." Would he take the hint and make his way home like a good boy—wagging his tail behind him?

I needed alone time to gather my wits and slap myself back to sanity.

"Sounds good. What time?"

"Soon." The sooner the better before I caved to temptation and mauled him.

"I probably shouldn't go wearing last night's clothes." He grinned at me. "We wouldn't want to give Brenda the wrong impression." He winked.

I winced. Way to remind me of my new sexual deviance. At least this time I'd not ruined his outfit, although it wasn't because I'd not wanted to. His clothes had almost gone the same route as poor Anthony's. And if he kept tempting me with those sexy boxers, he might end up leaving commando.

Here comes nympho Chloe, slut extraordinaire, destroyer of garments and champion stainer of difficult-to-find bargain sheets. If this kept up, I'd need an emergency fund to replace the goods I kept damaging. Or, at the very least, have a new rule for guys I brought home intending to fuck—*please disrobe before entering my apartment or I won't be held liable for damage.*

I almost snickered at the thought. Then couldn't help picturing it. My across the hall neighbor, Mrs. Goudry, would get such a thrill if she peeked out her spyhole and saw a parade of men—or at least two—stripping down naked before entering my place.

"Tell you what, baby. Why don't you shower and get dressed while I pop out and grab a fresh set of clothes?"

More commandments? I should have told him where to go. I'd shower and dress, if and when I wanted, thank you very much. The fact I planned to do so the minute he left had nothing to do with his instructions and more with the fact I needed to wash the scent of sex off my skin before I tracked it all over my apartment. Instead, I just said, "Okay."

"I've programmed my number into your cell, so if you need me, just call."

Presumptuous didn't come close to describing his actions and I would have told him so in no uncertain terms had he not taken that moment to approach me with a ripple of muscle that hypnotized me. I could only stare as he bent over and grabbed his discarded clothes.

He yanked up his jeans first, hiding his tool of pleasure. Sniff. I almost waved goodbye. Then on went his shirt, covering his male perfection. Next time, I'd have to work harder at destroying it so he'd have to go around shirtless.

Next time? Great. I already planned seconds. Hmm. Maybe thirds.

Finished dressing, Pete faced me. Seemed it

was my turn for a little attention.

"Damn but I wish we could spend the morning in bed," he growled. Well, at least that made two of us. His ardent gaze swept over my nude form and I'll admit I preened, arching my back to push out my tits and tilting my hips in invitation. Might as well act the wanton slut all the way.

He dove on me, ravaging me with his mouth, his hands roaming my body.

Yes. Yes. Yes.

"Any chance we can call Brenda and postpone brunch?"

Way to bring me back to reality. "No," I panted. BFFs did not blow off their Sunday morning rituals for sex.

Okay, not entirely true because my main reason for not blowing off brunch for sex was because my tummy needed fuel and MJ's served the best breakfast in town, or the best I could afford on my paycheck.

"We can't cancel." Look at me. Finally saying no.

Unfortunately, he listened.

A last heart-stopping kiss, a suck of my nipple, which left me gasping and writhing, a naughty wink, and away Pete went.

But he'd return.

I couldn't decide if the idea excited me, angered me, or frightened me. Whether I was ready or not, Pete the werewolf appeared determined to date me. Or fuck me. Or something.

I'd yet to figure out which category he fell in, but I should probably ask. Then I could lay some ground rules. Like no leaving me horny in the morning.

Seriously. What man kissed a woman breathless, teased a nipple, and then left before satisfying a throbbing pussy? It was wrong. Just plain wrong. I wanted to whimper with the injustice of it.

I should teach him a lesson by masturbating. Yeah. Take care of my own sexual needs. I didn't need a man to orgasm. But I did need one, apparently, if I wanted an earth-shattering one.

Sigh. Hard to settle for a little O when you knew with a little patience you could get the big one. Gulping the rest of my now cold coffee down, I hopped out of bed and glanced at the clock. I had just over an hour to get ready for brunch. It occurred to me to warn Brenda we'd have company, but given her humor at my expense the previous night at dinner, I thought screw it. I'd show up with my werewolf lover and, if I was lucky, she'd choke on her mimosa or spit it down the front of her shirt. Entertainment either way.

As I showered, I couldn't help replay events from the dinner, and despite the night spent with Pete and the planned morning with him, my mind kept straying to Anthony. Sure, he'd implied he'd call me again. That he wanted me despite his rivalry with another man. But that had been before I slept with Pete. Would he still want to pursue me if he found out? And if he did show up or call, would I tell him?

It seemed dishonest not to. So let's assume I did tell Anthony—*I slept with a werewolf*—and he didn't have a hissy fit and storm out. Then what? Could I seriously handle having two lovers? Could they?

The new laws encouraging threesomes didn't

mean men easily accepted them. Jealousy thrived, as did psychiatric practices, especially those specializing in couples counseling. Balancing the needs and emotions of a pair of people was difficult; add in a third person and it turned into a very fine balancing act. Many failed. It took a solid friendship to handle sharing.

My parents were a good example of when it could work. Brenda's forays into threesomeville, on the other hand, were a handbook on how it could go wrong. She kept the restraining orders framed on her wall as a reminder.

But why the hell was I even thinking of them in terms of three? One man was too many for me to handle right now. Two? Not in the cards. Who to choose, though? Seeing as how I'd not tried harder to ditch Pete, I was pretty sure I'd made my choice on the winner. *I think.* Or did I want Anthony? No, it had to be Pete. I worked with, well technically against, Anthony. Work and play didn't mix.

There. Decision done. I would keep Pete as my fuck friend. Nothing more.

Soaping, rinsing, shaving, and not just the legs, I erased the previous night from my skin while carefully avoiding rubbing too intently. My pussy was already swollen and sensitive enough without me compounding the problem.

I'd just wrapped a towel around my hair and another around my body when the knock came at my door. It seemed my wolf had returned already.

I didn't bother to peek through the hole before opening. Dumb. I know. City girls should always do things with an eye on safety, but then again, I didn't expect Anthony to come striding in holding a Starbucks coffee and a paper bag.

"Morning," he said. He took in my attire—towel, wet skin, and slightly dazed expression—and smiled. "A very good morning."

A spurt of pleasure shot through me. *He came back!*

Keep the judgments and speeches for someone else. Right or wrong, I couldn't help my happiness at seeing him, the heat in my crotch, or my increased pulse rate. I also couldn't stop myself from stupidly saying, "What are you doing here?"

"I felt bad about how the evening ended. So I brought amends." Apparently, he didn't mean the coffee or treat in the bag.

Only once his lips pressed against mine did it occur to me to protest. Occurred but didn't happen, as he once again melted my resistance, wiped away my reasoning, and made me reevaluate my decision to give him the brush off.

When he let me up for air, because he had to set his offerings down so he could make a proper grab for me, sanity reasserted itself.

I darted out of reach with a squeaked, "You shouldn't be here."

"Why?" He opened his mouth to say more then stopped. I think he sniffed, hard to tell because he'd partially turned away from me to face the bedroom. His entire body went rigid, and damn it all, if I didn't know he'd guessed who spent the night.

Forget the regular hand-caught-in-the-cookie-jar embarrassment. It didn't compare to pussy-caught-on-another-dick one. I blushed beet red when he faced me to say, "I see you didn't spend the night alone."

"I—um—that is…" Hold on one second. Why was I embarrassed or even thinking of apologizing? I'd made no promises to this guy. Hell, we weren't even dating. We'd fucked—once.

He'd invited himself to dinner.

He showed up with Starbucks—my favorite.

But those things didn't mean he owned me. Didn't make us exclusive. We were nothing to each other. Nothing except extremely compatible in the bedroom.

Chin up, I found my tits and my pride. "Pete spent the night." There. I'd said it. Take it or leave it. I refused to hide or pretend. Nor did I feel the need to excuse myself. Much.

I waited for a jealous outburst and readied myself to blast him with curse words not heard often outside a biker bar.

I prepared for him to stalk off, slamming my door in its frame. I even braced myself for possible tears. Not likely given Anthony's usually dominant attitude, but hey, you never knew. Sometimes the toughest guys ended up the biggest crybabies.

He did none of those things. Nope. The bastard went with option D and drew me back into his arms so he could kiss me. He didn't speak a word. Just kissed me and groped me. The next thing I knew, the towel hit the floor and his hand slid between my thighs, rubbing across my clit, making thinking almost impossible.

I retained enough wits to know we should stop. The smart thing to do was to move away. The sane option involved me saying no. Apparently, I'd inherited my great aunt Matilda's crazy streak because instead I rode his fingers on my way to nirvana.

It didn't take much for my pussy to get slick. My body, already sensitized by all the erotic attention I'd recently been the recipient of, plus the fact I appeared to have entered a late twenties sexual peak, all meant he found me more than willing to enjoy the pleasure he seemed intent on bestowing.

"Oh gawd," I moaned as he hissed, "That's it, come for me."

How I wanted to come. The forceful thrust of his digits, the thumb stroking my nub, the way his teeth tugged at my lower lip... The man knew just which buttons to push, what to do to turn me on. Add to that the fact that I stood there naked while he did this to me fully clothed. Say what you would, it added a whole other element to our tryst, a taboo one that made the whole thing even hotter.

In the midst of a moan, we gained an audience, shattering my almost-there orgasm.

I raised eyelids, heavy with passion, to see Pete standing nearby, watching.

Oops. I'd forgotten to lock the door. One would almost think I wanted to get caught.

Before things got really awkward, I opened my mouth to speak, to warn Anthony, but his lips claimed mine, stealing my voice. I pushed at his shoulders to get his attention, but his fingers found and stroked my sweet spot. Sweet heaven. I couldn't help myself from enjoying it, even knowing we had an audience.

My eyes closed for a moment as pure pleasure vibrated through me. When I opened them again, Pete still stared, his eyes glowing golden and his hand... Oh damn, his hand cupped his erection, evident even with his jeans.

As if he knew he'd caught my attention, he rubbed himself, matching his strokes to Anthony's finger thrusts. I'd never understood the attraction of voyeurism until that moment.

Having Pete watch as another man caressed me, the arousal evident in his expression, totally took my pleasure to another level. Heat roared through my veins and I crested, my whole pussy clenching around Anthony's fingers, my climax vocalizing itself in a shrill cry. Once again, my eyes shuttered themselves as I basked in the ecstasy. As my pleasure ebbed from my glowing body, the only sound was that of my panting, but in that silence, I could feel, with an instinct every woman probably owned, the tenseness spicing the air.

Pete broke the stalemate. "Sorry to interrupt, but I think we're going to be late for brunch if we don't get a move on."

Despite his seeming enjoyment of the impromptu porn show, Pete's tight, clipped tone threw an effective cold bucket of reality over my actions. Mortified—my throbbing pussy not willing to release Anthony's still flexing fingers—I stepped away from Anthony, who wore a smug smile.

I flushed. Red from head to toe because, really, what woman wanted to get found being finger fucked by the guy she'd literally just fucked—oh damn it all, this was getting too damned complicated.

Off I stalked, and I mean stomped, to my room, muttering under my breath about men with no boundaries and not forgetting to engage my locks. Probably not the brightest idea leaving much-too-pleased-with-himself Anthony in a room with a jealous and angry werewolf, but in my ire, I'd gone past the point of caring right into the I-hope-they-kill-each-other zone.

I totally felt like the rope in a tug of war. Yanked in two directions. Everyone wanting to win. Everyone wanting to a piece of me. No one caring if they stressed me and stretched me to my breaking point.

Screw that. If they wanted to play games, then they could play them with each other. I had a brunch to make and a gurgling belly to satisfy. Bedroom door slammed shut, music cranked so I didn't have to listen if they went at each other again, I dressed quickly. Armed with clothing and still annoyed, I didn't return to the living room. I didn't want to face or talk to either of them.

Grabbing my purse, which held my keys, I exited via my window onto the fire escape. I know, I know. Cowardly. I should face my problems and deal with them. Blah, blah, blah.

Maybe later when I felt more like myself. Currently, my tummy rumbled with hunger. My pussy griped it was still horny. And emotionally? I was totally annoyed.

I needed a mimosa, stat!

Down I clambered, the metal fire escape creaking and groaning, but, according to the report building management posted on the lobby corkboard, completely safe. Ha. I wondered how many greenbacks it cost them for that lie.

I didn't plunge to my death, the first good thing to happen that morning, and ended up in the alley. I trotted out from between the two buildings and peered up and down the sidewalk. I didn't spot either of the idiots stalking me.

Quickly, with a hand outstretched, I flagged a cab, not wanting to risk them spotting me as I walked the ten blocks to the restaurant. Diving into the back seat of a yellow death trap, which drove as if chased by the hounds of hell, I made it to the restaurant alive—but surely missing a few years of my life.

Entering the greasy spoon, I immediately spotted Brenda. She waved as I weaved through the tables until I reached her. Plopping into the seat across from her, I snagged her half drunk beverage. I downed it, despite her indignant, "Hey, that was mine!"

"I needed it more than you," I said as an excuse when I finished chugging it.

"Apparently. What the hell has you looking so frazzled?" Brenda asked after she'd mimed two more drinks to our waitress.

I held up an extra two fingers. One each wouldn't cut it. Not today.

At her raised brow, I explained. "Pete spent the night."

"Damn. You are on a lucky roll," Brenda exclaimed.

"Not really. When Pete left this morning to get changed, Anthony showed up."

"Say what?"

"Anthony showed up. Found out Pete had spent the night then proceeded to seduce me, which is of course when Pete returned."

Brenda's eyes widened until they rivaled the saucer that held the little packages of milk and cream. "Oh. My. God. What happened next?"

A peek show and an orgasm. Not details I felt like sharing quite yet. Or at least not until I'd had a chance to dissect why I'd let it happen.

"I don't know. I got dressed and left through my bedroom window."

My best friend blinked at me. "Did you say you left?"

"Yup."

Our waitress arrived with our four drinks and I ordered up some food. The hungry man—in this case nympho—special for me, a fruit salad for Brenda.

As soon as our server left, Brenda leaned forward and, in a whisper that was probably heard by everyone in the place, said "Are you telling me that you left a werewolf alone with the guy he caught you fooling around with?"

"Yup." When she said it so starkly, it didn't sound so smart. So I drank. The alcohol didn't make my choice sound any brighter, but at least my insides got a warm fuzzy glow.

"Oh, your poor apartment."

My forehead wrinkled. "You think they'll destroy it?"

"Don't you? Seriously, Chloe, how the heck did you get into this situation? I mean, two hunks, vying for your attention. And you decide to come here? Are you nuts?"

"What else was I supposed to do?" I grumbled. "I thought I'd keep Pete. Then Anthony showed up and kissed me. Next thing I know, I'm riding his hand and questioning my choice when Pete comes back. I panicked."

"I'll say you did."

"So what do you think I should have done then, smartass?"

"Both of them, duh."

"At once?"

"Come on. Don't tell me you've never had a threesome?"

"No."

An incredulous, "But your parents are in a triad," burst out of her.

"And? It doesn't mean they're into, you know, that kind of kink." And I'd really rather scratch my eyes out than imagine if they did.

Brenda laughed. "Oh, Chloe. You are such a prude sometimes."

"Am not. I'm very sexually open-minded."

"Yet it never occurred to you, that instead of running away from two men who obviously want you, to instead embrace the opportunity to have them both take you?"

"They don't even like each other."

"But they like you."

Not anymore, I was sure. By now, they'd probably caught on to my escape.

I drained drink number one and pushed the empty glass away. I tugged drink number two closer. "I'm not ready for a relationship. Especially not a complicated one."

"Oh, Chloe. I know you've got some trust issues because of what that asshole did."

"This has nothing to do with my ex."

"It has everything to do with him. You thought he was the one. You even used the M word."

M word as in moving in together. "Yeah,

well, that was before I caught on to the fact he was a lying, cheating asshole. I've realized since then I don't need a permanent man in my life. I'm perfectly content as a single gal. No one to eat the last slice of cold pizza. No one hogging the bed or remote."

"No one to hold you and tell you they love you."

"Then leave you right after so they can fuck the little blonde they hired as their secretary."

"Not all men are like that."

"But I have no assurance Pete or Anthony won't be."

"You can't spend the rest of your life assuming all guys are going to cheat on you."

"I'm not. But I can spend a few years just using them for sex before I make any rash decisions."

"Somehow I don't think you have that long."

"What's that supposed to mean? What do you know that I don't? Am I dying? Is the world ending? Has that space lab your dad works for discovered some huge meteor hurling our way, about to end life as we know it?"

"What? No. Nobody's dying."

"Then what the hell are you talking about?"

"Remember how you wanted to take a few years to decide what you want. Don't look now," Brenda whispered, "but my prediction is, like it or not, you're not going to get that long. It seems your men have teamed up and tracked you down."

She had to be mistaken. I'd not told them where I was going. I'd snuck out.

Apparently, I needed to work on my subterfuge skills.

The men, whom I thought I'd evaded, slid in on either side of me on the bench, squashing me between them.

This was going beyond determined to pursue right into freaky. Could anyone say stalker?

"How did you find me?" For one insane moment, I couldn't help picturing Anthony waving my dirty underwear under Pete's nose and then the pair of them loping off to hunt me, Pete playing the part of blood hound, nose to the ground following my scent. Disturbing, yet so vivid. Damn, the mimosas in this place were good!

"I texted your mother," Pete said, signaling our waitress and bursting my odd theory. "She very kindly let me know where you and Brenda enjoyed getting together for brunch."

Someone really needed to have a talk with my matchmaking mother. "And you just decided to show up? Did you not get the hint I needed some time alone?"

"Yes. But we chose to ignore it," Anthony answered, not sounding in the least repentant about the decision. "It occurred to us that we needed to speak."

"We? As in all three of us?"

"Yes."

"There's nothing to say." I yelped as Brenda kicked me under the table. "What? There isn't."

Brenda frowned at me. "I disagree. If you won't say anything, I will."

"Don't you dare." I glared at my best friend.

"I will dare because you're being an idiot. They're making an effort. The least you could do is hear them out."

"No one ever asked them to. And no, I don't have to listen. If I wanted to hear them argue about who gets to keep me, I would have stayed. Smarter men would have gotten the hint. I guess they let their little heads make the decision to follow."

"Am I the only one offended by the reference to little?" Pete looked around the table. "I've been called many things before, but little was never one of them."

"Fine. I stand corrected. You're not little in that department, either of you," I added pointedly when Pete threw a smug in-your-face look of triumph at Anthony. "Which is probably why neither of you are thinking clearly. Obviously, there's a lack of blood flow to the intelligent part of your body."

Brenda snickered. "Damn. You guys are good. Complimented and insulted in one fell swoop. But we're getting off track. Nice try, Chloe."

"What do you mean?"

"In case you hadn't noticed, your pleasant demeanor hasn't frightened them off."

No. It hadn't. Neither Anthony nor Pete showed any sign of budging. What would it take?

Or would my BFF do the job for me? Brenda would have made a great matador. She grabbed the bull by the horns and stopped it dead in its tracks.

"Let me ask you, boys, just what are your intentions toward my best friend?"

"Are you asking if we're going to propose?"

I almost choked on a mouthful of mimosa. "Good gawd no!"

Pete snickered at my exclamation and I elbowed him. As if I hurt the beast. He didn't so much as flinch.

Brenda forged ahead. "Nothing that drastic. Yet." She ignored my glare. "I won't go into details; I'll leave that to her. But suffice it to say, my BFF has trust issues. Big ones. Be that as it may, she still likes both of you. Or as much as she's capable of, given she's an ornery bitch who thinks relationships are for dumbasses."

Eloquently put except for the liking part. I did not like them. Much.

"Are you saying that after what happened last night we're not in a relationship?" Pete asked in a low rumble.

"Yes," I replied quickly. "Or do I mean no? I mean, no, we're not in a relationship."

"What about you, lawyer dude?" Brenda pinned him with a stare that might have looked menacing to a chipmunk.

Trust Anthony to make the dirty things we did sound snooty.   "I assumed given our coital relations that we were."

Was I the only one who knew the meaning of hook-up? "No we're not. It was just sex."

"I disagree," Anthony countered. "We might have let attraction initially bring us together, but having spent some time with you and your family, as well as having dealt with you on a professional level, I freely admit you intrigue me. I want to get to know you on more than just a sexual level."

"Ditto what he said," Pete added.

"I'm sorry, but did you just say in some roundabout way that you like me?"

"Yes. I like you. Very much in fact."

Thankfully, the restaurant didn't have any flies, or I might have caught a few with my gaping maw.

Rich, suave dudes did not just announce in greasy spoons that they liked a girl. Didn't their prep school handbooks have a rule against that? "I can't believe you said that."

"Said that I like you? What's wrong with that?" Anthony asked.

"Everything. We barely know each other and you're not supposed to just, I don't know, blurt it aloud, where people can hear it."

Pete snickered. "And how else would we do it? This isn't some romance novel or sappy movie. This is real life. We like you and we want you to like us. I guess we could have pretended to act all cool and shit. Maybe given you the runaround and kept you guessing, but frankly, I'm not into playing juvenile games. I know what I want and that happens to be you."

Don't melt. Don't melt. Don't melt.

"The dog might have put it rather crudely, but aptly. I don't see a need to play games or to hide my intentions. You seem like a woman who appreciates honesty and forthrightness. By declaring our intentions upfront, such as our intention to engage you in a relationship based on more than just coitus, we hope to gain your regard and trust."

"But I don't want a relationship." My sulky tone went well with my jutting lower lip.

"Perhaps not an emotional one as of yet, but that is only because we are in the early stages. The discovery stage, if you will. I, for one, wish to pursue it further."

"If you ignore the fact that I'm not as fancy as lawyer boy over there, then yeah, I think you're hot, but I also like the fact you're smart and funny."

"Don't you mean supercilious and sarcastic?" I retorted. "Or, in the words of my BFF, an ornery bitch."

Pete frowned. "I wouldn't use the B word. My kind doesn't like it. However, what some people call ornery, I label assertive and no-nonsense. It's a rare and attractive quality."

"As for myself, I enjoy the fact you don't simper or couch your word or actions. Do you have any idea how refreshing it is to meet a woman who is not afraid to be herself? To speak her mind? And, not only that, one with a passion that is unrestrained and really quite tempting?" Anthony tossed his two cents in, flustering me even further.

"We are not having this conversation in a restaurant," I moaned, laying my head face-first down on the table. Figured it was sticky. Great. Now I'd have a jam mark on my forehead.

"We wouldn't be if you hadn't scurried off," Pete said, scolding me.

"I did not scurry. I climbed." Yeah, way to tell them!

I pried my face from the table and chugged the rest of my orange drink.

"We noticed, hence why we followed."

"And found me." I spit on a napkin and scrubbed at the jam. I wished I could wipe the male problem sandwiching me so easily. "So where do we go from here? Flip a coin? Arm wrestle? Or have you already decided?"

"I don't think I follow."

"How do we decide which of you gets me?"

Dead silence.

"Well?" I asked. "Because I sure as hell am not choosing. I'm not the one who wants a relationship. You guys are. So how are we going to decide who gets first shot?"

Over the top of my head, Pete spoke to Anthony. "She expects us to choose?"

Duh. Hadn't I just said that?

Brenda sighed and shook her head. "Do I have to do everything?"

I shot her daggers. She didn't die on the spot.

"In case you haven't noticed, Chloe is uncomfortable with the whole doing-two-guys-at-once thing."

"So are we," Pete answered.

Anthony shifted beside me. "But, given the situation, the dog and I have agreed we could share."

"On a rotational basis, of course."

"Gee, how nice of you to make this decision without me," I snapped.

Brenda kicked me again in the same spot, making an already blossoming bruise bigger. I'd have to get her back later. Maybe by having a giant cake sent to her place and making her gain five pounds. I knew her weakness and I wasn't afraid to exploit it in the name of revenge.

"We're sorry about the presumption. However, given our rivalry seemed to make you uncomfortable, we came to an understanding."

"Did this understanding involve any violence that resulted in the destruction of my apartment?" I braced myself for the worst.

"We're not animals," Pete said with a chuckle. "Well, not all of the time at any rate."

Way to remind me. I still had so many

questions about the whole werewolf thing, but more pressing matters required my blunt attention. "So, let me see if I've got this straight. You're going to take turns, what, screwing me until one of you ends up a winner?" Sounded like fun. But they presumed a lot. "And what if I want neither of you?"

For some reason, that made them both rock with laughter. I didn't find my comment that amusing, but apparently, the matter was already decided. Like it or not, I had two men in my life. Men who would share me. Starting Monday.

When I pleaded for time to think, they graciously agreed to let me have the rest of my Sunday alone.

Of course, I regretted that the moment they left, each planting a kiss on my lips that made me want to forget I wanted neither and drag them back to my apartment.

If you asked me, they did it on purpose. Kissed me until I was turned on then leave so I couldn't say no when they came to spend quality time with me. So long as that time meant orgasms, I guess I'd have to tolerate it.

Damn, the things I had to put up with as a law-abiding citizen.

Chapter Eight

After my Sunday brunch—where under the disbelieving eyes of my new lovers, I proceeded to demolish the biggest breakfast on the menu plus several mimosas—I went home. Alone.

I spent the day doing menial things. Cleaning, cursing, laundry, kicking things, vacuuming, wishing certain someones would ignore my request to go away and call. Or show up. Or something.

No need to state the obvious. Anyone could have seen I was a contrary mess. On the one hand, I didn't want Pete or Anthony or what they offered. On the other, I craved the pleasure I'd found in their arms, craved them, which, in turn, scared and irritated the hell out of me.

I wasn't happy at how things turned out, yet, at the same time, what would I have changed? To deny myself either seemed foolish. Not to mention, I couldn't deny a certain excitement, a spark if you will, that my life had lacked before.

I'd gone from boring single gal to femme fatale with two men. Me! Boring Chloe, the nympho lover of a pair of hotties. Should I invest in a female version of Viagra to keep up with all the sex about to come my way?

Maybe later, because at the moment my body

seemed more than ready for the upcoming erotic marathon scheduled to start on Monday. Heck, despite two nights of wicked orgasms, I craved more. In retrospect, I regretted my hasty decision to demand some alone time, which those jerks graciously allowed.

In doing so, had I scared them off? If yes, then good riddance. I doubted it, though. They seemed pretty bound and determined to become a part of my life. But for how long? I mean, who was I kidding? Did I really expect these two hunks to stick the distance? To put up with all my foibles and mood swings, which even I could admit sometimes bordered on the irrational, especially before my period. Sure they liked my attitude now, but after a couple days of my mouthiness, a few bouts in bed, they'd get bored quick enough. Really, what did I have to keep a werewolf and a rich lawyer intrigued? Nothing but me.

Damn, that sounded deprecating. Low self-esteem be gone. I did have some redeeming qualities. I had to; after all, Brenda had remained my friend all these years, but then again, I'd had plenty of time to brainwash her into thinking I was cool. My mom also made really good cookies, which probably helped.

If I looked past those forced to like me—and those bribed with home baked treats—my track record bore some utter failures. I couldn't help but flashback to my last boyfriend and most serious relationship thus far in my life.

Stupid me, I thought I'd met *the one*. Similar interests. A decent sex life. Good conversation and everything else the books and articles claimed were the right ingredients for a lasting commitment.

I'd even contemplated the M word. Moving in together and sharing closet space and letting his toothbrush live alongside mine.

Wow, was I ever wrong about him. About us. I'd also taken a major hit to my self-esteem and my heart still carried a hefty bruise. Everyone said I'd get over him. And I had. If the apocalypse arrived, as the doomsayers predicted, and I had a loaded shotgun and a zombie was chasing him, intent on eating his brains, I'd save the bullet—I'd probably need it, given the asshat wouldn't feed the undead for long with his puny pea-sized noggin.

Nope, I didn't harbor any fondness for my ex and it wasn't that I didn't like men. I did. But, he'd left me with something—other than an STD.

Doubt.

If I couldn't keep my dork of an ex intrigued, then what chance did I have with hunks one and two? Once they got over the initial thrill, I could totally picture one leaving and without the rivalry to keep the other intrigued, I'd probably also lose number two and I'd end up single again.

Alone.

Only me and…no one.

Not even a cat.

How depressing. Maybe I should invest in my own set of lovebirds.

Was it any wonder I didn't want to let them into my carefully guarded heart?

Exhausted, I fell asleep early that night, but it didn't prove restful.

I found myself in the woods. How or why, I couldn't have said. I just was suddenly there. And I didn't like it.

City girls usually didn't prance around the forest at night. The lack of lights and traffic sounds made us nervous. Or, at least, it freaked me out, which was why I couldn't figure out how I ended up running in the woods not wearing a stitch of clothing.

Startled, I stopped my mad dash and ogled my nude body.

"Where the hell are my jammies?" Because I distinctly recalled putting some on. Cute ones too, with teddy bears holding hearts.

A crackle of dry leaves and twigs getting crushed made my head whip around. Not really reassuring, given my location and the unfriendly greenery surrounding me. Who knew what lurked behind the trunks and foliage? Rabid squirrels? Slavering chipmunks.

Don't laugh. They might be small but they had sharp, pointy teeth.

I squinted at the shadows around me. As if I could see a thing. Apparently, clothes weren't the only thing I'd forgotten to bring. A flashlight and a GPS would have helped. I figured I must be dreaming, but it didn't reassure, especially when a snuffling noise saw me turning and confronting a golden-eyed stare. The unblinking yellow gaze floated in the darkness as if disembodied, and I swallowed.

Dream or not, I couldn't help a frisson of fear. "This isn't real," I muttered.

The eyes came closer and a hint of musk, a male scent mixed with something animal-like, came to me. What had my subconscious conjured? I took a step back, the mossy ground underfoot tickling the soles of my bare feet. The eyes drew closer and a shiver swept me, leaving my nipples hard and my skin pebbled.

A low growl rumbled. I couldn't tell if it was a happy playful one or the I'm-about-to-eat-you variety. Nor did I really care.

Despite all the documentaries I'd watched advising against it, but unable to stop myself, I pivoted and took flight.

At least dream me could run, long-legged strides with barely a stumble, practically a miracle given I couldn't see two feet in front of me. I don't know why I thought I could outrun the predator stalking me, a wild creature who didn't mask his chase as he followed, his hungry snarl encouraging me to lift those knees higher.

Branches whipped my body and snagged at my hair. I ignored those minor discomforts, figuring I would feel a lot worse if whatever chased me managed to catch me and sink the surely big teeth it owned into my skin.

I don't know how long I ran, but eventually, I emerged from the forest into a starlit clearing. Fronds of tall grass provided no concealment, not for someone my size, and wading through them left a clear path.

And provided a soft landing.

Something slammed into me from behind, and down I went, my scream strangled in my throat as all my breath left me in a whoosh upon impact.

I squirmed and thrashed under the weight atop me, expecting sharp teeth to rip into me. For claws to rend my skin into bloody ribbons. For a certain horrifying and gruesome death.

It took me a moment to realize it wasn't a hairy beast that pinned me to the ground, but flesh. Hard, heated, naked, and distinctly male flesh—or so I assumed given the distinctive poke against my backside.

A strong hand gripped my wrists and pulled them over my head while another rolled me over until I lay stretched beneath a very masculine shape sporting a massive erection.

Talk about a scary dream taking an interesting turn.

I stopped fighting and took stock of my situation.

Golden eyes peered at me. A heavy body pinned me. A cock throbbed, squished between our bodies, showing carnal intent. I didn't fully relax until I heard a familiar voice say, "Hey, baby. Fancy running into you here."

Not enough he'd invaded my life and bed, did he also have to perturb my dreams? "Pete?"

"You know a lot of other werewolves who like to chase you naked in the woods?"

Um no. As a matter of fact, this was the first time anything had ever chased me naked anywhere.

Now that I was over my fear, it was actually kind of stimulating. I relaxed, even wiggled my hips a little to give myself a cheap thrill. My pussy hummed in pleasure, and the eyes watching me turned a deeper gold. "Taking yourself for a walk, were you?" I sassed.

Dark or not, I couldn't miss the wide grin displaying a mouthful of white teeth with pronounced canines. "More like going on a hunt."

"A hunt for what?"

He answered with a low chuckle and a grind of his hips. A pleased shudder went through me at the pressure he put against the apex of my mound. "Take a wild guess."

Too easy. Kind of like the new me. Dream or not, I wanted more than just talk, though. I let my legs part, settling him deeper between them. My nipples tightened as he repositioned himself, the hair of his chest tickling my breasts, the head of his cock nudging at my moist lips. When he didn't immediately penetrate me, I moaned and wiggled my hips.

His reply? His head swooped down, and he tugged a nub into his mouth.

Sweet heaven. The sensation sent a jolt right down to my pussy. As he sucked and devoured my nipples, I clung to his shoulders, arching my hips, trying to draw his cock into me, but he held off. What a tease! And, yes, it excited me. He played like this for a while, alternately sucking my hard nipples, his teeth grazing them and sending shivers along my nerves. My pussy tightened, hungry for something to fill it.

"Fuck me," I moaned.

"I want to claim you," was his reply.

It sounded so possessive, and while the awake Chloe shied from such a thing, dream Chloe craved it. Where was the harm in indulging? "Take me."

Magic words with immediate result. He flipped me to my stomach and hoisted me to my knees so that my buttocks were up in the air while my upper torso remained pressed to the grassy ground. Exposed to his view, I couldn't help but moan as he slid a finger down my velvety slit.

"So pretty and wet."

Try, so fucking horny I could scream.

Thankfully, dream Pete wasn't going to spend too much time waxing poetic about my girly parts. He sheathed his cock in one quick thrust, impaling me upon his length. I clawed at the ground, my buttocks rotating back in an attempt to draw him deeper.

Large hands gripped the sides of my waist as he withdrew until only the tip of his cock touched me. A whimper of need escaped me then a squeak as he slammed back in.

"Yes," I hissed as he set up a steady pace of thrusts in and out. "Oh gawd," I sobbed as he gave my pussy what it needed. A good hard fuck. A pounding. Unbelievable, animalistic pleasure.

A motion to my side drew my attention and I realized we weren't alone. Before I could scream, a voice spoke from the darkness, "Come for him, Chloe."

"Anthony?" Indeed it was my blue-eyed lover. From the darkness he floated closer, naked and aroused. Given I dreamed, I didn't find this the least bit odd, nor did I mind the fact he'd been watching. On the contrary, much like the voyeuristic episode of the morning before, I found it quite titillating.

"She's so fucking wet and tight," Pete growled as he continued to pump me.

"*Tasty* too," Anthony purred.

Try borderline orgasmic. Hypnotized by the sight of Anthony's hand working the length of his shaft, I panted and shuddered as my body tightened around Pete's thrusting cock.

"Harder," I begged.

"Harder," Anthony whispered.

Harder Pete slammed.

My orgasm hit and I yelled, my body quaking with the force of it. Pete came in a hot spurt and a roar that made my ears ring and ring and...

Fucking alarm clock. It shrieked me awake, the remnants of my erotic dream still coursing through my sweaty body and evident in the pulsing waves still quaking through my sex.

Awesome. I'd just had my first wet dream. Somehow, the sticky thighs weren't as sexy as I'd imagined, especially given, climax or not, I felt unfulfilled. Wanting. It seemed only the real thing could leave me feeling sated.

I dragged my butt out of bed, preparing for work while keeping an ear out for the ring of a phone or the beep of a text. Neither happened.

I got to the office a few minutes late and still hadn't heard from either of my suitors. Jerks.

Where was my sense of relief? I should rejoice they didn't crowd me and that they gave me some breathing room. Maybe I'd gotten lucky and they had given up altogether. Once again, though, I lived up to my feminine genes and proved my contrary nature.

I moped, feeling forgotten—and unwanted— at least until the huge bouquet of flowers—fake silk ones in deference to my allergies—arrived with a little card. It simply stated, *Thinking of you. See you tonight. A.*

Yeah, I grinned from ear to ear, unable to help myself. Had I mentioned in the past that I thought flowers were a waste of money? I mean, they died in a few days, contributed to organic waste, which in turn meant increasing my tax dollars to support the disposal of such a frivolous, unneeded item. Of course, that was before I got some. And besides, I consoled myself, these weren't the real kind. They were beautiful replicas that would last forever, keeping my eco conscience clear.

Every time I looked at them, in my makeshift vase comprised of a stainless steel thermos, which I bought for ten bucks off a coworker, I smiled.

Shoot me now. I was acting like such a girl. Brenda and my mom would have beamed in pride.

As for Pete, when I did finally hear from him, it was via the phone. But at first I didn't expect to hear his voice, not when I saw the call display featuring the police station number. Not unusual given my clients tended to have problems with the law. I wondered who'd screwed up this time.

Boy, did I get a shock.

It seemed my werewolf lover had gotten himself arrested and chosen me as his one allowed phone call. I didn't find it quite as flattering as the flowers.

"Hey, baby. How are you?"

"How am I? Shouldn't I be asking that of you? Why are you calling me from the cop station?"

"I'm in a spot of trouble. I need your help, baby."

"Duh. What did you do this time? And if you tell me you peed on your neighbor's flowers again, I am going to hang up on you."

"Um, it's kind of more serious than that."

"How serious? Because I don't really have the patience or time for frivolous pranks."

"Pretty serious and they haven't set the bail yet."

Bail? That didn't sound promising. "Were you actually arrested?"

"Yes."

Great. I was dating a jailbird. *Way to pick 'em, Chloe.* "What are you being charged with?"

"Murder."

Holy fucking shit. I sat up straight in my chair. "Who are they saying you killed?"

"The witch next door."

I leaned my forehead against my desk. I felt bad for doing it, but I had to ask. "Did you?"

"Did I what?"

"Kill her? No, wait. Don't answer that. Don't answer any questions. Tell them you want a lawyer. I'm on my way."

Guilty or not—although I hoped for not—Pete needed me and I couldn't say no.

Damn it. Things were about to get complicated. Our involvement meant I should recuse myself from his case and I would, after I figured out what the hell was going on and sprang him from the big house.

For a moment, I contemplated calling Anthony. Just a moment, then I vetoed it. For one, I didn't need to hear him gloat that his competitor was facing possible prison time. And secondly, I didn't want to give in to weakness. I didn't want to rely on Anthony in a crisis. I didn't want to rely on anyone.

The officers at the station recognized me and only made me sign in before letting me into an interrogation room, one I made sure had its camera turned off and no viewing window.

Even if they couldn't use anything said in this room against Pete, there was no sense in giving the police leads about where to look for evidence. Assuming, of course, that my werewolf lover was in fact guilty.

I sure hoped not. I'd hate to think I'd slept with a murderer. I wondered what evidence they'd gathered that pinned the death on Pete. I'd yet to hear the details of the crime; the detective in charge of the case was still at the scene of the crime, collecting clues.

The door to the room opened, and Pete shuffled in, cuffs clinking. Made of heavy silver, the wide bands circled his wrists and were linked by a thick chain so that he couldn't spread his arms. Leading down from his wrist restraints was another length of links, which looped down to the expanse of silver between his cuffed ankles.

The heavy-duty metal combined with the orange jumpsuit, I'm ashamed to say, made me swallow down a frisson of fear. I tried not to let it show on my face, but he looked dangerous. Like a man who could have killed his next-door neighbor. Yet, I knew appearances didn't mean squat. And this was America.

Innocent until proven guilty. Everyone deserved a fair trial. Yada, yada. That was the motto all lawyers should live by, but my jaded side knew the cops were fairly thorough. They might make mistakes, but when it came to the serious crimes, they tended to cross all their t's.

I waited until the door shut before speaking. "What happened?"

"To the witch?"

"To you. Her. The whole shebang. Tell me everything and don't leave a single detail out."

"Shouldn't the first question you ask be did I do it?"

The query I dreaded. Or was it the answer I feared?

Could the man who'd touched me so intimately actually be guilty of the crime? Had I slept with a murderer?

"Did you kill her?" I stared him in the eyes, wishing I owned a lie detector other than just my gut instinct.

He met my gaze steadily. "I did not kill her." He didn't hesitate or look away or do anything to indicate he said anything but the truth.

Perhaps it made me gullible, but I believed him. I sensed a weary resignation in him, as if he didn't expect anyone to take his side. But before I threw myself into his camp, I needed to find out more.

"If you didn't do it, then why do the cops think you did?"

"Because, apparently, when they found her, the body appeared as if a wild animal had torn it apart."

Ouch. "And they blamed you." I didn't phrase it as a question.

He nodded.

"On what grounds?"

"I'm a werewolf, and the moon was full last night."

"Oh." Uh-oh. Double, triple uh-oh. Given he'd just come up on charges of harassment, misdemeanors or not, I could see why they might assume him responsible. "Start from the beginning. What did you do after you left me yesterday?"

"I hit my gym for a few hours to work out. I had some pent-up tension that needed attending." A ghost of his boyish smile lifted his lips. There one second, gone the next. "After my shower, I did some groceries. Caught up on some laundry. Had a nap."

"Sounds like an exciting day."

"Well, it would have been if someone hadn't needed some alone time."

Sure, blame me for his lack of alibi.

"What about last night? Who did you spend it with?" If he said another woman, I'd walk out. "Did you meet up with some other Lycans, or did you change into your furball self alone?"

I'd read that many werewolves enjoyed sticking together. They called themselves packs. But I also knew, or so rumor said, that dominant males who didn't rule these so-called furry gangs tended to be loners.

Even among animals, too much testosterone in one place never boded well. Pete definitely struck me as the kind of guy who wouldn't take orders from another. Hell, he probably owned a T-shirt that stated, *Does not play well with others.* I know I did, in bright pink. A present from Brenda.

"I'm afraid I turned shaggy by myself. As usual. I just did my regular thing. Drove to the state park just outside the city. It's a great spot for a run. No hunting allowed, few humans to freak out. I stripped down, changed, and ran until just before dawn. When I got home, the cops were waiting for me. They arrested me on sight."

"You didn't resist?"

He snorted. "Yeah, like I'm going to argue with half a dozen trigger-happy cops toting guns with silver bullets. I hit the ground with my hands over my head as soon as they ordered me to."

"Good." Cooperation was a point in his favor. The guilty liked to run. "When did you find out what happened?"

"The detective in charge told me they were arresting me for the murder of one Meredith Heksen. I asked who that was and that's when I found out it was my neighbor."

"You didn't even know her name?"

"Why would I? She called me dirty dog; I called her witch. We never made it to the first name stage."

"So, then what?"

"They read me my rights as they cuffed me. Shoved me into the back of a car and brought me here to arraign me. And, let me tell you, they are thorough. I will never look at latex gloves the same." He shuddered.

I bit back a hysterical giggle. He probably wouldn't appreciate it, but having read the procedurals for a typical body search, which now included a cavity one, I could understand his discomfort.

"Have they questioned you yet?"

"They tried. I told them I didn't do anything. That I was gone all night and never saw her. When they started hammering me with questions, I demanded my phone call and a lawyer."

"And called me." I slumped. "You do realize I can't represent you."

"Because we slept together? So what? You're

the one I trust. I want you as my lawyer."

"The state will never go for it. Public defenders must not have a personal relationship, current or prior, with their clients."

"So I'll hire you privately."

"I can't just quit my job to work for you." His shoulders sagged and he turned soulful brown eyes on me. "And don't you dare use those puppy dog eyes on me."

He grinned. "It was worth a try."

"This is not a time to joke. This is a serious accusation. You know the laws are harsh to those of your kind who harm humans." As in, an eye for an eye. Kill a human and get found guilty? There was no appeal.

"I didn't do it."

"But we need to prove that. With no alibi to account for your whereabouts, we're going to have to rely on the autopsy report and DNA tests. If we're lucky, whatever did kill her will have left traces behind. Hair. Saliva." A wallet with photo ID.

"What if they don't find anything?"

"Let's cross that bridge if we reach it."

"How long until we know?"

"Hours. Days. Weeks. It all depends on the backlog." And the priority given to the case. Given the media jumped all over anything to do with the Lycans, I figured they had a rush on the tests.

"I hate waiting."

"Join the club."

"So what do we do in the meantime?"

"We?"

"Yes, we. You are going to help me prove my innocence, right?" Puppy dog eyes had nothing on those of a man who'd given you numerous orgasms who looked at you as if his whole world rested in your hands. In a sense, it did. Damn him for chipping away at my cold heart.

A heavy sigh blew past my lips. "Of course I will. Lucky for you, they don't know," yet, "that we've slept together, so I'll get the paperwork started on your bail. Any idea when you are going in front of the judge?"

"Sometime this afternoon."

Not much time for me to figure things out, but enough to get some balls rolling. "Okay. For the moment, I want you to sit tight. Don't say anything. To anyone. Not without a lawyer present. And might I recommend that you hire one if you can afford to, instead of relying on a court appointed one?"

"Don't you know of anyone good in your office?"

Not good enough to trust with Pete's life. The only one with enough skill would probably end up as prosecutor. *Unless…*

I stored my backup plan for later. First, I needed to track down the detective in charge of the case and find out what evidence they'd gathered. Then I could come up with a scenario to help my werewolf lover, behind the scenes of course.

Because walking away wasn't an option.

Chapter Nine

The lead investigator on the case made me sit and wait.

And wait.

In a time before cell phones and tablets, this might have annoyed people, but I used those minutes to make some calls and gather intel.

First, I dug up which judge would end up hearing the charges and set the bail, as well as who the prosecutor's office had delegated to stand in.

Anthony of course. What a surprise. Not. It looked as though I might have to employ my evil plan to undermine the prosecution's case.

Oh judge, I'm afraid you're going to have to replace the DA's number one guy because I've seen him naked. Sure, we'd both get a slap on the wrist at the admission— maybe a stern talking to by our bosses, a spanking by Anthony later for being a bad girl—but if we wanted to prove Pete's innocence, then we needed to remove Anthony from the equation.

He was just too damned good at his job, not to mention he had a vested interest in keeping Pete behind bars.

By the time the detective called me in, I'd lined up some possible lawyers for Pete, and my email hummed with incoming messages as I gleaned what I could from outside sources—i.e., the newspapers and rumor mills. Even before I spoke to Detective Jefferson, I knew the case was weak and circumstantial at best. I could only surmise they'd succumbed to pressure from some higher-ups to have a suspect behind bars so the public wouldn't panic at a possible maniac at large.

The papers had already given the case a name. Indecent Werewolf Exposure Leads to Murder. Oh yeah, they'd dug up the previous charges and were now having a field day with their assumptions.

The frazzled policeman in charge of the case sat behind a desk piled with folders and a scratched-up laptop with a sticker on the back stating, *God made policemen so firemen would have heroes.*

My laptop also had a sticker—*Warning: I have PMS and GPS, which means if you piss me off, I will find you.*

"Detective Jefferson, thank you for seeing me." I held out my hand and shook his soft-skinned, pulpy one. A man who'd let himself go, he strained the buttons on his poor shirt and pants.

"Ms. Bailey. Please have a seat."

"Thank you." I seated myself gingerly on the worn plastic chair, checking it first for puddles.

Don't laugh. The morning after a full moon, the cop shop fairly bursts at the seams and the drunker patrons didn't always get up to use the washroom. It had taken only one ruined skirt and a scalding bath to soak myself, followed by several bottles of antiseptic—just in case—to train me to look before I sat.

"What can I help you with?" he asked

As if the detective didn't know, but I played

the game. "I'm here on behalf of my client, Mr. Cavanaugh."

"The werewolf who killed his neighbor."

"Alleged." Nothing like reminding him of the law.

"Not for long. Forensics is working on the trace evidence right now and the coroner is examining the body, but I'd say it's a pretty clear-cut case."

"How do you figure?"

"It's documented that he and his neighbor were involved in a dispute."

"One that never involved violence. Just minor misdemeanors."

"Which escalated."

I arched a brow. "And you're basing this on what?"

"After pleading guilty to those charges, your client went on to have the victim's cat picked up by animal control. A clear act of retaliation. Ms. Heksen confronted him about it, in her backyard, but chose an unfortunate time, as the moon was full. While arguing, Mr. Cavanaugh shifted into a wolf and proceeded to savage the victim. He ran off and Ms. Heksen bled out. A clear case of homicide."

Alleged, dammit! I held my tongue as I mulled over his words and quickly honed in on one aspect of it. "You say this happened in the yard."

"Yes."

"And you have a witness to this supposed argument?" Highly unlikely given the thick hedges surrounding the properties. Unless actually present, no one would have seen anything.

"No. But the evidence—"

"Shows that a wild animal may have attacked Ms. Heksen. No one heard or saw anything." Before he could reply, I went on. "When you arrested my client, did he have any blood on his body or clothing?"

"No. But he could have showered and changed. Then left to dispose of the clothing."

"I assume you've pulled all the drains from the sinks and showers for analysis."

"Of course. This isn't my first crime scene."

"Just asking. The medical examiner will be taking dental molds?"

"Yes and your client will have to provide records of his teeth. Two sets. One while human and the other when he's a dog."

"Lycan, if you please. To call him otherwise is derogatory."

Detective Jefferson scowled. "Sorry, I meant to say Lycan."

"I am sure you did." I smiled sweetly. "The grapevine says very little blood was recovered at the scene."

"Who told you that?"

"I don't recall, but it was someone with a uniform." I batted my lashes in an attempt to look innocent.

"It could be that the blood soaked into the ground."

I kept drilling. "I thought her body was found on the patio."

"Between the stones then."

"You're of course pulling up those stones to look, right?" Placating smile? Yeah, he didn't fall for it. His scowl deepened as I poked holes at his supposed air-tight case.

"Forensics is handling it."

"Have they found any fingerprints?"

"No."

"Hair belonging to my client?"

"They're still analyzing it."

A bulldog when it came to details, I didn't relent. "The time of death was estimated at just past midnight, correct?"

This time, he didn't ask me where I got my intel. "According to the on-site specialists who measured the temperature, yes."

"And yet didn't the moon rise sometime just before nine p.m.?"

"I don't know."

"But didn't you just say that during the argument my client supposedly engaged in with Ms. Heksen, that the moon rose, and in the throes of anger, while in his shifted state, he killed her? How do you account for the three-hour time difference between the attack and her death?"

"Maybe she didn't die right away."

"But yet, initial reports state she suffered deadly gashes to her person, several of them severing arteries. That would seem to imply a quick death, not a lingering one."

"Maybe we got the time of death wrong."

"Or maybe she didn't bleed out." Which left the disturbing question of where did her blood go?

"Since you seem so well informed, why are you here, Ms. Bailey?" For a moment, the man he used to be shone from his eyes. He pinned me with a hard gaze.

It didn't intimidate me.

"Just getting my facts straight. You know how rumors can be. I'll require a paper copy of the case."

"I'll have it sent to your office within the hour."

Sure he would, and he'd start going to the gym and follow a healthy regime. Not. However, I'd heard enough.

I stood. "I'd appreciate that. Thank you for your time." I shook his hand again and didn't show my contempt.

A case based on blind ignorance by a lazy detective quick to jump to the most simple, yet erroneous, conclusion.

I'd gleaned enough information to surmise Pete didn't kill his neighbor. A relief, I'd admit, but, at the same time, that left us with a more disturbing prospect.

Somewhere out there walked a murderer. One who not only liked to tear his victim apart, but who, if my sources were to be believed, ate parts of them and drank their blood. A rather disturbing fact the detective neglected to mention, probably out of respect for my feminine sensibilities. Good thing I wasn't relying on just my local policeman for info.

Springing Pete would end up easier than I'd first thought, but it'd also put the cops back at square one, without a suspect. The public wouldn't like that. Hell, I didn't like it because either we had a rabid shapeshifter on the loose, a sick, cannibalistic human, or the world was about to find out if vampires or zombies really existed—I mean, who else fit the profile?

Time to load the shotgun with silver shot,

stock up on holy water, and sharpen some stakes. I, for one, wouldn't get caught unprepared.

Nothing wrong with channeling my inner Buffy. But I drew the line at the short skirt and pompoms.

Chapter Ten

Apparently, the detective I'd spoken to paid more attention to my dissection of his case than I credited him for.

I wasn't the only one to come to the conclusion Pete hadn't done the crime. Before we even set foot in front of a judge, they'd released Pete. According to the grapevine—ahem, Brenda—we owed it all to medical science, better known as "the creepy guy in the morgue."

The coroner's initial report stated there was no way a human or Lycan had left the marks on the body; the dentition impressions just didn't jive. Nothing they had on file matched the marks.

Creepy because it meant whatever had killed the witch remained at large and a mystery, a mystery that intrigued the whole office, which buzzed with inane theories.

My two cents? Didn't know and didn't care.

Sticking my nose into a case involving a dead body that somebody had taken a chunk out of and chased down with a slurp of blood wasn't something I considered necessary for my mental or physical health.

With my late afternoon court visit for Pete cancelled, I stuck my nose to the grindstone—surfing

Facebook and reading the latest scandal on TMZ.

It was too late in the day to tackle anything new or intensive, although I wouldn't have minded taking to the floor my unexpected visitor.

Pete showed up at my office bearing a grin and a box of donuts. It was a toss-up which I drooled for more. Having worked through lunch, donuts won.

The jerk held them out of reach until I'd given him a kiss on the lips. The things I did for sugar.

Breathless and hungry for more than just jelly-filled goodness—the bakery kind, not the sausage—I sat down and gestured for him to take the seat across from me.

While I chewed, he crowed. "I told you I didn't do it."

"I never thought you did."

A snort escaped him. "Yeah, right. Admit it. For one teensy tiny moment, you wondered if I had."

"Well, you did pee on the woman's flowers."

"I also like to write my name in the snow with urine and chase my tail in circles."

"You have a tail?"

"No. I'm just messing with you. Although…wanna check to make sure?" He wiggled his brows, and I bit my lip so as not to laugh. He truly looked adorable.

"I'm good." Besides, I'd already seen his fine ass. It was tail free. The only appendage down there jutted from the front, and it bobbed rather than wagged. It also dipped, but I tried not to think of that, lest we entertain my coworkers too much when my old desk broke under our combined weight. "But, tail or not, you do get hairy, with big teeth and claws."

"I do. I've got great big fangs." He grinned widely at me with his perfect white smile. "It doesn't make me a killer."

"Not even when you're in your wolfman shape?"

"Depends on what you call a killer. Am I more primitive? Yes. Do I hunt? Again, yes. But I hunt animals. Small creatures like rabbits and squirrels. I don't, however, eat them." He shuddered. "I might like my meat red, but even I prefer it singed on both sides, not raw or from the source."

"Good to know." Because how did you tell a man you didn't want to kiss him for fear of gagging on blood breath or spotting rabbit fur between his teeth?

With him in such a talkative mood—and for once not shutting me up with his tongue in my mouth, a pity that—I decided to assuage some of my curiosity. "So you're in control when you're shifted? Fully aware of what's going on?"

"Of course I am." He rolled his eyes, as if to imply the mere suggestion otherwise was ludicrous.

"No need for the sarcasm," said the pot calling the kettle black. "I was just asking."

"Sorry. There's just so many erroneous assumptions out there about our kind, the most prevalent one being we turn into slavering mindless beasts who will kill anything that moves. Totally untrue. We retain all of our morals and intelligence, no matter our shape. Which is more than I can say for some people who are fully human."

"True enough." I knew I turned into a gnarly

beast when PMS time came around.

"Anything else you want to know about Lycans?"

"Does silver really weaken you?"

"Is it our kryptonite? No. Shoot us with anything, and it will hurt. But we are harder to kill than an unenhanced person. Our regenerative capabilities are much more evolved than that of humans."

I knew all about his power of recuperation. My pussy could testify to it.

I crossed my legs. "Is there anything about you that is normal?" Too late, it occurred to me how that sounded. Cheeks heating—a rarity I assure you—I stammered. "I mean— That is—"

Judging by his laughter, he didn't take offense. "Don't apologize. I already told you, I like your no-bullshit attitude. As to your question, there's plenty about me that's normal, such as the fact I'm a slob, suck at math, and love to watch sports."

"Do you play any?"

"No. I wasn't allowed because of my special side." He pouted. "Apparently, Lycans are considered on par with steroid users. So unfair. I would have made a great linebacker."

I would have said more of a tight end, but then again, I was biased when it came to his delectable ass. "I suck at sports."

"Not all of them." The wink said it all.

I squirmed again, and the grin on his face widened, no doubt on account of my panties were getting uncomfortably damp. Damn the fact it was too early for me to leave work. I could have used an early dinner. Speaking of which…

"Thanks for bringing me the treats." I gestured to the mostly empty box. Having skipped lunch, I'd needed the sustenance.

"My pleasure. I wanted to thank you in person for coming to my rescue this morning. I know I put you in a tough spot, what with us being involved and all."

"Yeah. Yeah." I waved his thanks away, even if secretly pleased at the acknowledgement. "I'm just glad they saw reason without me having to make them look stupid. Any idiot could see there was no way you'd done it."

"However, it begs the question, who did? Do the cops have any leads?"

Normally, I wouldn't have discussed an ongoing police case, but given he'd just gotten off the hook for the crime in question, I thought he had a right to know. Besides, Twitter was abuzz, and the newspapers were reporting things left and right. "None. But I've heard a few hushed-up theories. Crazy ones."

"How crazy?"

Should I mention them or not? Some seemed so farfetched, yet, having gleaned more facts on the murder since the morning, even I could admit to being stumped. Nothing made sense.

"Don't laugh; however, I've heard the word zombies tossed around." I waited for his laughter and didn't get any.

A serious mien to my nutty answer, Pete shook his head. "Not likely. A witch would have lit up a corpse before it got close. And zombies enjoy organs, not muscle or flesh. They also don't drink blood."

I blinked. "Excuse me. Tell me you're kidding."

"I don't joke about the undead."

"But you're implying zombies are real."

"Not implying. Stating."

Hot damn, the things I wished I didn't know. "They're real? Real, as in shambling, decaying, I-want-brains real?"

"Yup." I stared at him while he munched away on the last of the treats he'd brought. He paused in his chewing, a bit of sugar at the corner of his mouth tempting me. "What? Why are you staring at me like that?"

He really had to ask? "Because zombies don't exist. Dead things don't come back to life. I mean, come on, if they did, wouldn't we know?"

"Oh, plenty of people know. Including our government and the police. It's the general world at large that hasn't gotten the memo yet. The lawmakers are secretly working on a bill to categorize and limit zombie creation before going live with the news."

"So why are you telling me if it's a secret?"

"Honesty, baby. I promised to tell you the truth. Zombies exist, and that's the truth. I do, however, expect you'll keep this to yourself. No need to cause a world-wide panic."

"Of course." Feeling faint, I grabbed the sweet concoction out of his hand and bit down. Perhaps the endorphin release from the sugar rush would take away the lightheadedness. As I chewed, I mulled over his words. "What did you mean by creation? How do you make a zombie?"

"Not so much make as animate an already

dead corpse. I'm not sure of the magic involved, spells and potions and what not, but from what I understand, there are a handful of necromancers in the world and some voodoo types who practice the art of raising the dead."

"I swear, Pete, if you're fucking with me, I will rip your dick off."

"It's the truth. Scout's honor." He placed his hand over his heart.

"You were never a scout." More like the long-haired bad boy in the cool jean jacket who convinced girls to visit the spot under the bleachers.

He chuckled. "Nope. But it sounds good."

I still found it hard to wrap my mind around that fact. Mental note to self: get a shotgun, with lots of ammo. The elephant-sized kind. No use taking chances. If I shot anything, I wanted it splattered into pieces.

"Zombies exist." Saying it didn't make it feel any more believable.

"They do."

"But they didn't kill your neighbor."

"Not likely."

"So what killed the witch, I mean your neighbor?"

"Dunno. What else have you heard on the grapevine?"

"Pack of rabid squirrels."

Pete snorted. "No way."

Thank gawd. My parents had tons of them running rampant through their yard. Just the thought of them attacking in a pack made me glad I lived in a condo with no pets allowed—except for a hairy lover. I tossed out the next theory. "Vampire."

"They don't eat meat, and they never drink from witches. Or so I've heard. Apparently, their blood disagrees with their digestive system. Something about the magic tainting it."

It didn't surprise me at this point that he'd claim vampires existed. I, however, was still on the fence about whether to believe him or not. I mean, come on, just how many hidden species did he expect me to believe existed under our noses? Then again…

I glanced at the werewolf across from me. Maybe not so farfetched.

"Let me guess, vampires are waiting to come out too until they get their own laws."

"Those old geezers? Nah. They like living in the shadows and have no intention of letting the world know they truly exist."

Finally, a fairy tale that stayed true to form. I'd hate to think my childhood crush on Edward was misplaced. "Are the legends about them accurate?"

For some reason, he seemed less keen on this topic than the zombie one, or so it seemed as Pete shrugged a massive shoulder. "Dunno. Don't care. You'd have to ask one."

If I knew one. Which I hoped never happened. Becoming anyone's dinner or snack didn't rate high on my bucket list.

"The last option I heard tossed around was that she summoned a demon and lost control of it."

"Unlikely."

Not, "Oh no, demons aren't real." Could this day get any more seriously fucked up? "Why unlikely?"

"Aren't you going to express disbelief they

exist?"

"Are you mocking me?"

"Would I dare do that?" The innocent look on his face didn't fool me.

I gave him my best evil eye. He didn't curl into a whimpering ball begging for mercy. Apparently, I'd have to work on it.

"Assuming demons exist, what do they look like? Are they like the horned devils we see and hear about in religion and on television?"

"Depends on which one is called."

"Called as in…"

"Demons don't exist on our plane per se. They have their own realm."

"Because, of course, Heaven and Hell are real." Hello, sarcasm, my old friend.

"No."

"Excuse me?"

"Now you're just being silly. There is no such thing as Heaven or Hell. Or even limbo."

"Like fuck. You mean to tell me all this other shit exists, but the one thing pretty much every religion agrees on doesn't?"

"I didn't write those bibles. Humans did. Misinformed ones. There are other planes of existence, or so I've been taught. They're just not a place souls go to after death."

"I'm too sober to handle theology right now," I mumbled as I rubbed my forehead, wishing for a bottle of Advil chased down with a few ounces of vodka.

"Good because we're getting off topic. We were talking about demons. You know, now that I think of it, the signs do point to them possibly being the culprit. Most of them enjoy killing, and they do have a varied diet, again, so legend states. I don't know anyone who's ever actually met one."

"So they don't live among us?"

"Not that I know of."

"Then where do they live?"

"In another dimension. They can only set foot in ours if called via some fucked-up ritual. The question is, who would be dumb enough to summon one?"

"So find the guy who knows how and we find the demon who killed your neighbor."

"I wish it was that easy. Summoning a demon is a lost art. The church spent a lot of money and man-hours hunting down every single text pertaining to demons. After the great plague, brought upon by the demon of pestilence, they banned demon grimoires. As a matter of fact, they burned them. Burned the books, scrolls, and even those with the knowledge, in a massive purge to ensure no one could do it again."

"This whole purge thing is great and all, but all it takes is one idiot hiding the instructions for future use. The method or whatever to summon one could have survived." Of course it could have. Just look at how many people on the Antique Road Show discovered relics in their attic when their great-great aunt Petunia died.

"It's definitely possible."

"What does a demon look like?"

Pete spread his hands. "No one truly knows. As I said, the church destroyed all the information, leaving us only with fables and old wives tales. But, if I had to wager a guess, I'd say ugly with fucking big teeth."

"You're not being very helpful here."

"What do you want me to say? I'm not a scholar. I'm just telling you what I know."

"Well, you seem to know enough to think the crime looks demon-related."

"Because from the legends I've heard handed down among the Lycans, only demons drink human blood and partake of the flesh. But, of all the theories, even if it fits, it's the craziest. There hasn't been a documented demon case in hundreds of years."

"That you know of."

"That I know of," he admitted.

"So it's possible." I hammered at him and he sighed.

"I guess. Are you going to tell the cops?" Anxiety made his brows pull together.

He needn't have worried. "No fucking way. I don't need them labeling me as a lunatic. It's bad enough I came to the rescue of the wolfinator."

"The who?"

"Wolfinator, your nickname at the station. As in the wolf who pees." Too many coffees and donuts led to the brilliant combination of urinate and wolf. Not the most original of names, but one all the men seemed to find hilarious, including Pete.

A snicker escaped him. "That explains a lot of the jokes I heard."

"What jokes?"

"Never mind. They're not fit for a lady's ears."

How cute. He mistakenly took me for a lady. Did he not recall the wild sex we'd had less than two days ago?

"So how do we recognize or stop this demon thing? Or whoever it was that killed your neighbor."

"We don't. And you're not going looking for it either."

My turn to laugh. "Look for it? Are you nuts?"

"Then why all the questions about it."

"Simple curiosity and wondering how I can protect myself. I'm not Nancy Drew or some leather-wearing, ass-kicking Amazon heroine. I feel no need to go out on my own and fight crime or find murderers. I'll leave that to the pros and idiots with a hero complex, thank you very much. Me, I just want to know what weapon to buy so, if anything comes after me, I can at least maim it long enough for me to run away screaming." Eyeing Pete—his muscles, his white teeth, his size—it occurred to me he made the perfect defense system. And he gave great orgasms. "Speaking of screaming...what are you doing tonight?" No, I hadn't forgotten my date with Anthony, but with a killer on the loose, a girl needed to keep herself safe. Big bad werewolf or rich lawyer in a suit? No brainer.

I'd expected him to jump on the chance to spend time with me, especially given his speech the day before at the diner. Instead, he squirmed in his seat, and did I detect a hint of red in his cheeks? "I might be a little busy over the next little bit, which will make it hard for me to see you. Not because I don't want to," he hastened to add. "Something came up at work that requires my undivided attention."

His work? He was a bloody gardener. What

was more important than plowing my field? "You got a big contract or something?"

"You could say."

I frowned at his evasive reply. "What happened to honesty?"

"I haven't lied to you. Have I not answered all your questions, even if you mocked some of them?"

"You did. So tell me about this big job."

"Do I have to?"

"Does it have to do with yard work?"

"Not exactly."

I fixed him with my sternest glare. "Pete. Are you or are you not a landscaper?"

He caved. "I am. Most of the time."

"And the rest of the time?"

"I'm the idiot hero who goes looking for monsters."

His sheepish grin, and admission, might have made my jaw drop, but it didn't stop the laughter. Pete had even more layers than I'd given him credit for. I'm not ashamed to say, it totally turned me on.

Good thing I knew of a broom closet off a little used hallway.

Standing up, I came around my desk, all too aware of his heated gaze, which said without words that he'd caught my erotic interest. "Follow me," I ordered.

"Where?"

"You'll see." I leaned out of my cubicle and peeked around, mostly because I feared Brenda lurked. I knew my BFF. If she saw us sneaking off, she'd probably sing a dirty ditty and ruin the mood.

Coast clear, I dragged Pete down a hall lined

with conference rooms to a door marked maintenance. He caught on to my devious plan and kicked the door shut as soon as we slipped in. Then he effortlessly shifted a metal shelving unit across it, removing any worry about interruptions.

When he turned back to face me, I swear his eyes glowed. No doubt, he didn't mind my impromptu need or less-than-romantic spot.

Screw finesse. I threw myself at him, hands grasping at his hair, tugging his face down to mine so I could suck at his lips. He tasted sweet from the donuts, and I moaned in pleasure as I devoured him. Big hands cupped my ass, squeezing and massaging my cheeks as my tongue slid along the seam of his mouth. His lips parted, and his tongue joined mine in a sinuous dance that lit even more of my senses on fire.

Like teenagers in the first throes of passion, we rubbed against each other, our clothing providing friction and giving it that extra element of taboo. I knew we shouldn't be doing this, not in my place of work.

"I can't believe I'm doing this." I panted. I'd never done anything so wild. What if we got caught? It cranked my desire up another notch.

"I think you're wilder than you think," he replied in between fervent kisses. "Would it help if I told you that the entire time we were talking, all I could think of was how much I wanted you? How much I missed tasting you?"

Words to melt me into a puddle. I sagged against him, the rush of heat from his words making my knees weak.

But he wasn't done. "All I could think of was

how I wanted to get under that desk, hike your skirt, and lick you until you came on my tongue." Brazen words, which he matched with action as his hands inched up the pleated fabric of my skirt and, with a firm grip, tore my wet panties free.

I just about came at the decadence of it then squeaked as he cupped my mound, a sound he caught with his mouth. His hand covered my moist flesh and I quivered as he rumbled. "You are so fucking hot."

Ditto. Not that I managed to say it aloud, not with his thumb rubbing against my clit. I clutched at him, head thrown back, gasping for air as he played with my swollen nub. Gawd, how I wished he would suck on it, run his tongue across my heated flesh, make me clutch at his hair and scream his name, like he'd done to me a few nights before. The closet I'd dragged us into didn't have that kind of room, though. Fuck, it didn't even have a wall for him to prop me up against. Dammit. How would I get him inside me? I wanted him so bad.

Screw the logistics. I'd worry about the "how" later. Confined space or not, I needed to touch him. Stroke him. Have him panting as hard for me as I was for him. I fumbled at the zipper for his pants, managing to get them open enough that his cock sprang forth. Hot, hard, and heavy. For me. What an empowering feeling to know I could make him so wild.

Back and forth I stroked him, our pose kind of awkward but passionate as we both tried to caress the other to a higher state of pleasure. But I grew frustrated, needing more.

I wasn't alone.

"Fuck this." With deft fingers, he unzipped my skirt so that it pooled around my ankles. A moment later, I was aloft as he palmed my buttocks and hoisted me. Then impaled me.

No wall to brace myself. No bed to dig my nails in. Just Pete. Big and strong, holding me up like a dainty little gal, fucking me like I'd always fantasized about. I clung to him, practically sobbing as he bounced me, up and down, a jiggling rhythm that seated him so deeply, each jounce, each thrust, each poke butting against my sweet spot. Fuck. Fuck. Fuck me, it felt good!

I practically bit him in my enthusiasm as I tried to hide the noises I made. He didn't seem to mind my savagery. I think it actually turned him on because his tempo got faster, his cock thicker, until I shattered. And by shattered, I mean I creamed his cock with a bone-crushing orgasm. My pussy had never convulsed so hard. Never milked a dick with blissful waves and shudders like I did his. And he loved it. Loved it enough he bloody well howled when he came.

A little disconcerting to say the least, but it also put a smug smile on my lips. What could I say? It wasn't every day I made a werewolf lose control enough that he howled practically in public.

Sweating, smelling of sex, and limp as a noodle, I still managed to muster a giggle when I heard the distant exclamations asking what the hell had made that noise.

Nympho Chloe had struck again. Lucky for me, Pete and his wonderful ability to scent if people were around made it easy for us to escape without getting caught. We would have gotten away with no one the wiser but for one thing. Make that one person.

Brenda.

She cackled as she handed me my purse and coat in the parking lot where Pete had parked. Bitch. Wait until she needed me to cover up her sexcapade at the office. Then again, knowing her, she'd probably already had one, or two. She did so enjoy doing the naughty in public places.

As for me, with my werewolf lover free of charges, my pussy sated for the moment, and my belly full—because he stopped for food—I was happy as a human girl could be.

I should have known it wouldn't last.

Chapter Eleven

Somehow, we managed to make it to my place without ripping each other's clothes off and having sex in Pete's truck.

Barely.

By the time we reached my condo, we were ready for a quickie up against the wall before he took off to do his secret werewolf stuff.

A more curious girl would have asked to go along. I preferred to remain the alive girl and not the stupid one in the movie who sticks her nose where she shouldn't and ends up either dead, or kidnapped and tortured by the bad guy. To think, people thought watching too much television was bad. I'd have never learned this important life lesson if it weren't for marathon horror flicks.

Television might have just saved my life.

It didn't, however, give me someone to cuddle with or do anything to abate my worry over Pete. A behemoth such as him could probably handle anything that came his way—short of a Mack truck, and even then, I'd place bets on my werewolf lover.

As for the fact I fretted over his safety? It didn't mean a thing. Nope. I'd worry about anyone hunting a murderer who liked to eat his victims.

The reminder made me queasy. So, as a

snack, I stuck to a salad that night—without any bacon bits.

Around nine o'clock, while dressed in my comfiest jammies—adorned with pink sheep jumping over fences—a knock came at the door. Grabbing my biggest kitchen knife, I peered through the viewing hole. Someone, or something, blocked it.

"Who is it?" I asked in my best, I'm-not-afraid-of-you voice. It kind of sounded like a squeaky mouse on helium.

"Open up and find out," was the gruff reply.

"Ha. Not likely. Go away before I sic my really big boyfriend on you."

"You mean the one who left a few hours ago?"

Shit. Who the hell was at my door? And why were they watching my apartment?

My grip on the knife handle got slick with sweat. I eyed my cell phone on the living room table. For some reason, I feared moving away from the door, as if by moving it might suddenly fly open and let in whoever threatened on the other side.

"Open up." Said in a low cajoling voice.

No way was I listening. I wouldn't even open it if they said they had candy. "No."

"You do know that if I was a real bad guy, you just put yourself in a vulnerable position for attack," the unseen speaker mocked.

"Says you. I say this door is reinforced, bullet-proof steel on the best hinges available. Short of a stick of dynamite, no one can get in."

Leaning against the door, I added my weight to the barred portal. As if it needed it. My fathers invested heavily in security when I bought my downtown condo. Nothing short of a bomb would let anyone in that door. My daddies made sure their little girl was safe.

"Is that a dare?" The voice purred and goosebumps prickled my skin.

"It's a fact."

Click. Jingle.

Eyes wide in disbelief, I took a few steps back from the portal as my dual deadbolts and safety chain moved, on their own I might add, unlocking my door.

Either I was dealing with ghosts or magic. Either way, it was an oh shit moment. As if my life wasn't messed up enough already.

Where was a werewolf to hide behind when you needed one?

I raised my knife—wished for a gun with serious firepower—and aimed at the opening.

The door swung open, and Anthony grinned at me. "Evening."

I caught flies with my open mouth.

"You fucking, jerk!" I yelled. "You scared the crap out of me."

Speaking in a voice I recognized instead of his I'm-A-Psycho-Killer one, and completely unrepentant, he said, "Good. I wanted to see if you were smart enough to not answer blind."

"I didn't, and yet you managed to get in. How the fuck did you do that?"

He waggled his fingers. "A parlor trick."

I glared.

"Would you believe I possess a sexy magnetism?"

Yes, but I still glared some more.

"What if I said magic?"

That didn't remove my glower at all because if he had magic then he had some explaining to do.

"Is this where I apologize for scaring you and tell you I brought candy?"

Not completely mollified, I still took the peace offering of Belgian chocolate in the pretty gold box.

I ate a piece—the rich, dark chocolate melting on my tongue, releasing my tension—and sighed in pleasure before asking, "What are you doing here?" Because I'd assumed when I didn't hear from him all day that he'd cancelled our Monday night date.

"I came to spend quality time."

"You could have called."

"Why would I do that when we already had plans? Or did you already forget about the schedule we devised yesterday at brunch?"

Ah yes, their plan to share me. "I didn't forget, but it's not like you told me a set time. I think it's logical for me to have assumed you'd canceled given the hour."

"The hour? It's not late."

"You do realize it's after nine?" Working girls, despite what television portrayed, went to bed at reasonable hours on weeknights so they could drag their asses out of bed for work the next day.

"Is this a hint we should hurry to bed?"

Heat invaded my veins and I couldn't help a shiver at his implication.

Stepping into my apartment, into my personal space, Anthony approached me as I moved back. Despite him not touching it, a rapid heartbeat later, the door slammed shut.

More magic.

Or ghosts.

The latter I could call a priest about, the first…Why could Anthony suddenly do magic?

"You are seriously freaking me out." And then he really scared me because, between one blink and the next, Anthony disappeared from sight. What the fuck!

Arms encircled me from behind. My knife, which I'd forgotten I held, went flying and bounced hilt first on the couch. Before I could scream, I found myself spun and thoroughly kissed.

As embraces went, it was actually rather nice, hot even, and it totally turned me on. Not that I let it sway me. When Anthony let me breathe again, I lost my mind.

"What the hell is wrong with you?"

"Nothing some time with my girlfriend won't fix." He had the nerve to smirk.

He called me his girlfriend!

Cute, but I was way too wigged out still to appreciate it. "First, I am not your girlfriend." Fuck buddy, yes. Anything more, no. "Second, you scared the pants off me."

Down he peered. "I wish. Is that flannel?"

"Yes, it is, because I wasn't expecting company, especially not company who gets his kicks frightening women and then does some freaky-ass thing to my door."

"Didn't you get my note with the flowers? I told you I was coming over."

Yes, but in the meantime, I'd helped my other screw buddy get out of jail, had sex twice, showered, and convinced myself that no one would dare kill a girl in pink flannel jammies adorned with fluffy sheep. I'd also thought Anthony changed his mind.

"It's late. I thought you forgot. And don't change the subject, mister. What the hell was that whole freaky-stranger routine at my door?"

"I was testing you."

"For what? A heart condition?" Good news. Blood pressure was up, but I'd yet to fall to the ground paralyzed or twitching. I'd however probably lost about ten years of my life.

"I just wanted to make sure you were practicing some safety. With a killer on the loose, not to mention other innumerable criminal types, I wanted to make sure you would—"

"What? Answer the door and invite a rapist in?" As my pulse slowed, my caustic tongue took over.

"Maybe my plan was ill advised. I apologize. However, perhaps now you'll see my concern. You are not as safe here as you think. And really, a knife? As weapons go, you should have a firearm at the very least."

So I was beginning to grasp. Calmer now, it occurred to me to ask how he'd managed to open my door. "Who gave you a key to my place?"

"No key."

"But the locks. You undid them. And the chain too. Was it really magnets?" Some kind of new break-and-enter technology? Because my initial impulse to blame it on magic just couldn't be true. Suit wearing, perfectly coiffed hair, hot shot DAs did not go around opening doors with forces I did not believe in.

"Would you believe I used my mind?" He

tapped his temple with a finger.

"Bullshit." The expletive slipped from me, and the corners of his eyes crinkled.

"The truth. Watch." He turned to face my door. Without him touching or making any movement at all, I could only stare in disbelief as the deadbolt tumbler turned, clicking into place while the chain rose like a sinuous serpent to latch itself in the slidebar.

Oh my freaking gawd. Or not. Didn't Pete say Heaven didn't exist?

"How did you do that? Are you some kind of magician? Do you have telekinetic powers just like an X-Man?" Did he fight crime wearing a tight leather suit? And, more important, could these special powers come in handy during sex?

"Slow down. I'll answer everything if you but give me a moment."

"I will not slow down. I want to know what the heck you are. You told me I could trust you. That you wouldn't lie to me."

"And I haven't."

Putting some space between us, I planted my hands on my hips. "You have special powers."

"Yes, of a sort."

"No, not of a sort. You do and you didn't tell me. That's lying."

"No. That's not spilling all my secrets at once. If you'd asked me directly, I would have told you."

"Don't you dare argue semantics with me." Because I didn't need a repeat of court, where he argued me into a corner and won. "You're avoiding the question. What. Are. You?"

Stepping back from me, Anthony swept me a

bow and under a sweep of hair that fell over his eyes said, "I am Maelruanaidh Mor mac Tadg, descendent of the kingdom of Loylurg, known in this century as Anthony Vanderson. Day-walking vampire at your service."

Good thing I stood near the couch because I sat down hard. "A vampire." My words emerged faintly. "Oh, good grief. Please tell me you're kidding. This is a joke, right? You're pretending to be a vampire because you can't handle the fact that Pete's a werewolf. You know this isn't a competition. You don't need to one-up him. I like you just fine as a human."

"No joke, I'm afraid."

Judging by his serious mien, he meant it. Fucking great. I wasn't just shagging a werewolf; apparently, I was also screwing the undead, and I'd not even suspected it. I really needed to tone up on my people skills.

"Why are you telling me this now? I mean, you had to know I didn't have a clue."

"Before our relationship went any further, I felt it was time you knew the truth. Pete mentioned he'd—"

"Wait a second. You talked to Pete. When?"

"After his release and his meeting with you. He called and told me you'd taken the news of the existence of other beings quite well."

If by quite well he meant I'd not started drooling and banging my head off the wall while humming, then I guess I had. But hold on a second. Something he said penetrated my shock.

"You mean Pete knew what you were and didn't tell me?"

"It wasn't his secret to divulge."

Maybe, but it didn't mean I wouldn't kill him. Okay, not kill him kill him, but he'd hear about my displeasure, loudly and in very unladylike terms.

"Great. Just freaking great. It's not bad enough I have a werewolf determined to date me, now I have a bloody vampire too. This all makes sense now."

"What makes sense?"

"The reason why you're interested in me. I should have known I couldn't attract nice, ordinary *human* men. Oh no, lucky me, I get the freaks. The wolfman and the bloodsucker." I buried my face in my hands. "Why couldn't I just have a normal life?"

"Normalcy is overrated."

The sofa cushion alongside me sank as he settled at my side. I didn't resist the arm he placed around me. I didn't shy away. Vampire or not, I didn't fear him, nor did he repulse me. On the contrary, he might have gotten even sexier. Totally turned on or not, I did have an important question.

"I have to ask. Have you sucked blood from me?"

"Yes."

"During sex?" While leaving behind that hickey, I'd wager.

"Yes."

The nerve. I'd not agreed to being a blood donor or a free buffet. I should have shoved him away at that point. Socked him the gut at least. Ordered him to leave then chowed down on some garlic to keep him from coming back.

Instead, I queried, "So how do I taste?"

His lips teased the lobe of my ear as he

whispered the answer. "Like ambrosia."

"That's good, right?"

"The best. You are better than any fine wine. More decadent than any treat. Tasting you as my body thrusts into your welcoming sex is the most heavenly sensation I've ever felt."

Mmmm. Okay, that sounded way hotter than it should have, hot enough that my blood stirred. "You're exaggerating."

"I don't lie. Your absolute exquisiteness is one of the reasons why I'm willing to put up with the fact you have a werewolf lover."

"So you're with me because I taste good?"

"I'm with you because you've turned my dull existence around. Since the moment I met you, you've intrigued me. Your sharp mind. Your forthright tongue. Your splendid body. Your confident attitude. Being around you is a pleasure in and of itself. For the first time in centuries, I feel *alive.*"

I dare any woman not to melt a little at a declaration like that. I didn't prove immune. Turning my head, I caught his gaze, trying to ascertain if he jested, but his steady blue stare didn't waver. And, this time, when his eyes flashed an electric blue, he didn't turn away, and I couldn't blame it on a trick of the lights.

"Your eyes…"

"Glow when my emotions are especially strong. Most of the time, I can control it, but around you, I am like a fledgling again. Prone to intense sensations that overwhelm."

Me? Sasquatch-sized Chloe with the sharp tongue made an ancient vampire lose control? *Move over, Edward, I have a new vampire to crush on.* "I've got to confess something."

"What?"

"I've always had a thing for vampires." I honestly did. Or at least sexy ones who didn't appear as cadavers and didn't want to kill me.

"You're not appalled then."

"At this point, the only thing I am is horny. So unless you feel a need to dissect my emotions or give me lessons on being a vampire, I'd suggest you strip out of that suit before I demolish it."

"I have more suits."

Who could resist an invitation like that? I don't know who dove on who first. Who cared? Fabric ripped, teeth clashed, and flesh slapped against flesh as we came together in a passionate rush, my limbs locked around his waist while he thrust into me. I clung to him, my nails digging into his back while he sucked on the hollow of my neck. I could have easily come. My body was more than willing. To my annoyance, he slowed his frantic pumps then withdrew entirely.

I whimpered. Lucky me, Anthony wasn't done. He just had something different in mind. I lay splayed on my couch, my body naked and rosy with passion. Anthony knelt between my legs, his blond hair tickling my pale skin as he rubbed his cheeks against my inner thighs. His blue gaze caught mine as he lowered himself to lick my clit. I sucked in a breath. He lapped again, his tongue swirling and dancing, leaving me panting with pleasure.

"So tasty," he murmured against my slick flesh.

"More," I begged.

He complied. He worked my clit like a musician with an instrument, making it sing, pitching it to heights only a master of his craft could achieve. He brought me to a teetering apex of taut bliss, stringing it out until I thought I would die then retreating, ebbing me back down, just enough that I couldn't crest. When my clit couldn't handle anymore, he lapped at my pussy, spreading the moist lips, penetrating me with his tongue, spearing me with it. In my wantonness, my hips jerked, pressing against his mouth, demanding more. I needed something in me. Fingers, cock, anything. Something hard to fill the aching need he'd created.

As if sensing he'd driven me to sanity's edge, he finally poised himself over me. I gazed up into his mesmerizing blue eyes, the inner glow so alien and yet sexy. He didn't try to hide the tips of his fangs any longer, and they peeked from between his lips, their sharp points a sexy reminder of his vampire status.

A thrill went through me. *My very own vampire lover.* The dreamer in me, the romantic girl who'd once devoured everything to do with fanged lovers, shivered in anticipation.

"Bite me," I whispered. "Bite me and fuck me." *Show me the pleasure and bring my fantasy to life.*

A shudder went through him.

"You are a divine creature, Chloe," he murmured.

Yeah, I knew that. But we could talk about that later when I wasn't so horny. I locked my legs around his waist and drew him into me. His head went back, and he groaned. I squeezed his length, loving the thick feel of him in my sex. His cock answered with a pulse.

Down he came, his body covering mine, his lips catching mine in a torrid kiss as he began to thrust into me, rhythmically. In and out, a steady pace, one that made me gasp each time the head of him sank deep.

His mouth left mine and travelled, devouring the edge of my jaw, toying with the lobe of my ear, and I tracked his movement because I knew what was coming. Knew and wanted it. When he finally bit me, a tiny pinch that I was waiting for, euphoria swept through me. Unlike our previous encounter, I was fully aware he sucked on my blood. That he fed from me. It was even better than expected. I urged him on. How could I not, with ecstasy pouring through me, energizing me, driving my pleasure to heights only before imagined? I opened my mouth in a silent scream as I came, my body trembling and squeezing around his driving cock, milking him until, with a final thrust, he came within me.

Chests heaving, bodies entwined, we lay in a mess of limbs on my couch.

"Wow," I gasped when I regained the power of speech.

He chuckled. "Is this where I say you're welcome?"

I slapped him lightly. "Hey, I played a part."

"You were the entire sum of the reason for the pleasure. Never doubt that."

Shifting himself, he tugged me until I sat upon his lap, our legs extended on the couch, my head resting back against his chest. Cradled thus, I could feel the thump of his heart and found myself brimming with questions. First and foremost, "Why don't you seem dead?"

A rumble beneath my head made me vibrate as he laughed. "Because I'm not. Vampirism is a genetic change. A cell mutation if you will. I am just as alive as a human. I breathe. I bleed. My heart beats. All of my organs function pretty much the same as before."

"But?"

"But vampires are something more than human. Think of vampirism as a virus. It invades the body, but in this case, it changes the cellular structure. Improves it. As soon as we go through the change, aging is stopped. Our ability to heal increases a thousand fold. We become sensitive to ultra violet rays and hunger for the nutrients found only in fresh blood."

"Hold on a second, if you're so sensitive to ultra violet rays, how come you can go outside? Shouldn't you, like, burn to a crisp?" Did he have to invest in super-duper sunblock?

"I would burn alive were it not for a magical binding placed upon me."

"Magic?" There was that pesky word again. For a girl who hadn't known magic existed a few days ago, I seemed to come across a lot of examples of it lately. "You mean you have a spell that makes you immune to the sun's rays?"

"A very costly, but well worthwhile, spell. You've seen the tattoo on my back?"

I was almost embarrassed to admit I hadn't. Last time I was with Anthony, I found myself more focused on other things, such as how quickly I could get him inside me. "Flip around and show me."

Dumped off his lap, I sat on the couch as he

stood, long lean lines moving with a grace I found utterly sexy. Where Pete was all raw, animalistic masculinity, Anthony was elegance personified, every motion calculated and fluid. Turning around, he laced his fingers behind his head, pulling the skin of his back taut. "Wow." Once again, my massive vocabulary sprang from my lips. But, really, I don't know if there existed a better word to describe the art on his back. And it was art, of the most incredible kind.

Where the skin of his body was pale all over—with good reason as it turned out—his back displayed a colorful canvas. There, in glaring relief, from one shoulder to the next, from his neck down to the crease of his buttocks, was an intricate tattoo, a plethora of odd symbols and raised, ridged flesh. I peered closer at the almost Egyptian-like images and squiggles done in a rainbow of colors, trying to make sense of the abstract art.

Reaching out, I traced some of the scar tissue, and he shivered. "This must have hurt."

"It did. The spell took three days to craft and cost me a fortune in gold and jewels."

"I'll bet. How did you know it would work? I mean, weren't you scared the first time you stepped out into sunshine that you would light up like a torch? That the spell would fail?"

"I was terrified actually, although, if you tell anyone, I will deny it." He grinned at me over his shoulder, a boyish expression that I would have never expected from him. "But the joy I felt when, for the first time in five hundred years, the sun bathed my face in its warmth—"

I ogled him, mouth hanging attractively wide

open. "Whoa a second there, buddy. Did you say five hundred? Just how freaking old are you?"

"Old."

"As in Christopher Columbus old or older?"

"Older."

I wrinkled my nose. "Doesn't that make me young enough to be like your great times a million granddaughter?"

He laughed. "Probably. However, keep in mind, our longevity isn't something vampires dwell on. If we only made friends or lovers from those our age, we'd find ourselves very lonely, given our sparse numbers. When choosing those we will associate with, we prefer to make our choice based on personality rather than actual age."

"Still, though, don't we seem immature? I mean, the shit you've seen. Experienced. I'm like a baby compared to you."

"Again. We don't look at things the same way. We can't."

"So you never date other vampires? Only humans?"

"I could date another such as myself, if any intrigued me, I suppose."

"I smell a but."

"As mentioned, we are few. Of those walking this earth, many are jaded, disillusioned with humanity and life. Others are into practices I prefer to abstain from."

If it made him grimace in distaste, then I probably didn't want to know what these other vampires did. However, I did ask, "Does this mean you're going to ditch me when I get old? I mean, if we stay fuck buddies and all."

He grinned at my slip. "I am not with you because of your looks or youth, but because of you."

"Still, though, in a few years, I'll start showing my age while you'll remain young."

"Or not. There are ways of extending your life and appearance. You could even make the choice to attempt the change."

"Me, a vampire?" I couldn't help but laugh at the idea.

He arched a brow. "Why the mirth? Aren't you tempted by the concept of immortality?"

A good question. I pondered it. Would I want to live forever? Just imagine the things I could see. Experience. Maybe I'd live long enough to see a space shuttle make it to Mars. Or colonize other worlds. What a thrill to be around when they got the cure for cancer. Or cloned a dinosaur.

However, as the world turned and history got made, its inhabitants would move with it. Immortality meant I'd have to watch as those I knew and loved aged and passed on. Things and people I took for granted would change. Get old. Die. Become obsolete. I would have to hide who I was.

Heavy thoughts. Definitely not a decision to take lightly. One I wouldn't have an answer to today or even tomorrow. When it came to making decisions about forever, I'd have to make sure I had all the facts, pondered all the ramifications.

And make the choice while not tempted as I currently was, cuddled naked and face to face with my lover who'd resumed his seated position on the couch. Straddling a hot, aroused vampire was not the best position in which to make life-altering choices. But I could ask questions.

"First off, I'm not too crazy about the idea of a blood diet."

"You can still eat everything you do now. You would just require extra sustenance."

"So I wouldn't have to give up donuts?"

"You could eat as many as you liked and never gain a pound."

Ooh, I liked that. "Would it make me pretty?" Because vampires were universally attractive. Just read any vampire romance, it was a known fact.

"You are already beautiful."

"Good answer."

"The truth."

"I've never liked the idea of a tattoo, but I love the sun."

A shadow crossed his face. "Unfortunately, you would have to give up daylight as the art to day walking was lost centuries ago when the church got rid of the mages."

No sunshine. Ack! I didn't know if I could live for centuries never again experiencing the warming touch of the sun's rays. "There's got to be an instruction manual somewhere."

He shook his head. "Those who hunted the magically inclined were thorough."

"The demon purge," I stated.

"I take it the werewolf told you about that. Yes. The ones with the knowledge needed to cast such a spell died during that time, their tomes burnt to eradicate their teachings. I've not heard of anyone since who's managed to replicate the process."

"Sounds like the pros and cons are balancing out. I don't know. You said it yourself. Until I came along, life sucked. Or is that unlife?" I cackled at my bad joke.

He poked me in the ribs and turned it into a squeal as I fought his ticklish fingers.

"Enough!" I gasped at one point.

"Promise you won't make any more bad undead jokes."

"I promise, *old man.*" I smirked, and he let out a bellowing laugh.

The serious and disturbing turn in our conversation faded as we indulged in a full-blown tickle fight. Turned out he didn't have any squirmy spots, but I still enjoyed attempting to find some and he most definitely enjoyed the exploration. Especially when I rode him cowgirl, and he hissed, "That's the spot."

One way or another, I managed to make him scream for mercy. And when he came, despite the countless lovers he must have entertained over the centuries of his life, he yelled *my* name.

Chapter Twelve

Waking the next morning, once again alone in my bed, I couldn't help but begin to get a complex.

Did vampires not like to cuddle?

Did I snore?

Was my morning dragon breath that bad?

Would I need to invest in some cuffs and keep Anthony shackled to my side so I could at least experience one morning where I could roll over and snuggle, maybe get me some vampire nookie to start the day?

Kicking off my sheets, I splayed out on my mattress, fully naked, and indulged in a bone-cracking, muscle-wrenching stretch. I couldn't believe after the Monday I'd had that I'd woken before my alarm. And to such a glorious, sunny day.

I froze mid-stretch and craned my head to peek at my clock. Ten o'clock.

Oh shit! I'd overslept.

Jumping from bed, I ran for the bathroom to turn the water on then headed to the kitchen to grab a cup of coffee while the shower warmed up. I skidded to a halt in my living room as I saw who stood behind the breakfast bar and who sat at it.

"Morning," my pair of suitors said.

Ever wish you'd thrown on a robe and run a

brush through your hair, maybe rinsed with some mouthwash, before dashing out like a crazy person?

Apparently, I didn't have a fairy godmother standing by to grant my wish. Lucky me. Instead, I ended up stark naked, rumpled, and beet red in front of the guys vying for my body.

If ever there was a time I wished I possessed the cool nonchalance of a cat, now was that time.

Embarrassed—kind of horny because damn did they look good—and annoyed, I snapped, "Okay, which of you wise guys shut off my alarm?"

Anthony raised his hand. "Guilty." And not appearing repentant one bit.

I planted my hands on my hips, trying not to think of how incongruous I must appear. "Why did you do that? I have to work today."

"Not anymore you don't."

"What's that supposed to mean?"

"As of today, you are on a two week vacation."

I blinked. "Vacation? But I don't have any vacation time banked." Not since the drunken cruise Brenda and I had taken in late March. Good times, I was sure, or so the pictures indicated. Myself, I didn't remember much of it.

"It's an unpaid vacation."

"Unpaid?" I gasped. "Excuse me? I don't think I heard you right. Are you saying you not only booked me off, but that I'm not even getting paid for it?"

"Yes."

Good sex or not, vampire or not, I blasted him. "You have a lot of nerve. You know, some of us have to work to make ends meet. It's how I pay the rent, buy food, you know the normal stuff us poor folk have to do."

"You don't have to worry about any of those things. I'll make sure you're covered."

He did not just say that. I straightened my spine and shot him a haughty glare. "I don't want your money."

"I'm not giving you my money. I'm making you work for it."

I gaped at him. "If you think you're paying me to have sex—"

The shock on his face was clear, even to me. "What? Good grief, no, woman. Why would you think that?"

Heat made my cheeks hot enough to melt butter. "Well, the only work I've done with you was of the um…" Tapering off, I glanced at Pete, who struggled to hold in a grin.

He waved a butter knife at me. "You can say it aloud. I know you're having sex with the vampire."

Way to remind me of his omission when we'd had our heart-to-heart the previous day. He got the full force of my cold glare as well.

"Fine then. I will say it. I might be having sex with you, but I draw the line at being paid for it. Even if I am that good. I might be a slut where you both are concerned, but I am not a whore." It sounded a whole lot better in my head.

Pete lost the battle and burst out laughing while Anthony scowled. "Woman, you are sometimes too forthright, not to mention quick to jump to conclusions. I am not talking about paying you for sex. When I said work, I meant real work. Work where you will use your mind and wear clothes."

I flopped onto the couch, noted the interest the guys displayed in the shadowed vee between my splayed thighs and crossed my legs then grabbed a pillow and hugged it to my lap. "I think I need a coffee."

Pete rounded the counter with a steaming mug before I'd even finished my sentence. "I've got bagels toasting. Cream cheese sound okay, or do you want something else?"

"Just butter," I muttered as I wrapped my hands around the warm cup.

"Coming right up."

I closed my eyes as I sucked back a mouthful of coffee. Instead of my usual bitter brew, a rich flavor tickled my taste buds and I inhaled deep. "Is this French vanilla?"

"It is. I took the liberty of gathering some essentials."

I peered at Anthony with one eye. "You're a vampire. How is fancy coffee essential?"

"Just because I require blood doesn't mean I don't eat or enjoy a fine beverage."

"Wow, do the vampire books have their shit wrong." But I didn't really care. I kept drinking my caffeinated ambrosia, aware of the thick silence, interspersed by the sound of traffic outside.

Pete broke first. "How did you sleep?"

I snickered. Then outright laughed. "Really? That's what you're going to ask me? How did I sleep? Fine. Just fine. As a matter of fact, my whole world is fine. Dandy even. I'm dating a werewolf and a vampire. I'm out of a job, looking at becoming homeless and having a conversation, naked, I might add, with two men who are eyeing me like a piece of steak."

"I'll have you know I never get a boner when I see my steak." Pete's grin and wink made me giggle again, but this time with real mirth.

Some of my tension eased. No point in acting the role of bitch, or at least not until I knew exactly what Anthony needed me for. Besides, with java running through my veins and my belly about to get filled, my mood improved by leaps and bounds. Pete handed me a bagel, toasted and buttered, on a paper plate. Apparently, I wasn't the only one not into doing dishes.

"Are you having one?" Pete asked Anthony as he returned to his spot in the kitchen.

"I'm not hungry, thank you," Anthony replied.

"What, not even for a hemoglobin snack? Bag of blood? Big juicy steak?" I added in between mouthfuls of toasted perfection. Brownie point for Pete. He knew how to tame my morning grouch.

"I'm actually vegan," Anthony stated.

Half chewed bits of bagel went flying as I snorted. "Excuse fucking me? A vampire vegan? Isn't that like against the natural order of things?"

"Not really when you think of it. When you're used to drinking blood, warm and rich from the source, meat, of any kind, pales in comparison. I'd go so far as to call it disgusting. It's dead flesh. Refrigerated for days or, worse, frozen then thawed." Anthony shuddered. "Even the smell of it is nauseating."

"So you don't eat meat of any kind?"

"Not entirely. I do enjoy sushi so long as the

fish is prepared on the spot from live specimens. Lobster is also a favorite of mine."

I wrinkled my nose. "Eew. That is just way too fresh and raw for me. I like my animals dead and cooked. Or at least singed at any rate." I preferred not to think of the process in between them munching on hay and ending up on my plate.

"Grilled and red inside, the bloodier the better," Pete added. "But I'm pretty sure Chloe here isn't interested in our diet so much as what you meant by getting her to work."

"Actually, I'm most interested in knowing who gave you the right to screw with my life?" Food to tame my grumbling belly and time to think over Anthony's actions didn't make them any more acceptable. How dare he make decisions for me? "Sleeping together does not give you the right to book me off on holiday. I mean, seriously. We are fuck buddies—"

"Lovers."

"—and, as such, there are ground rules. One of them is, don't mess with my job."

"You could do better."

Anthony's assessment gave me a warm feeling inside. I squashed it. "That's not the point. The point is, it's my life. My choice. Did it ever occur to you to ask?" *So I could say no.*

"As if you would have agreed. Don't forget, I'm getting to know you."

"Then you should have known this would piss me off."

"I did."

"And yet you did it anyway?"

"I had to. You would have never agreed and I

didn't have time to argue. I need your help and work would have interfered, so I did what was necessary to ensure I had your undivided attention."

Wow, someone sure showed his age. Didn't he follow the news at all? Women were no longer chattel. We had rights and made our own decisions now. "What if I don't want to work for you? Did that ever occur to you?"

"Yes."

"And?"

Anthony shrugged. "I am, as you put it, ancient, which makes me old-fashioned. As you are my woman, I made an executive decision."

"Your woman?" The feminist in me took affront. The woman in me…yeah, she might have creamed herself a little.

Pete chuckled in between his consumption of bagels, a plateful from what I could see. "Dude, I can't believe you said that and didn't end up with a stake in your heart. She must like you because I'll bet anyone else would be crying for their mother right about now."

Oh, how sweet. My werewolf did know me.

"Don't try and sweet-talk me, furball. You're obviously in cahoots with him."

He didn't deny it. "I am. Wanna punish me?" He raised a brow and quirked one corner of his mouth.

Yes, I did want to punish him. With my tongue then pussy. However, given I didn't know which of them I wanted to punish more, the only one suffering was me because now I was hornier than ever. *Great. Just great. Naked and aroused with two men over, and I can't do a damned thing about it because if I choose one to take care of me the other will end up offended.* A pity I couldn't just do both.

I am such a slut. One way of looking at it. On the other hand, though, one could say taking them both on showed my practical side. Heck, it even catapulted me into the caring category, sacrificing my morals to please both my lovers at once. As if they'd ever go for that scenario. Hold on a second, since when did I think three-way sex was a viable option?

Brenda and her whacky sexcapades must have rubbed off on me more than I expected.

Mmm, rubbing...

I mentally slapped myself. "Stop distracting me and get to the point. What is it you both expect me to do? I mean, the only skills I have are courtroom-related, and neither of you are in jail."

"The day is young," quipped Pete.

I bit my inner cheek to prevent a smile. Damned guy was really too comical.

"Actually, it's what you do before you make it to court that I need," Anthony answered. "I need your investigative skills. There was another murder last night."

"I didn't do it!" Pete announced, lifting his hands in the universal gesture of innocence. "And I have an alibi this time."

An alibi that wasn't me? I narrowed my eyes as I asked, "Who?"

"Put the green-eyed monster away, baby. I was with three other Lycans. Male ones. We were trying to see if we could sniff out a trail from the witch's house."

"Did you find one?"

"Nope, but we did discover a great pizza

joint."

At least with Pete around, I'd never go hungry. The man appeared to love his food. "Back to the new murder. I take it the body was found in the same state as Ms. Heksen?" Brownie points for me, I didn't mistakenly call her the witch.

"Bodies this time. A pair of them. Male and female," Anthony replied. My brows rose at this tidbit. The killer had expanded his repertoire. He continued. "And, yes, they both showed signs of being eaten and drunk from."

"Were they found in the same place? Or killed apart?"

"Apart. And both, like the first victim, were magic users."

"Witches!" Pete growled.

"Down, boy. No need to get your hackles up, although, you can bring me another bagel." Turned out I didn't mind being fed by a hot guy.

"I am not your dog," he rumbled even as he moved to fulfill my request.

"And I am not your bitch," I retorted. "Glad we got that clarified."

Having shut him up, I mulled the news as I waited for my bagel. "So, there was another killing. Not sure why you need me. I'm not a detective. I never met these people who died and I am most certainly not a witch."

"I don't know about the witch part, you've certainly cast a spell over me." Anthony, more than five hundred years old Anthony, used the corniest line ever.

I still giggled. "That was so bad it was cute."

Frowning, Pete handed me a plate with a

freshly toasted bagel.

Mmm. Bagel... I might have sounded a bit like Homer Simpson and drooled a little.

Pete's turn to smirk.

Look at me, the bone of contention between two men.

It was seriously as annoying as it was hot.

Anthony adjusted his cravat. From perfect to, still perfect. It totally gave me an urge to run my fingers through his hair and ruffle it.

So I did. Standing from the couch, dropping the pillow, plate in hand, I made sure to walk past him, even if it made my path to the kitchen longer. My hands slid through his blond strands, making it lose its pristine perfection.

His eyes widened. He sucked in a breath he probably didn't need.

I walked past, realizing I was the object they stared at.

They. Stared. At. Me.

And it feels so good.

Sure they saw the naked Chloe, the hot siren version of Chloe, but that was only part of why they kept coming around.

They wanted me.

Dropping the plate, I snagged the cold bacon he hid from me.

I wagged it in the air. "I can't believe you were offering me bagels when there was some salty protein for me to eat."

Too late.

I only realized my mistake once the words escaped my lips.

I'd just tossed down the dirty innuendo

challenge in front of a pair of alpha men.

They took up that dirty glove and spanked me with it.

"I've got some fresh meat with a salty finish if you're really in the mood for something to eat," purred Pete.

"Why would you expect her to do the work for you? I'd prefer to give her any kind of protein she needs. Give while she receives."

They both seemed to think their offers were more appealing than the bacon.

In that moment, the bacon won. I sashayed back to the couch with my salty offerings. Plopping down, a fresh pillow covered my lap. Best to not overwhelm them with my attributes.

They'd see them soon enough again at this rate.

"So people are dead. Witches. Cops are baffled."

In between bites and chewing, I mused the situation they placed in front of me. "I still don't get what you expect me to do."

Anthony finger combed his hair. Naughty boy. Did he seriously try and tempt me to rise again to muss it.

He held my gaze as he explained. "We need you to do what you usually do. Dissect the evidence. Find the trail to the real criminal."

Actually, I usually preferred to find evidence convicting other people. Usually, though, it didn't bode well for my client. Even worse, I couldn't exactly hide what I found from the prosecution.

But in this case, Pete was already innocent. I wasn't defending anyone. Still, though, I was the one who lost in court. Against Anthony at any rate. Would he want me. "Why are you investigating the evidence? You'll probably be the one trying to put them away," I asked.

"This isn't about putting them away after they're caught, though, but finding them in the first place."

Pete interrupted. "The problem is, we can't smell what it is killing them."

"You've been to the crime scenes?" I asked.

"After the fact. Any scent trail that might have existed is too compromised to easily follow."

The idea of smelling someone out reminded her of what Pete was.

A wolfman.

Can he smell me now?

It made a girl yearn for a shower, especially to wash off the damned crumbs sticking to her skin between her boobs. Rubbing or flicking them off would draw attention to her stellar eating skills..

"You're asking me to get involved in an active investigation, without permission from my office. I am a girl who follows the laws." At Pete's snicker, I amended. "Most of them."

"I won't deny this might compromise you from being involved in the case if it goes to trial."

"Why won't you?" she asked.

"Because it would be seen as initiative. Being prepared to put away the bogeyman killing citizens."

A rude noise escaped Pete. "Now he's stylizing himself a super hero."

"Just don't wear a cape." I'd seen *The Incredibles.*

"If we're done joking, perhaps we should

concentrate on the task at hand. We need to find out what's targeting—"

"Don't you mean who?" We were dealing with person. Right?

Right?!

"We can't be sure what's dong this," Anthony replied, confirming my fear. "Could be a demon, or something else, targeting these magic users. Doesn't really matter what it is, though, we need to stop it before it starts going after others."

"You mean others as in humans?"

"Yes. Can you imagine the panic if the population got wind of these attacks, and what was behind them? They'd make the Salem witch trials seem like a walk in the park."

In today's electronic age, vigilantes were quick to blame, and once things hit the Twitter-verse, they lasted forever. Out would come the twitchforks, and no one with a supernatural gene or a funny-looking mole or a third nipple would survive.

"This isn't going to put me in danger, is it?" Always best to look out for number one. I never aspired to being a heroine—unless it was in cartoon form, and I had the most kickass bodysuit ever, with bitching boots.

"You'd better not be in danger," Pete muttered with a sharp look at Anthony. "Fang boy over here promised you would just be looking over case files. As far as I am concerned, you are not to go near any of the crime scenes, nor will you interview anyone we deem a risk."

"How reassuring." My sarcastic tone was in fine form this morning.

"You will also not be alone at night,"

Anthony added. "Demons, much like vampires, have an intolerance in their natural form for sunlight. Either Pete or I will spend the nights with you. We will not leave you unguarded."

"Backing up a second." I held up a hand. "Exactly why would I be in any danger? Do you know something I don't?"

"Of course you're not in danger," Anthony said in a soothing tone.

I held up my fingers in a cross. "Don't you be trying to spell me with your incredible eyes."

"What are my eyes?" Pete growled.

"Don't you start," I snapped. "I am still trying to find out why I'd be in danger enough to need you bodyguarding me." One on either side would work.

"Consider it a precaution."

"We won't do anything that risks your safety," Pete added. Then he grinned and winked as he said, "You never have to worry when I'm around. I'll eat anyone who even looks at you sideways, baby."

Over-protective, kind-of-disturbing threat, but hot nonetheless. "Is this a ploy to have nookie and sleep over because I thought we'd clarified that already. I'm okay with the whole sex thing. Just don't try and make it into something more."

"Even without the demon running around, you wouldn't be spending your nights alone." The blue light in Anthony's eyes told me, without words, what we'd do when darkness fell.

I shivered in delight. "I feel like I should throw out the fact that I am not a person who does danger."

"And yet you do me." Pete's leer earned him a dirty look.

Anthony shook his head. "How you could sleep with one so crass…"

"Oh stuff it, ivory. You might have mesmerized her into thinking she likes you but—"

"I did no such thing."

"Sure you didn't."

As they argued about who was the better man—something I'd yet to decide since they both appealed to me in different ways—I wrapped my dignity around me, which did nothing for my nudity, and stood from the couch. Time for a shower, which, as luck would have it, ran cold. I'd forgotten to turn it off in my mad dash to get ready for work.

The icy thirty-second sluice-off did wonders for my mood and, even better, killed my arousal. But it did nothing to quell the hurricane of questions in my mind. My thoughts whirled in circles.

What could I do to help find a killer? Despite Anthony's confidence, I wondered what I could add to their investigation. And, more importantly, did I really want to dig deeper into this murder/mystery with an honest-to-god monster at its core?

While I mulled that over, I also wondered what I should do with my two lovers who seemed determined to crowd me. On the one hand, I found their attention flattering—another word for arousing yet, at the same time, discomfited because there was just something wrong, laws or not, about having two men casually talking about sharing me.

Did I need to devise a schedule and install a revolving door so my men didn't hit each other coming and going from my bed?

To think, only days ago, my biggest problem was finding clean underwear because I'd forgotten to do the laundry again.

When I emerged from the shower, shivering and no closer to an answer to any of my problems, it was to find Pete lounging on my bed. I ignored his evident interest in my damp body and dressed. "I take it you pulled guard duty?"

"Anthony had to go and meet with some people. He left you a USB stick with the case files. Said to call him if you find anything. He'll be back around dinner time to take over for me."

"So you're just going to sit here all day babysitting me?" I didn't think I could handle him hovering over me all day unless he planned to do it naked with his cock buried deep. But it would make reading and concentrating on the task at hand difficult.

"Actually, I planned on napping. I didn't get much sleep last night. Wake me if you *need* me." The curve of his lips let me know what kind of need he preferred. The fact I'd thought about indulging in his innuendo didn't mean I caved to the allure. I was still mad at him. At them both.

They'd taken it upon themselves to make executive decisions about my life. The fact that they did it for altruistic reasons didn't make it right. I'd help, but only because I didn't want to see anyone else die. However, if they thought they'd get any nookie after the stunt they pulled, well... They probably would, but they'd have to work for it, dammit!

Ignoring his puppy eyes, I waltzed out of the bedroom—with a swing of my hips that made him groan—and shut the door. Before I could get to work on the case, my phone rang. BFF alert, or so the ring tone of "The Lady is a Tramp" informed me.

"Where the fuck are you?" Brenda asked.

"At home," I answered.

"Are you sick? Someone said you took two weeks off. What the hell? And why didn't you call?"

Uh-oh, hurt feeling warning. Time to soothe some ruffled feathers. "I'm not sick, and I was going to call. I just didn't have a chance. It was kind of sudden. Blame my stalkers. They took it upon themselves to place me on a working holiday."

"Sex isn't supposed to be work, Chloe."

"Gee, Brenda, talk about a one-track mind. I meant real work." Never mind the fact I'd assumed the same thing.

"Rewind and explain."

I gave her the nutshell version without demons, implying I did it to help out Pete and his Lycan buddies from getting the blame. I didn't enjoy lying; however, still coming to grips with the secrets I'd been given, I fudged the truth.

"Chloe, sex pot detective. Fighting crime alongside her lovers. I like it. It will make a great story to tell your kids one day."

"Would you stop that? I am not in a relationship with Pete or Anthony."

"Whatever. Let me know if anything exciting happens. And, by exciting, I mean if you finally get naked and wild with both."

I hung up as she started to give me pointers.

Booting up my laptop, I inserted the memory storage unit Anthony had left me of the case and perused the contents. It didn't take long for me to get sucked in to the mystery.

The guys had summarized the scenario pretty accurately.

The newest bodies were found around the same time, one by the victim's girlfriend as she came off her night shift, the other by a passerby who noted feet hanging out of the bushes. Their times of death were estimated to have happened within hours of each other, one around elevenish, the other about two or three a.m.

In both cases, none of the neighbors admitted to hearing anything. Odd, because I know if I was getting ripped to shreds and siphoned, I'd probably scream my face off.

I jotted a few notes.

Do demons have the power to hypnotize? Why don't the victims call for help? Are there signs of them being gagged? And why are these murders occurring outside?

What drew these witches from the relative safety of their homes to meet with the monster in the first place?

As I read through the reports, nothing jumped out at me, so I put them aside to go through the dozens of digital images taken at the homes of each of the victims. Witches or not, they lived just like any regular person would.

Ugly mismatched furniture. Knick-knacks ranging from a collection of glass figurines to baseball caps. Definitely not rich magic practitioners, so the murders weren't financially motivated. Unless they all had big life insurance policies going to one person, which led to me make another notation.

Motive? Why kill them? They had magic in

common.

Did the victims know each other? Maybe they all belonged to the same club? Or was that a coven? Could the three of them, or more, have gotten together and summoned the demon? Did they cause their own demise by dabbling in things better left alone?

Another thought struck me. How did one get rid of a demon? Could we kill it, or would we have to use a spell to banish it?

Oh and skip the *we*. No way was I going anywhere near any of the danger. Or at least smart Chloe said that. Brave Chloe, however, the one who now slept with not one but two guys outside of the human realm, wondered what it would be like to swoop in and play the part of heroine.

My inner sleuth longed to put on her sexiest crime-fighting boots—thigh-high black leather of course—and hit the pavement in search of clues. What a rush it would be to find the crack that broke the case wide open. To know I'd played a part in saving lives and making the world a safer place.

A great fantasy if we were dealing with something normal. Something human. But a demon? Maybe I'd hold off on fulfilling my inner crime-fighting fantasy for a case fraught with a little less supernatural danger.

Now, if only I could convince my lovers to do the same.

Alone, I could at least admit to myself that I didn't like the fact Anthony and Pete seemed hell bent on inserting themselves in the midst of the danger. Despite my annoyance with them and their determined involvement in my life and business, I didn't wish them ill. Actually, the thought of them getting hurt didn't sit well with me at all.

I preferred not to dwell on what that meant. As far as I was concerned, I cared for their safety and welfare the same as I would anyone who put themself in danger. Lying to myself sucked, especially since I was a horrible liar.

No way was I falling for them. Nope. Not me. Great sex. That's all we had. All I wanted. Nothing more. No matter what they seemed to think, or want.

Back I went to the pictures, needing distraction from dilemmas best left alone. Panning through them, I noted food bowls and water dishes on the floor in all of them. Flipping back through the reports, though, only one mentioned they'd found a cat.

Ms. Heksens's infamous black kitty, found calmly sleeping on the front porch in a wicker chair. Odd because Pete told me he'd had it picked up by animal control. The victim must have sprung it before her demise.

The other two victims, while showing signs of owning a pet, didn't have mention of one by the cops investigating. I shelved it under not important. No itty-bitty cat had torn these people apart.

But…

Inspiration hit. Off the couch I bounded, and I skipped into my bedroom. I'd no sooner set foot inside saying his name than Pete rolled from my mattress and sprang across the room, one hand tucking me behind him, his tense body filling the doorway as his head swung from side to side.

I tapped a shoulder, noting his rigid

muscles—*and is he sniffing the air?* "Uh, Pete?"

"Yeah. What is it, baby? Did someone knock? Did you get a funny feeling?"

I had a feeling all right; it was anything but funny.

Call me insatiable, or fickle, I didn't care. A man who instantly thought to protect a girl, using his own body as a shield, totally turned me on. Forget my earlier irritation. With one sexy move, he'd redeemed himself.

And fired up my libido.

I slid my arms around his muscular frame and said in a husky murmur, "No danger."

He turned to face me, his hands coming to rest on my hips, pulling me against him, showing me without words that my proximity didn't leave him untouched. Something appeared very happy to feel me.

"If we're not under attack, then what has you rushing in here? Did you find something?"

Oh right. The case. Concentrating proved hard when all my thoughts involved him and me, naked, sweaty and panting.

"It's probably nothing." I toyed with the ends of his hair, tickling his nape. The tips of my nipples pointed as he tucked me closer to his bare chest.

"Sometimes the smallest clue can solve a case," he murmured. His eyes fairly smoldered as he stared down at me.

"Just an idea. About why we keep finding the victims outside."

"We wondered about that too. Most witches have magical protection around their homes preventing entry to the uninvited."

"You mean demons can't go in?"

"Demons. Vampires. Fairies."

"Lycans?"

"We're too human for it to work." He grinned at me.

However, while still aroused, my brain was mulling over this new information, which actually made my theory even more viable.

"So, the demon knows he can't go in the house and kill these witches." Oops. "I mean victims. So how does he lure them? They're obviously not going to answer the door and invite it in. The demon could skulk around, waiting for them to come out at night. Or he could create an opportunity."

"What are you thinking?"

"All of these people owned cats or pets of some sort."

"Familiars."

"Whatever." Not all of us were up to date on the latest terminology in the witching world. "If the victims were anything like my old neighbor, they wouldn't go to bed unless Fluffy or Fido was inside, where they're safe."

Pete's hand dropped from my hips and he paced before me, catching on. "The demon kills the cat—"

"Or cages it."

"The owners come looking for it, stepping outside the house and the boundary of their protective spell. Then wham. Instant dinner." He snapped his teeth and pretended to chew.

I recoiled. "Okay, that was gross."

"Sorry."

How surprising. He didn't look repentant.

"It's one theory. But it could be wrong."

"Easy enough to check."

"How do you figure?"

"Find the cat and sniff it."

"You know, I really wish you wouldn't say things like that."

"Why?"

"Because it's disturbing." No one liked to think of their boyfriend sniffing an animal. Ack. How did that word boyfriend sneak in there? I'd mentally castigate myself for it later. Pete was still talking.

"We should get out to the crime scenes and check it out while it's still daylight."

"Hold on a second. What's this *we* business? I don't do danger, remember?"

"You'll be perfectly safe with me."

"I'm also perfectly safe here. I don't need to go."

"I won't leave you unprotected."

"Don't be silly. Anthony said demons roam at night. And besides, I'm not a witch. The demon or whatever is doing these things doesn't even know I exist. I'm perfectly safe."

Ever challenged a testosterone-laden werewolf with an overdeveloped protective instinct? It resulted in great sex. After we finished fighting.

Stepping away from him, I crossed my arms over my chest. "I'm not going."

He growled, and I could practically see the hair on his body bristle. "Don't challenge me, baby."

"Not challenging, telling."

"Same thing." He invaded my personal space. "I don't like it when you argue. Not when it's about your safety."

I placed a hand on his chest. "If you don't want me to argue, then stop acting like a caveman. And don't use my safety as an excuse. We both know it's a flimsy one. You said it yourself. It's daytime. The thing we're hunting doesn't like sunlight, doesn't know who I am or where I live. By all accounts, I'm in no immediate danger."

In one ear, out the other. "You're coming with me."

"Did you hear a word I said?"

"Yup."

"And?"

"Wasted breath. You are coming with me."

In a fit of girl pique—my first ever—I stamped my foot a la Brenda. "I don't recall giving you the right to give me orders. You don't own me."

"But I'd like to."

Well, that took me aback. It also gave me a cheap thrill that would have appalled most feminists. "Um, excuse me. But this isn't the Middle Ages. Women aren't objects anymore, you know."

"I do know, but it doesn't stop how I feel. I want you, Chloe. Want you as mine." He growled the last bit.

"I thought we said no commitment." The words emerged high-pitched and nervous.

"I never said that. You did."

"Yes I did say it, which means you need to——"

Apparently ignore it. That or he was just tired of talking. Whatever the reason, he silenced me with a hard kiss and, despite the fact that my logical side knew he was doing this to prevent me from arguing, I didn't stop him.

Instant passion flared between us. Flames stoked to life, flushing my body with heat and desire.

We tumbled onto my bed, where he made quick work of my clothes, and his. Never once did his lips leave mine, not even when he drove into me. I was more than ready, though, my slick pussy welcoming his urgent thrusts. Arguing with him, even over his caveman tactics—which, despite my protests, I found quite flattering—made me horny. I'd never had someone so ardently pursue me. So determined to have me. So eager to fuck me.

Which was why I kept pushing back. I still couldn't come to terms with the why. Why did Anthony and Pete want me so much? What did they see in me that brought out the alpha in them? The gallant protector and ardent lover? Did I dare trust it? Trust them?

Dear gawd, Pete hit my sweet spot, and all thoughts swept right out of my mind except for one—need.

Perhaps I couldn't allow myself to express how much I enjoyed his perseverance in stalking my heart. My qualms over their intentions might prevent me from succumbing wholly to their advances, but when it came to the sex, I gave in to that whole-heartedly.

Bodies fused. Hot moist breath mingled. Hearts raced as we joined together intimately. In this perfect instant, I could and did let myself go. I basked in the climactic moment, urging him on, my nails raking at his broad back, my heels digging into his spine, my pussy devouring every hard inch of him.

When it came to the fucking, we both gave it

our all and yelled our pleasure for the whole condo complex to hear.

I blamed my still addled wits for how I found myself getting dressed only moments later. Somehow, between our arguing and screwing, I'd agreed to go with him to the crime scene despite my better judgment.

I made token arguments as I pulled on my underpants. He stroked a finger over my still trembling pussy, and I nodded at his feeble excuse that he needed an extra pair of eyes.

Next thing I knew, I sulked in a corner of his truck.

"Are you going to ignore me the whole way there?" he asked, placing his hand on my knee.

I shoved it off. "I didn't want to come."

"That wasn't what you screamed a little while ago."

I glared at him.

He chuckled. "Ah, ease up, baby. Don't pout. You're too cute when you do that, and we're already late as it is."

"I still don't see why you needed to drag me along. I thought you said I wasn't going near any of the crime scenes."

"I hadn't meant to, but that thing you said about the pets. I had to check it out, but I wasn't leaving you alone."

"Then you could have dropped me off somewhere. Somewhere public."

"Probably."

"So why didn't you?"

"Because I like having you with me."

I wouldn't melt. Wouldn't melt. Wouldn't...

Damn him and his seductive smiles.

We hit the male victim's house first. Crime scene tape surrounded the property, as did a few cop cars and gawkers. Exiting Pete's truck, I frowned, not because he laced his fingers through mine, though.

"Um, Pete. How are we supposed to look for the cat? No way are the police going to just let us waltz in there so you can have a sniff."

"Don't be so sure."

As he tugged me along toward the house, someone in a suit emerged from the house. The sun caught his golden hair and brought out red highlights I'd never noted before. My heart skipped a beat as Anthony came to meet us.

"What the hell are you doing here?" he snapped. "I thought we agreed to keep her out of this for her own safety."

"Exactly what I said. Being here is not my idea of a good time. Blame Captain Caveman." I jerked a thumb at the lover I threw under the bus.

"Chloe had a theory about why the witches ended up outside. I wanted to check it out. Have a look around."

"Is this true?" His blue eyes lost their frost glare as they turned to me.

I shrugged. "Maybe."

Anthony grinned. "Such humility. How unlike you."

My lips twitched.

"So what is this theory that couldn't be relayed by phone? A wonderful invention even us old timers have learned to master?" Anthony asked, his sarcasm directed at Pete, who let it roll off his massive back.

"Missing pets."

I could almost see the light bulb flash as Anthony groaned. "Of course. Their familiars. What else would draw a witch from the safety of their home? I can't believe I missed that."

"I could be wrong." Modesty, who knew I had any left?

"I somehow doubt that. It fits. While our canine friend here has a sniff for the missing pets, why don't you come with me and we'll do a walk around? Maybe something else will strike you that didn't show up in the pictures."

Being asked by a dude I thought super slick and smart in the courtroom for my opinion warmed me. While the world was becoming a better place for women to work, being recognized as an equal, being asked to participate, meant the world.

I pulled away and Pete let go of my fingers with reluctance while Anthony adopted a cool expression of self-satisfaction.

Still competing.

For me.

Still felt wrong, but in a good and squirmy way.

Tucking my hand into his, Anthony led me onto the property while Pete did his thing.

"Won't the cops wonder what he's doing?" I asked.

"Not these ones. The men you see are part of a special police branch. Some have worked with Pete, or those of his ilk, before."

"Oh." Well, at least I wouldn't have to worry about bailing him out for snooping. "Any leads?"

"None, which is why I'm glad I brought you

on board."

Compliments, gotta love them. "I don't see how knowing he uses pets as bait to lure witches helps us catch the guy."

"Thing."

"So you're sure it's," I lowered my voice, "a demon?"

"Very. Lab reports, specials ones I might add, on the hush hush, have come back with preliminaries. Some of the tissue samples from under the nails of the first victim confirmed it."

Eew. I tried not to shudder. "How can you be sure what it is if there've been no demons around in hundreds of years?"

"You seem awfully well-informed. Who told you that?"

"Who do you think?"

"The wolf, of course." He shook his head. "In a sense, he told you the truth. According to human annals and Lycan history, there are no known demon appearances."

"But according to vampires…"

"Keep in mind we are much longer lived. We've seen and heard more in our lives."

"Meaning?" I prodded.

"Given our records are somewhat more thorough, we have access to certain info the other races don't, such as samples of preserved demon tissue, which we used for comparison." Anthony's shoulders lifted and fell. "It came back positive for demonic DNA. It would seem a demon has managed to breach the planes and cause havoc on earth."

A demon. Said without the hysteria it deserved.

A fucking demon. Probably with claws and teeth. Lots of teeth that enjoyed chewing on soft flesh.

My lips turned down. "Would it sound weird if I said I was kind of hoping for a crazy cannibal or a zombie?"

Anthony laughed. "Not weird at all. There are many who would prefer we deal with anything but a demon. They are hard to kill."

Hard but not impossible. Good to know. Was it too late to invest in sword fighting lessons? I wanted something that could chop a head off.

Decapitation was one of the most sure ways of killing things in the horror movies.

And once again, in a span of days, my marathon scream fest watching came in handy.

"What I want to know is why anyone would ever think it's a good idea to summon a demon if they're so hard to keep in line." Like seriously, what fucking idiot did that?

Anthony, of course, had a reply. "Why do people do anything? Power. Greed."

I grimaced. "Good point. So do we have any leads on why these magic guys would call one?" Human versus demon. Pretty easy to guess who would win.

So why, in all that was fucking holy, would a human, even a witch, call one?

The idea stumped me.

"None. We've gone through their books. Notes. Computers. So far, nothing on demons has popped up other than the basic warnings found in all magical primers."

'Which is?"

"Do not summon."

Good advice. If only the victims had heeded it. Because why else would the demon target them, unless a rival witch was taking them out.

Did witches have gangs that fought for territory? And if they did, why resort to demons when lobbing fireballs and lightning would make much cooler YouTube videos?

"Other than not summoning, what other wonderful words of advice can you give? Something along the lines of don't feed the demon after midnight, or throw some salt to shrivel him up." It worked for blood-sucking leeches.

Oh no, would this mean I'd have to get rid of my chip habit? But I needed my salty treats. Perhaps I could buy something to prevent vampire anaphylactic shock.

"Hiding is probably your best solution."

Hiding? Didn't that usually involve a shadow stopping right in front of the spot you chose? And then the door opened...

I shook my head. *Maybe time to stop watching those movies.*

Back to the actual crime scene. The quicker I analyzed the hell out of it, the quicker I could get home.

I did wonder, though. "If my theory about the dead witches getting caught while popping out to fetch Fluffy is right, then what happens next? You can't exactly bring that to the cops."

"The humans will know nothing. A warning will go out to the magical community."

"You mean you have a bulletin board for witches?"

"Of a sort, but it encompasses more than just sorcerers. We already sent out one alert about being careful. Now we'll update it and inform those of the magical persuasion that they are not to step foot outside after dark, not even for their pets."

"A curfew? I doubt they'll like that."

Anthony's lips thinned into a tight line. "Not my problem. If they want to live, then they'll obey. If not..."

They'd end up possibly as the demon's next meal.

But not me, oh hell no, I had plans with the pizza I'd make them grab me on the way home and Netflix.

With the curtains shut.

Chapter Thirteen

Searching the house of the dead witches, no furry carcasses were found hiding in the bushes or under any porches. Neither did we locate any of the pets. Whatever living creature the witches had owned had disappeared and left no trail behind.

This in and of itself was suspicious. Or so Pete claimed as we left Anthony behind to converse with the detective in charge, although before I made my escape, he managed to drag me into a private corner and kiss me senseless, making me eager for his promised, "We'll finish this later."

Piling into Pete's truck, we headed back to my place, stopping along the way to grab cartons of Chinese food. Not pizza, but the leftovers would taste just as good, so I allowed it.

Settling ourselves at my kitchen counter, we discussed our findings, or lack of.

"There's something weird about the animals missing," Pete said in between bites of General Tao chicken.

"Not all of them are gone," I pointed out. "The cops said they saw your neighbor's cat sitting on the porch when they arrived."

"And not a single sighting since."

"So the cat wandered off."

Pete snorted. "You've obviously never owned a cat or dog."

"Nope. My dad is allergic." And I'd never felt a burning desire to own something furry that liked to mark its territory—until I met Pete.

I quite enjoyed petting the hair on his chest, which arrowed down to his python. I bit my lip so as to not snicker as Pete explained his reasoning.

"Animals tend to stick close to home where they know they'll be fed."

Shoulders rolling in a shrug, I swallowed my chow mein mix before replying. "So the demon ate the cats." Which is what each of the trio had owned, according to the niblets left behind in the food bowls.

"Doubtful."

I wanted to slap him upside the head. "Okay, Mr. Negativity. Since you're having such a good time shooting down my theories, mind telling me why?"

"First off, there's no scent trail. It's like the kitties disappeared into thin air. Damned if I know what happened to the felines. The only thing I am sure of is that the creature we're hunting didn't eat the cats. And the reason I know this, before you ask, is simple. A demon who is eating human flesh is not going to ruin its palate with a cat. It would be like mixing spam with your porterhouse. It's just not done."

Somehow, my appetite vanished, and I pushed my carton of Chinese food away. "That is a really disturbing comparison."

"Yet an apt one. So, again, I have to wonder, what happened to the cats?"

"Honestly. I don't care." I didn't.

Maybe they'd wandered off. Maybe something else ate them. They'd been run over. Aliens beamed them up. Or a neighbor took them in. Who knew? Who cared? We'd only gone on our fieldtrip because Pete wanted to understand why those people left the safety of their homes and he forced me to go along. Now we knew, or assumed. On to the next question.

"We're still no closer to discerning the reason they were targeted," I pointed out as Pete continued to scarf down his portion and mine.

"It has to tie in to the fact they were all witches," he mumbled around a mouthful. Talking while eating was a lot sexier when it was my flesh he chewed on.

"Give the dog a bone!"

Coming from behind, Anthony's voice, so unexpected, startled me, and I screamed. "Holy fuck, stealth man. What the hell are you doing sneaking up on us?"

"I knew he was there," Pete retorted, tackling the last egg roll.

"And didn't tell me?" Evil eye meet the guy who treated too many things with nonchalance. He'd pay for that later when I told him about the head he would have gotten had he done the chivalrous thing and not abetted me almost wetting my pants.

"Sorry. I forget sometimes your hearing isn't as good as mine."

Ignoring the apology, I spun sideways in my seat and peeked up at Anthony. Looking disheveled with the top button of his shirt undone and his tie loosened, tired or not, he nevertheless bestowed a smile upon me before leaning down to give me a thorough kiss. "Good evening, Chloe," he murmured when he finally let me up for some much-needed air.

"It is now."

He grinned at my reply before seating himself beside me, which earned him a scowl from Pete, who'd chosen the spot across.

"Any luck finding clues after I left?" I asked.

"Actually, I found the answer to what you were discussing just before my arrival."

"You know the connection?"

"I do. It seems those three witches, plus four more, were part of a local coven who met once a month on the full moon."

"Of course they did." Everything happened on that night. Just ask any EMT or cop.

"Have you found the others and warned them they might be in danger? Or, even better, asked them what they did to piss a demon off?"

"I would if we could find them. Either the demon already got to them, or they've gone into hiding. We've paid visits to their homes, but no one answered. Calls to their known friends and places of work have netted no results."

"Can't we cast like a spell or something to find them?" For a girl who'd only discovered witches and magic a few days ago, I had no problem transitioning and seeing if we could make it work for us.

"Already being attempted. The TDCM—"

"The what?"

"TDCM, the Thaumaturgic Department for the Concealment of Magic, has some interdepartmental wizards working on it, but the members of the coven hid their tracks well."

"More witches?" And why was I not more surprised a secret agency existed? Probably because it was a lot less crazy than realizing I dated a vampire and a werewolf.

"Wizards."

"There's a difference?"

Anthony grinned. "According to them, yes."

Pete snorted. "One goes to university to gain the title and the right to wear a pointy hat and robes; the other dabbles at home. It's all the same in the end. They play with things best left alone."

Intriguing as they sounded, I had more important things to concentrate on. "You say these wizards couldn't find them? Does that mean they're dead?"

Anthony shrugged. "They couldn't answer that either. Hell, they wouldn't even confirm it was demon DNA we found in the sample under the witch's nails."

"I thought we'd already ascertained it was."

"By scientific means. It has yet to be confirmed by esoteric ones."

In other words, we were dealing with useless idiots. Nice to know even the magical underground had issues getting straight answers from publicly paid employees.

"Okay, so locating the rest of the coven is a dead end at the moment. Has anyone checked out their last meeting spot to see if they left any clues as to what they were up to?"

"That is the plan, once we figure out where it is."

I didn't miss the pointed glances my way. "Let me guess. You think I can find it."

Turned out they were right. Around one a.m., while sitting on the couch, my feet in Pete's lap—getting an awesome toe-curling massage as he absently watched some gory movie—and while Anthony sat across from me perusing some paper files, I caught the break we needed—a receipt found stuffed in the pocket for one of the bodies to have shawarma delivered, but not to any of their homes or places of work. A delivery that coincided with the full moon and appeared every month, regular as clockwork on a credit card statement.

To double check, I cross-referenced the delivery dates with my list of the dates for the last six full moons. They matched.

"Got it!" I crowed, adding for modesty's sake, "I think."

"What did you find?" Anthony asked, ditching his pile of papers with a rustle so he could kneel at my side and peer at my screen.

"An order for the family platter of shawarma, once a month, on the full moon, delivered to a warehouse at, get this, six hundred and sixty-six Hells Alley."

Pete emitted a disparaging sound. "Seriously? How can anyone in this day and age still believe that number has any meaning?"

"Not the number of the devil I take it?" was my dry reply.

"Nope. He's unlisted."

I shot Anthony a look, but his expression was blank. I shot my suspicious gaze back at Pete, who didn't even crack a grin. I wondered if he pulled my leg. On second thought, I preferred not to find out.

"I'll call it in," Pete said. He lifted my feet

from his lap so he could stand. A shame, the man had magic hands. Lucky me, he'd opted to spend the evening at my place since we had no leads. I wondered if armed with this new information he'd now go out. A part of me hoped not. I didn't like the thought of him possibly encountering danger. But then again, having both of my lovers here would severely curtail my chances at nookie.

Cool fingers brushed the hair from my cheek. "Good work," Anthony murmured.

I blushed inwardly at his praise. "You would have found it." Eventually. I just found it faster. Yeah, I'm not ashamed to admit I did an invisible fist pump. "Are you going to check it out?" I asked.

"Not tonight," Anthony replied.

"Got other plans?"

"Most definitely."

A part of me wanted to inquire if I figured in those plans, but that smacked too much of something a girlfriend would ask, and I didn't want that title. Or maybe I did.

"Do your plans have you staying or going?"

"Depends. Would you like me to stay?"

Before I could reply—with a resounding yes—Pete hung up and returned. "They'll send a team in the morning. No one wants to chance possibly walking into something ugly while it's still dark. We'll reconnoiter right after dawn. Case the joint for danger and suspects. If it looks feasible, we'll go in during daylight hours and see if we can find any clues."

"Do they think the demon might be hiding there?" Again, my worry over Pete's safety rose, making a liar of my attempts to keep him properly at arm's length.

"We don't know, hence our caution."

Caution good.

"Lucky you. I get to spend the night."

One man too many sleeping over? Bad.

Something of my chagrin must have shown because both my guys adopted looks of concern.

"Something wrong?" Anthony asked.

"Nope, nothing." Other than a case of hungry pussy. Even I wasn't gauche enough to take one to bed while the other languished on the couch. "Just tired. I guess I'll go to bed."

That might have been the moment they both clued in that their plans for sex were also screwed. As Pete and Anthony indulged in a silent staring match, I slipped away.

Brushing my teeth and hair, I railed at the injustice of having two drop-dead gorgeous men, who were also excellent lovers, in the next room while I went to bed alone—and horny.

The injustice of it all. Crawling under the sheets, I wondered what they did out in my living room. I heard the low murmur of their voices. No thuds, though, signaling violence. I also didn't hear the sound of my door shutting as one of them got the hint and left or lost the coin toss. I sighed.

Shutting my eyes, I tried to go to sleep, but it eluded me. I tossed. Turned. Threw off my sheets. Flung my arm over my eyes.

The creak of my door opening had me holding my breath. Had my lovers come to an agreement? Tossed a coin? Which of them would spend the night with me? What would I bite on so as to not scream and make the other jealous he'd not won the battle to grace my bed? Or would the winner just choose to snuggle? Would—

Having not moved my arm to peek, I was completely taken aback when not one but two bodies slid into bed with me. A male on either side. Naked. One cool, one hot.

They'd both come.

Damn.

I didn't dare speak. Didn't want to question. Hell, I almost forgot to breathe as they rubbed against me, their hands laying claim to their respective sides, cupping my aching breasts, their purpose similar, yet their touch worlds apart. Where Anthony skimmed my skin with smooth fingers, Pete kneaded with rough ones. The frisson on my left as soft lips nibbled at the skin of my neck contrasted deliciously with the rough stubble and harder intent of the mouth to my right.

I arched under their combined erotic play, my body coming alive and singing with pleasure, the yearning between my thighs resulting in warm moisture and a clenching of muscle as my arousal built and begged for more.

Slender yet long digits found my velvety slit, sliding in and stroking me. I gasped, a soft sound caught by demanding lips, my resulting moan happening around a hot, insistent tongue. While Pete took possession of my upper body, Anthony moved lower.

What had happened to my determination to sleep with only one man at a time? To not get involved in a threesome? Awash in sensation, any protest I might have had at this new experience vanished. If they could handle sharing me, then how could I deny myself the pleasure they seemed intent on bestowing?

I laced my fingers around Pete's neck as I kissed him back with passionate fervor. A rumble of contentment shook his frame. His callused hands grasped at my breasts, squeezing the globes. Pinching and rolling my nipples, he sent zings of sensation through me, and my breathing came faster.

But it was the tongue applied to my clit that had me crying out. With my legs spread and draped over his shoulders, Anthony lapped at my core, alternately flicking my clit and penetrating me.

Not to be outdone, Pete ended our hungry kiss, only to suck on my straining nipples. Tug. Suck. Wet slide. More sucking. Holy fuck.

Too many sensations assailed me. My pleasure built and built, a teetering wall that toppled all too soon. I bucked hard and screamed as I came.

"Oh, fuck. Oh, my." Coherence was beyond me. And the bliss wouldn't stop. Fingers joined Anthony's tongue, plunging and spreading me, taking the wild trembling remnants of my orgasm and building it again. It was too soon. I was still recovering from my first climax. I...

The coiling tension within me mounted. Flipped onto my stomach, with no warning or announcement of their intent, I finally found some words. "No, don't stop," I begged. Not with nirvana peeking at me.

As if they'd leave me hanging. Apparently, they had a plan, and it involved them too. How decadent. A plump cock pressed at my lips, Pete's familiar size demanding entry. I opened wide and took him in, sucking at him with eagerness, all too willing to give him what he desired. While I lavished his dick with attention, Anthony pulled my hips up, positioning me so I knelt on my knees, ass in the air, thighs spread.

It didn't take a porn expert to guess what he planned next. Expected or not, I still cried out when Anthony rubbed the head of his shaft against my trembling lips. I waggled my butt, a silent demand not to tease me. He slapped my greedy pussy with his cock. Pete reaped the benefit of my excitement as I sucked at him hard. His fingers clutched at my hair, guiding me up and down his length, his hissed and growled, "Yes, baby, that's it. Deeper. Fuck me, that's good," an added enhancement to my own enjoyment.

Seemingly impatient suddenly for his own delight, Anthony sheathed himself in me. A hard, deep thrust.

Yes!

I rocked back, dragging the edge of my teeth along Pete's length. Anthony withdrew and then slammed back in, pushing me forward. Oh, gawd.

We seesawed in this manner for a blissful eternity. Flesh joined, we fucked, I sucked, and our pleasure mounted. Pants, groans, and moans accompanied the sound of my slurping and flesh slapping. So fucking decadent. So amazingly good. So...

Incredible.

Pete's cock could only keep me distracted for so long before the rapid thrusts in and out of my pussy made me lose my rhythm. I hummed as my body braced itself to come. Sensing my dilemma, Pete took over and pumped himself into my willing mouth as Anthony upped his tempo.

Caught between the two, I became the point that joined us together. The focus of the pleasure. The one who came first.

I don't know if it was my vibrating scream as I came that proved Pete's undoing, but he quickly joined me, spurting hotly into my mouth. As for the lover between my thighs, he yelled as he dug his fingers into my cheeks. Thrust. Thrust. Pound. In. Out.

"Yes!" He gave one last mighty heave before coming.

And then we were still and silent but for our harsh breaths. Our bodies remained joined. And awareness returned.

It brought along its friend embarrassment.

Chapter Fourteen

What should a woman say or do after experiencing something so climactic? How did one thank two lovers at once? *You were both great,* seemed a tad trite. The burning question of the moment, though, the one which had me the most flummoxed? What happened now?

Things had changed. The dynamic had shifted. No longer could I say with any definitive vehemence that I didn't believe in a ménage lifestyle, or at least in the bedroom. *That was too fucking amazing for me not to want to try it again.* Forget choosing between them. I wanted them both. But did they feel the same way? How would the men handle themselves now after such intimacy? How did I now feel about them after sharing such a climactic experience?

"You're thinking too much," Anthony murmured as he slid from me and placed a kiss at the base of my spine.

"I guess she's allowed one fault," Pete added as he also shifted, freeing my mouth—which for once did not have a sarcastic reply.

As they aligned themselves on either side of me, it occurred to me that they intended to both sleep in my bed, a queen-sized bed that no longer seemed so large.

What just happened?

My first threesome, duh.

But how? I didn't do threesomes. Bad enough I'd taken on two lovers. I wasn't into kink. Then again, we hadn't done anything really kinky unless one counted the fact an extra person was involved. Was this going to become a regular thing? Could I handle it? Could they? I wanted to ask them what this meant. I wanted to analyze what I felt. I wanted to—

"Sleep," Anthony whispered against my ear.

I fought the word, but the jerk must have laced it with vampire mojo because next thing I knew, I woke to sunshine.

Alone.

"Gawdammit!" I yelled at the ceiling of my bedroom.

"What's wrong, baby?" Pete answered my cry of frustration from the doorway to my room, appearing delicious and at home in low-hipped track pants that would have looked better on my floor.

"Nothing is wrong," I grumbled. How to explain that for once I'd like to wake up snuggling, preferably with a cock buried in me. I'd gone to bed with two men. Two! And still couldn't get no satisfaction.

"I think someone is feeling lonely," Anthony replied, astute as ever. He crowded in beside Pete and tempted me to muss up his perfect appearance, replete with perfectly combed hair, pressed suit, and tie.

Did the guy have a personal assistant at his beck and call, ready and available at all times to deliver him clothes? If yes, then I'd admit to total jealousy.

"Would it kill you to stay in bed with me so I don't wake up alone?" I complained, finally letting them in on my pet peeve.

It wasn't a whine, more of a valid grievance. For men who professed affection for me, they didn't understand my need for morning nookie or cuddling. But they'd learn. If I kept them around.

"I'm an early riser," Pete explained. Apparently, judging by the fact that while still shirtless, he was freshly showered and shaved. And was that coffee and bacon I smelled?

"I don't require much sleep," was my vampire lover's excuse.

"You both suck." Mature? No. Did I care? Again, not really.

Their laughter earned them a glare. "We'll try harder to ensure you don't feel neglected in the morning," Anthony promised.

"Want me to come back to bed?" Pete offered. "I can make the squad wait if you need me to."

Put my selfish needs ahead of a job? I wanted to, but couldn't. "No. I'll live." Barely.

I watched, with only a little chagrin, as Pete yanked a shirt over his head, covering his impeccable chest. As for me, I remained naked and brazen about it, especially once I noted—when arching and stretching—how their gazes kept straying to my body. Evil of me? Yup, and not ashamed of it.

Redemption, for them, came in the form of a shower already piping hot, a warm towel when I stepped out, and breakfast. But as for company over said meal? Not the male one—which I hated to admit—I looked forward to.

"Sorry, baby, I gotta go. We're hitting that warehouse this morning."

As for Anthony. "I've got some things I've got to deal with. I won't be gone long."

Disappointed at their abandonment, especially after the night we spent, I almost asked to go along. Hadn't they, after all, not wanted to leave me alone?

As if reading my mind, Anthony said, "We don't like leaving you by yourself, but we're both needed elsewhere. With the sun blazing bright, you should be safe enough. Just in case, though, I've got some security positioned outside your building at the entrances to keep an eye out for suspicious characters. And, for entertainment—"

"They got me!" Brenda announced, flouncing into the kitchen, apparently let in by Pete. "And lucky you, I brought a little something from our favorite bakery." She shook a paper bag, and although I'd already eaten breakfast, I drooled a little. There was always room in my tummy for pastry smothered in icing.

I made a feeble token protest. "What about work?"

A raspberry blown through perfectly pinked lips said, with eloquence, what Brenda thought of that. "I took the day off. Screw the office. My BFF needs me."

I certainly did. I needed her to tell me I'd not turned into a slut or caved to the government's wishes. For so long I'd bucked the ménage laws, and now, I seemed to embrace them, succumbing to the allure of two men with nary a fight. I hoped the tax break was worth the certain headache—and heartache—I suspected loomed in my future. Perhaps now was a good time to buy those Ben and Jerry stocks I'd had my eye on. Sales of the decadent ice cream could shoot through the roof if my relationship went south.

With Brenda present to keep me from killing myself from boredom, my men prepared to abscond.

"Remember not to leave your apartment," Pete said before he left, his kiss leaving me breathless.

"Yes, daddy," I mocked.

His low growl and heated look made me smirk as I waved goodbye.

Anthony, on his phone in the corner of the living room, waited until my werewolf was gone before bestowing his own instructions. "It's very important you not exit this place. I had a TDCM defense specialist place a ward on your condo. In the very slim chance the demon decides to show up here, he shouldn't be able to come in."

I reeled back from his words. "Excuse me, but why would he show up?" I wasn't a magic user or part of the coven. And, despite all the sweets I liked to eat, didn't think of myself as a particularly tasty treat, for demons at least.

"If he's been watching the scene of the crimes or visited them, it's possible he saw or scented you."

"You mean I could be a target?" I didn't squeak, but it was close.

"Not likely. You're not a witch."

"But I am a bitch," I muttered.

"Good thing I like that about you," Anthony teased.

Brenda just about choked.

Casting a dirty look her way, which she replied to with a grin and double digits waggling, I thoroughly kissed my man and indulged in an ass grope. He left flustered. Brenda turned green with envy, and I ate some glazed donuts in the hopes of curing my worry.

With nothing better to do, I relayed the events of the past few days to my BFF. Did I leave anything out?

Nope. Some secrets needed sharing. Besides, if I suddenly went missing, turned pale with a penchant for blood, or began to eye Brenda with something other than friendly intent, I wanted her forewarned. I knew I could count on her to stake me if I went all vampy and got out of hand. Just like I promised to chop off her head if she ever got an urge for brains.

It was nice to have someone to count on, although, if my lovers could be believed, that number had increased by two.

Speaking of which, "What should I do?"

"What do you mean?" Brenda asked as she took over my couch, sprawling lengthwise.

"Now that I've slept with them both at once, what happens next?"

"Great sex every night."

"Apart from that." And no, I didn't succeed in stopping the blush heating my cheeks. Acceptable or not, admitting aloud that I'd fucked two guys and loved it wasn't an easy feat.

"Have you talked about it with them at all?"

"No. It just happened last night. Do you think we'll be doing that every night? Or will it be once-in-a-blue-moon kind of thing?"

She shrugged. "How the hell would I know? You could ask."

I goggled her. "Ask? Are you freaking nuts?"

"Hey, you asked. If you're too chicken to be direct, then I guess you'll have to wait and see."

Therein lay the problem, though. I didn't want to wait. Waiting meant thinking about and reliving the pleasure, over and over again.

"What do I do if they decide to make it permanent? Are they gonna make us all move in together?"

I almost picked some eyeballs up off my floor, Brenda's stare got so wide. "How did we go from 'how will I survive screwing two hotties' to 'shacking up'?"

How had I? An answer eluded me.

"Chloe, is there something you're not telling me?"

"I don't know what you mean."

"A few days ago, you reluctantly agreed to let them have sex, no strings attached. Take it or leave it, even though they professed to want something more. Now, you're talking about living together, making the situation permanent. This isn't like you. You never make quick decisions like this."

No, I didn't.

"So, let me ask you again, in words you might understand. Do you love them?"

"I can't."

"Why not?"

"As you said, it's too soon." I barely knew

them. We'd met only days ago. Already I couldn't imagine life without them.

Fuck me, I was so screwed.

"Too soon, yet you're talking about moving them in."

"See what I mean about them messing with my mind? This isn't like me. I swear, Brenda, they must have cast a spell on me."

"Or you've met your soul mates." She clutched a hand to her breast and sighed.

"That only happens in books."

"Does it? You wouldn't be the first woman to fall in love at first sight."

"Fall in lust, you mean."

"And just how do you think most relationships start?"

"This is different."

"How?"

How to explain it just was? I didn't understand it myself. In such a short time, they'd managed to turn my world topsy-turvy. To make me feel things I'd thought existed only in romance novels. Being with them brought me *alive*—mentally, emotionally, and sexually. I longed for things I'd eschewed—their presence and companionship, their humor and sharp wit, the way they took care of me, and not just in the bedroom. The protective circle they placed around me as if I was a precious object. Their jealousy implying the same. I wanted them, and not just occasionally or to scratch a sexual itch. I... I...

Nope. I wouldn't think the words. To think them was to make myself vulnerable. I wouldn't place myself at their mercy. I wouldn't give them the power to hurt me. It was too soon for me to make decisions. Sure, on the surface, everything seemed to indicate smooth sailing and a happy ending, but Brenda did make one valid point, a point I agreed with. It was too soon.

The walls of my condo were stifling as my dilemma closed in on me. "I need to get out of here," I muttered.

"Say what?"

"Why don't we hit the second-hand store down the street and see what new junk they've got?" You never knew the deals you'd find. People dropped things off on consignment there all the time. Besides, shopping was a great way to take my mind off things.

"You heard what your boyfriends said. We shouldn't leave your condo."

"Bah. I'm not a witch. And you heard them. The thing doesn't like sunlight. We'll be perfectly safe."

Turns out my decision to disobey might have saved our lives.

Chapter Fifteen

Keeping an eye on the time, I made very sure Brenda and I didn't linger on the streets as late afternoon crept toward twilight. No way was I getting caught outside after dark. Moment of defiance or not, I drew the line at taking chances with our lives.

As we hightailed it back to my place, I figured we were safe from discovery. I'd not received any texts or calls from my overprotective lovers, which meant we could sneak back in with no one the wiser except my credit card company, who had borne the brunt of my escape.

How naïve of me to think our excursion had gone unnoticed. Brenda and I returned to absolute chaos, and not just the people kind. Not that I espied the mess at first, but I sure heard it.

Given his size and demeanor, I had already pegged Pete for the kind of guy whose bellow would carry, so I wasn't surprised to hear his shouted, "What the fuck do you mean you saw nothing?"

Oops. Caught.

Assumption? He berated the guards left behind to watch me. Guards who knew nothing about the numerous ways in and out of the condo complex.

I'll admit my boldness in defying their orders didn't extend to me flitting past them in grand gesture. More like I skulked and hid around corners as we made our dash for freedom.

Now someone paid the price for my victory. Brenda and I exchanged a guilty look as we strode up the hall laden with our shopping bags. Poor guys. I'd not meant to remain out so late, but we'd hit a bar for lunch and given the hour—past one o'clock— had indulged in a few liquid aperitifs. Time kind of flew after that.

Of more surprise than Pete's cursing and vocal rampaging was Anthony's booming, "Where the hell is she?"

Damn. I'd ruffled the usually collected vampire. I hastened my step, stunned at the level of worry, and shouted out an "I'm here, sorry—"

My words died in my throat as I reached the doorway to my condo and caught a glimpse of the destruction.

And I mean destruction.

Think of a tornado let loose in a small space, bouncing off the walls, maybe adorned with razor-sharp claws, and you'd get an idea of the wreckage left in its wake.

Except this wasn't Kansas.

My poor condo.

My disbelieving eyes roved the devastation. I wanted to ask what had happened, who the hell was responsible for the sabotage, but I could only stare in utter shock.

Not for long. My feet lifted from the ground as I found myself caught up in a bear hug—or was that a wolf one?—of epic proportions.

"Thank fuck you're safe. Where have you been? Are you all right?"

Before I could answer, another set of hands grabbed me and enveloped me in a second, equally bone-crushing embrace. Anthony murmured, over and over, "Thank God."

How ironic that a blood-sucking creature of the night should invoke a deity. I didn't ponder that incongruity for long. I couldn't with my teeth rattling as I was shaken.

"I thought we told you to stay put."

Having regained a few of my wits, I managed to retort, "I didn't feel like it. Anyone care to explain what happened to my condo?" I swear, if I found out the boys did this when they discovered me missing, I'd dump their asses. Good sex or not, if this was how they reacted to me disobeying their caveman orders, then I didn't want them in my life.

"By all indications, the demon showed up, and when he didn't find anyone, had a bit of a temper tantrum."

It took me a moment to digest his words. Icy fingers tickled my bravado, threatening to tear it away.

I fought back with a caustic, "A bit? I'd hate to see what the place would look like if our demonic friend was actually pissed." Which reminded me, did my insurance have a clause to cover hissy fits by nonexistent demonic creatures?

When in a state of shock, resort to stupid musings. It helped keep the brain numb a moment longer.

Anthony didn't appear amused. Good, because despite my words, I certainly wasn't. "What happened to staying in the condo and not letting anyone in?"

"By the look of things, it's a lucky thing I didn't."

Judging by the sour look in Anthony's face, he didn't appreciate my logic. Neither could he refute it, though.

"Good point. But if you weren't here to let him in, then how did it happen? There are spells around your place. Or there were. Nothing of his ilk should have been able to enter, not without invitation."

How sobering. Especially since no one had an answer; not Pete, not Anthony, nor any of the magic specialists who showed up. They did all agree on one thing, though. I was lucky to be alive.

My decision to disobey had likely saved mine and Brenda's lives. I also got a great deal on shoes. Good thing because I'd need them.

Nothing survived in my place. What wasn't torn to shreds stank worse than roadkill left in the sun. I called the odor eau of demon piss; they gave it some fancy sciency name that wasn't cute at all.

The odor ruined everything, and the only thing left to do was abandon my shit.

My stuff. Ruined. Everything I own.
Gone.

At the knowledge, I finally broke down and cried. Yup, I turned into a pathetic weeping damsel.

I'd worked hard to create my home. Scrimped, saved, and hunted estate sales to furnish and turn a simple condo into somewhere I could relax and call my own.

As for my clothes, I'd bargain shopped for

years to build a respectable wardrobe suitable for a woman who spent a lot of time in court dealing with suited lawyer types.

In one fell swoop, some fucking asshole, a creature that didn't even belong here, had destroyed it.

I'd earned my right to a meltdown, and no one begrudged me it or told me it was all right, that it would be okay. Or that things weren't as bad as they looked. Good thing or I probably would have bloodied their noses. It wasn't okay. There was no silver lining for this catastrophe.

Under usual circumstances, I would have wailed all over the equally shell-shocked Brenda, but to my surprise, I had a chest to sob on. Make that a pair. Pete and Anthony took turns soothing me. They didn't care that the other agents on site saw them. They didn't seem to mind how my salty tears soaked their shirtfronts. Or the fact they'd essentially announced to all present that we were a threesome. I needed comfort, and they gave it.

Cocooned in their protective embraces, I gave in to my tears. Cried for the loss of my treasures. Sobbed my fear and frustration.

Lost in my melancholy, I didn't take much notice of what went on around me, not until I realized they'd led me from the devastation down to street level and Pete's truck. I dug my heels in. "Wh-where are we going?"

"Pete's house for now. He's got some stronger, more established wards."

It was then I noted Brenda's absence. What about my BFF? Having associated with me, was she also in danger?

Panicked for her safety, I cast a frantic glance around, looking to spot her. "Brenda? Where is she? She needs to come with us. What if this thing goes after her?"

"Don't worry about that little spitfire, baby. She's not alone. I called in some favors, and she's gone to a pack safehouse under the guard of a few Lycans. They won't let anyone harm a hair on her head."

Brenda surrounded by a group of virile, hairy men? I worried more about their safety. Nothing energized my best friend like a brush with danger, and when her adrenaline got going, nothing with a dick was safe.

Assured of her wellbeing, I allowed myself to be led to Pete's vehicle. Anthony boosted me into the front seat of the truck while Pete slid behind the steering wheel. Sniffling, I peered with surely red-rimmed eyes at my vampire lover.

"Aren't you getting in?"

Anthony shook his head, his usually well-coiffed hair mussed and his expression taut. "Not quite yet. Fear not. You should be safe with the wolf."

"What about you?"

"I require some items from my home. I won't be long."

"We should go with you." For some reason, the thought of being separated raised my anxiety levels.

Lifting his hand, Anthony tenderly stroked my moist cheek. "It's not safe. The people I have to entertain and work with have made it so my home is not guarded by the necessary spells. I'll be along as quickly as I can manage."

On impulse, I leaned over and kissed him softly. "Be careful."

"Why, Chloe, don't tell me you're starting to become fond of me?" he teased.

Instead of a reply, I kissed him again, a more heated embrace that probably said more than I intended to admit.

With an expression of regret, Anthony pulled away and shut the passenger door. I stared at him standing on the sidewalk, wondering if I'd see him again, a knot of foreboding hurting my stomach.

A warm hand landed on my thigh and squeezed. "The vamp will be fine. It will take more than a demon to kill him."

"How reassuring."

"Get used to it. You've entered a whole new world with your association with us."

"So I should expect demon attacks and threats on our lives on a daily basis?"

"No. This is a unique situation. However, given what we are, and what we strive to do, sometimes events spiral out of control."

Massive fail with the pep talk. I wanted to hear how they'd never place themselves in danger again. How I'd never have to feel this awful sensation of helplessness and fear, not just for myself but them. "Not helping here, Pete."

"Just being honest."

"Yeah, well, the truth sucks."

"I'm sorry this happened to you, baby."

I sighed. Me too. But the only way to erase the events was to rewind to a time when I didn't know Anthony and Pete. Oddly enough, I preferred the destruction of my condo to the idea of never having discovered what I could have with them.

Not wanting to dwell on what this might mean, I changed the subject. "With everything that's happened, I never asked what you found at the warehouse."

Pete shrugged. "Nothing to tell. We showed up and surrounded the place. We were just about to invade when the fucking joint blew up. Kaboom!" He lifted his hands from the steering wheel in emphasis, and I dug my fingers into the seat.

Thankfully, we didn't swerve off the road. His truck had great alignment.

"It blew up? You're kidding."

"Nope. Lucky thing for us, we were running behind schedule. Had we gone in when we were supposed to about five minutes before, we would have been caught in the blast. As it was, only a few agents got injured, minor burns and cuts."

"Are you okay?"

"I'm fine." He flashed me a toothy white grin. "Wanna do a full body check?"

Yes, but while he drove probably wasn't the most prudent time.

I did throw him a bone. "Maybe later." Oh, how I loved the way his expression turned instantly smoldering. "So did you find out anything at all?"

"Nope. Not a single thing. By the time the firemen put out the flames, everything was burnt to a crisp. Any clues we might have discerned were gone."

"He's covering his tracks." Yes, I'd begun to refer to the creature as he. Only a male would kill my poor, defenseless collection of shoes.

"Maybe. I find it hard to picture the demon being so meticulous. It seems more likely someone else is involved."

A frown creased my forehead. "What do you mean?"

"Someone had to have tipped off the fact we planned a raid. The timing of the bomb is too coincidental to ignore."

"Or the demon saw you guys surrounding the place and set a trap."

Pete shook his head. "The bomb was set on a timer. He knew what time to expect us."

Out came the defense lawyer in me. "Circumstantial. Another possibility is he set the timer and gave himself enough of a head start to get out of the blast zone."

"You seem awfully keen on trying to disprove the possibility of a traitor."

"And you seem determined to find one. Don't let paranoia cloud you to other scenarios." But his hypothesis chilled me.

Could someone on our side actually be in cahoots with the demon? It seemed impossible. Farfetched even. Who would betray their kind like that? Then again, I had only to look at the history books with their gruesome details of war to admit to myself that it didn't take much. A lust for power, a greed for riches, even simple revenge, it didn't take a lot for some people to eschew common decency and turn to the side of evil.

Pete sighed. "I can't help my suspicions. Being alert is what keeps me and my kind safe. If it means wearing tin foil hats, we'll do it. If it means investigating people I consider coworkers and friends, so be it."

"Does that include fuck friends?"

"I know you had nothing to do with it."

Such certainty. It warmed me to know he didn't consider me a suspect. "I know I didn't, but I have to play devil's advocate and ask, what makes you so sure?"

"You would have never let me leave this morning, not knowing a bomb waited."

I snorted. "Are you implying I like you too much to kill you?"

"Nope, I'm stating it." His smug grin earned him an elbow in the ribs. He laughed.

I scowled. "I do not like you."

"Are we still pretending that?"

"Okay, I like you, but only because the sex is good." Really, *really* good.

"And I'm handsome."

My lips twitched at his lack of modesty. "Cute."

"Puppies are cute."

"Exactly."

Again, he chuckled instead of taking offense. "Fine. Be a chicken and don't admit it. I'll say it for you. You like me, Chloe Bailey. And one day, I hope you'll trust me enough to say it. Maybe even come to love me."

Biting my tongue, I held back the words, *I already do.*

Arriving at his home—a brick two-story with a curved bay window, a single car garage, and not a piece of shrubbery out front taller than two feet—I noted the crime scene tape still plastered around his neighbor's place, a grim reminder that danger lurked and had me on his list of things to kill. It reminded me I should really work harder at completing my bucket list.

Item number one—start an actual list.

As Pete unlocked his front door, I asked, "So how do you figure staying here, next door to the scene of the crime, is safer than say, hightailing it to some obscure tropical island?"

Some R&R with a half-naked werewolf in Speedos would go a long way to restoring my good humor.

"If the demon's got you on his radar, there is nowhere you can go that will protect you forever."

"Nowhere?"

"Okay, there are a few places, but somehow, I can't see you taking the vows necessary to become a nun. Or living in a catacomb several levels underground."

I eyed him askance, but he didn't even crack a grin. Someone was taking lessons from a certain vampire in controlling his facial expressions.

Stepping into his home, I found myself, as expected, in a man's cave. The living room, a decent-sized space with scratched hardwood flooring, had one big comfy-looking couch and a pair of worn, leather La-Z-Boys, flanking, you guessed it, one big-ass flat screen television.

"Good thing I've seen your dick, or I'd wonder if someone had inadequacy issues," I quipped.

"Like it? I got a smoking deal on it. High definition. Surround sound. And every channel cable offers."

"Ooh, I can't wait to see that new chick flick that came out on pay-per-view on this. We can watch it together." To his credit, Pete didn't cry, but the pained expression on his face said it all. I burst out laughing. "Just kidding. I hate girly movies. But I warn you, I have a penchant for horror and cheesy B movies."

"That I can live with," he said with obvious relief.

"Going to give me the grand tour?"

"My pleasure."

More like mine.

His idea of a tour ended in the bathroom with its massive tiled shower with six rotating showerheads and my clothes on the heated marble floor. I didn't complain about the brevity of the visit; I couldn't with his tongue in my mouth.

Standing under the hot, streaming water as he soaped my body, I closed my eyes and basked in the attention. I loved the feel of his coarse hands on my body. Loved how he knew just where to stroke me, how to fondle my flesh, how to get me aching for his cock.

As he washed away the stress of my day, the tension in my body eased, and I opened my eyes to see him smiling at me wickedly, his golden orbs alight with the passion I'd come to expect when we were together.

"I'd say penny for your thoughts, but I have a feeling you're going to show me instead of tell," I said.

"Show you. Pleasure you. Suck you then fuck you." The dirty words slipped from his lips, each one a pleasurable jolt to my already fired-up libido.

Despite the pouring water, he knelt on the tile floor, his hands gripping my hips. I leaned back and spread my thighs, eager for what he planned. Too eager. I grabbed him by the hair and tugged him toward my hungry core. With a strength I couldn't help but love, he held back, teasing me, his lips close enough for him to blow hot air upon my clit. My sex contracted, anticipation as arousing as the act. With a gentle flick of his tongue, he touched me, and my whole body shivered.

"Yes," I sighed happily.

Again, he stroked me, back and forth, wet laps across my already swollen clit. No matter how many times I got oral, I don't think I'd ever tire of the incredible sensation. Shudder after shudder went through me as my pussy reacted to the stimulation. I dug my fingers into his scalp, urging him on. He placed his whole mouth on me and sucked, his tongue delving between my velvety folds and slipping inside.

Moans filled the bathroom, mine as I couldn't help but express my pleasure. My flesh throbbed, my inner sex tightened, my nipples pebbled, rock hard and begging for an erotic touch. He slid his mouth away from my heated core, and I whimpered as his lips worked their way up my body, gliding over my rounded tummy, tickling my navel, slithering around my nipples. I gasped when his teeth bit down on one nub, the tiny spot of pain an aphrodisiac that enhanced my bliss.

"Would you stop teasing me?" I asked. He ignored. But I didn't take offense. I knew he'd take care of me—in his own sweet time. Down I reached, grasping his cock, stroking the head of it. Two could play this game.

It was his turn to moan and hip thrust as I pumped his hard and heavy shaft. With my second hand, I fondled his sac, kneading them through my fingers until they pulled up tight under his cock.

"Enough," he panted.

I laughed. He growled. I shivered. Gawd, it was so sexy when he did that. Under the slick spray, he fucked me, lifting me enough to ram his dick inside my willing pussy. Wrapping my legs around his waist and my arms around his neck, I hugged him and ensured his cock stayed where it belonged. Buried deep within me. We stood together that way for several moments, intimately joined, his cock a throbbing presence inside my pussy. I clenched my pelvic muscles, and a shudder went through his mighty frame.

"You are so fucking incredible, baby," he breathed against my ear.

"I know." I smiled when he chuckled, the soft rumble shaking us both in a way that added to the intimacy of the moment. But we could only cuddle for so long before need claimed us.

With his hands gripping my full cheeks, he pumped me, pressing me back against the tiled shower wall, sharp thrusts into my tight sex. The sluicing water made me seem tighter than usual as it rinsed away my natural lube, but I enjoyed the gripping feel. Loved how he had to work harder to shove his thick shaft into me. My whole body quivered in time to his rhythmic strokes. My nails raked his shoulders as he brought me to the edge of bliss. And when he bit my neck, on top of the same spot Anthony enjoyed when we coupled? Over the edge I flew, the shudders of my orgasm milking him until, with a cry of my name, he spurted hotly inside.

Not willing to separate quite yet, I clung to him, leaning my head into the crook of his shoulder. He sensed my need, or also craved the closeness, because he tightened his arms around my torso, locking me into place. In that moment, I knew I was fucked. Not literally, that was a foregone conclusion. I meant more heart-wise.

I could deny it all I wanted. I liked Pete. Liked how he made me feel. Liked how safe and cherished and sexy I felt in his presence. All things I also felt with Anthony. Which left me where exactly? Was it time to take things to the next level? Was I ready? Were they?

Later, sprawled on his bed, king-sized of course, I mustered up the courage to ask him some of the things I'd talked over with Brenda over the course of the afternoon and under the influence of alcohol.

"Let's say, hypothetically of course, that I was to decide to take things past the fuck friend level to the next, what would happen?"

"Whatever you feel comfortable with."

"Which is?"

Pete rolled onto his back and manhandled me until I sat astride him. His eyes caught mine in a gaze so serious it was like being in bed with a different man than the one I thought I knew.

"Baby, I get that things are moving fast for you. Quite honestly, I feel like I'm riding on a roller coaster too. Just a week ago, I was a carefree bachelor, running around pissing on neighboring witch's roses, the next I met this beautiful woman who told me I was a juvenile idiot and that I needed to smarten up."

"I did not say it like that."

"Not in so many words, but the implication was there. And I didn't mind it. I actually loved it. Do you know how rare it is to meet a woman willing to stand up to a guy like me and tell it how it is?"

"Oh, please. As if any woman is going to be scared of you."

"And you've just proven my point. You don't see me as a threat. Other women, while titillated at the thought of sleeping with a big scary wolfman, would run the first time I said boo!"

"Why would you say boo? Shouldn't you like howl or bark?"

"Impertinent wench," he growled good-naturedly as he dug fingers into my ribs, tickling until I squealed for mercy.

Panting and flushed, I draped myself across his chest. "Where were we?" I asked.

"I was telling you how I fell for you the moment you told me to grow up. I knew then and there I had to get to know you better."

"Yet I turned you down when you asked me to dinner. If not for that accidental encounter at the marathon, we'd have never seen each other again."

"Or so you think."

"Explain."

"Despite your rejection, I had every intention of seeing you again. And it wasn't hard to arrange. I saw your calendar on your desk. You had 'volunteer for the cancer marathon' penciled in great big letters."

"Hold on a second. You ran in the marathon

because of me?"

"Yeah." Hot, confident Lycan or not, ruddy color suffused his cheeks. "I did it on purpose to run into you. Meeting your parents and getting invited for dinner just ended up being a stroke of luck. Some of the elder Lycans would even call it fate."

"Fate." I snorted, but couldn't help a spurt of warmth. "And here I thought I'd made it clear I wanted nothing to do with you."

He tapped his nose. "Good thing for me I smelled otherwise."

Bless his sense of smell. "Still, you couldn't guess at the time I'd want you for more than sex."

"Aha, I knew you'd eventually admit you wanted me for more than just my hot body."

No wiggling out of the verbal trap I'd stepped in. "I never said that."

"Nice try, baby. You like me. You don't have to say it aloud. It's enough for now to know you do. Which brings me back to your original question of what happens now. I'll admit I didn't factor in the possibility of sharing. Anthony was an unexpected addition."

"No kidding."

"However, unlike humans who are still coming to grips with polygamy, Lycans have lived with that lifestyle for centuries. We've had to, given our numbers were never great to start with."

"I assume these relationships were with your own kind, though. I'm human."

"As are many of our mixed couples. To promote a healthy gene pool and prevent inbreeding, it is encouraged that we not only seek partners within our packs but outside too."

"I thought Lycans were born. Wouldn't marrying humans deplete your numbers?"

"Nope. Children have a fifty percent chance or more of inheriting the gene. And even those who don't get it can pass it on to their progeny to a lesser degree."

"So if that's the case, why the need for threesomes?"

"Female Lycans tend to have a voracious appetite for sex when they go into heat, not to mention things can get rough. They often prefer sticking to our kind in multiples to satisfy their needs."

"Why does it seem I'm the only person who is struggling to adjust to the idea of living a threesome lifestyle?"

"Because you're worried about getting hurt. Two lovers in your life means twice the risk."

Since when was jocular Pete so damned perceptive?

And now we got to the hard questions. "If you and Anthony fight, I'm the one who ends up stuck in the middle."

"Yup. So that means we'll have to do our damnedest to get along. I'm not saying we won't have our moments. However, despite our differences, we'll do our best to ensure we don't let them affect you."

"Kind of hard to avoid if, and that's a big if, we were to come to a cohabitation agreement."

"Only a lawyer would use that word. If we shack up," he arched a brow to match his rakish grin, "then we'd obviously set some ground rules. Rule number one, no fighting in the house."

"Whose house?"

"Doesn't matter to me so long as you're in it."

Good answer. "Okay, I'll play along. What's rule number two?"

"No secrets between any of us."

Couldn't argue with that one either. "Three?"

It took him a bit longer to come up with that one. "No leaving our dirty socks and underwear on the floor?"

I snickered. "Oh, I'd be so screwed then. I'm awful when it comes to tidying up."

"Maybe we'll have to borrow Anthony's butler, or maid. I get the impression the guy's a bit of a neat freak."

"Speaking of which, shouldn't he have arrived by now? Night's fallen." And I didn't like the idea of him alone, outside, not with a demon on the loose.

"He's fine. Don't you know vampires are like cats? They always land on their feet and have way more than nine lives. Let's keep hammering out the rules, so by the time he arrives, we've got a list."

"He'll probably want to add some of his own."

"If you insist."

I laughed at his feigned pout. I saw what he did. Tried to lighten the mood so I wouldn't worry. Appreciating it, I played along. "I have a rule. No leaving the toilet seat up."

"Ah and here I was looking forward to your screech of indignation the first time you fell in and got your ass wet."

My playful slap at his chest just made said torso shake harder with mirth. "No shedding in the house."

"Awww."

"Or coming in with muddy paws."

He initially chuckled, but as if struck by a thought, he quickly turned somber. "I almost hate to bring this up, but have you ever seen a Lycan in his wolf shape up close?"

"Nope. The closest I've come is watching it on television." I shrugged. "It's not like you all run around shifting into your animal selves baying at the moon."

"For your information, I rarely howl at the moon. I do, however, like to chase squirrels."

"Why does that not surprise me?" I tempered my remark with a smile.

"Would you like to see my wolf side?"

He said it hesitantly, and as I stared into his eyes, I discerned wariness, even fear. Fear of what, though?

Then it hit me. *He's worried about my reaction.* A valid concern. It was one thing to talk and joke about what Pete truly was, another to see it. Touch it.

Could I handle the fact my boyfriend—yes, boyfriend, we'd obviously gone past the line separating this from a sexual relationship to a real one—turned into a tail-wagging, shaggy beast?

Only one way to find out. "Show me."

"Here? Now?"

Apparently, he'd not counted on my acquiescence. "Yes, now. Might as well get this over with. I should know what I'm getting into if we're going to be boyfriend and girlfriend."

There. I'd said it. Aloud. No taking it back now, not when super-duper-hearing boy caught it.

Beaming because of his small victory, he forgot for a second what I asked. I knew the moment he remembered, though, because a crease marred his brow.

"Are you sure?"

"Fairly sure." A small waver of uncertainty made my voice wobble.

"What's worrying you?"

"I don't need to worry about you eating me, do I?"

"The only nibbling I do will be in bed, and you'll like it."

Mmm. That I did. "You won't do anything gross like sniff my crotch or hump my leg?"

"No!" Such indignation.

"Then let's go. Time's a wasting."

Pete rolled me off his snuggly chest. I nestled in his sheets, soft linen that bore his scent. Trying hard to hold my trepidation in check, I watched him as he stood alongside the bed in all his naked glory.

Am I ready for this? Ready to see him for who he truly is? I hoped so.

Back went Pete's shoulders, determination glinted in his eyes, and he said, "Just remember, no matter what, I won't hurt you. I would never hurt you."

"I know you won't." My soft admission rang with truth.

"Here goes." He closed his eyes and took a few deep breaths in preparation.

A motion outside his window drew my attention, allowing me to see the hideous face that plastered itself against the glass. And I mean ugly.

I screamed.

Chapter Sixteen

"Shit, baby, I haven't even started," Pete exclaimed, his tone rife with wounded male pride.

"It's not you. The window." I shook my finger at the now empty glass. "There was a face. Right there. Pressed against the glass." Did I mention we were on the second floor of his house?

"What?" My lover whirled on one heel, but whatever peeked in on us was gone.

I shivered, cold even under the covers. "What was it?"

"I didn't see it. Can you describe it?"

Did malevolent cover it all? "Reddish, glowing eyes. Fat yet kind of flat nose. Big fucking teeth with dark, pimply skin."

"Demon." Grimly spoken and not surprised.

Great. It didn't take long for the thing to find us. "What's it want?" Other than the obvious—my plump and juicy human body.

"I don't know, but whatever it's doing here can't be good. I'll call it in."

"Won't the guards outside have seen it?" Wards around the house or not, they'd assigned a pair of guards just in case the demon showed up. I wasn't reassured by the knowledge they'd obviously not seen or shot at the thing.

"If they're alive. This creature is wily. Best not leave anything to chance."

His cell phone was in the bathroom, in the pocket of his pants currently lying on the floor. But I wasn't staying alone in his bedroom while he went to fetch it. One flimsy pane of glass and a supposed spell weren't enough of a shield for me.

Yanking off the sheet and wrapping it around me toga style, I followed Pete to the hall and stood there, shaking, as he retrieved his phone.

As soon as he had it in hand, he dialed. Bracing it against his ear with one hand, he drew me in with the other, sharing the warmth of his body as he explained to whoever answered that we'd caught a glimpse of the missing demon.

My fearlessness in court in front of a judge didn't extend to freaky life-or-death situations. Apparently, I wouldn't make a good ass-kicking heroine who went out slaying creatures of the night for the good of mankind. Nor did I want my boyfriend doing it either.

Or so he learned a moment later when I screeched at him, "What do you mean you're going outside to confront it?"

"I can't let it get away."

"But you're alone. With no weapon."

"I am my own weapon."

His teeth and claws against the monster I saw? Sorry, but my gut said it wouldn't be a fair fight.

"Can't you at least wait for backup?" None of the assigned officers were currently answering their communication devices. No one needed to tell me that didn't bode well.

"If I wait, we might lose his trail. I'll be okay,

baby." Famous last words. Right along with, "Hold my beer and watch this."

Even a torrid kiss couldn't stop him. Stupid hero complex. It always made men do the most dangerous things.

It also left me alone, in a house I didn't know, listening to unfamiliar creaks and groans. I hurriedly dressed, determined not to meet my maker in just a sheet. But once that was done, I fidgeted upstairs, standing well clear of windows, of course.

A weapon. I needed something to defend myself with in case the so-called magic around the house failed. What to use, though? I didn't see a sword or a machine gun anywhere.

Why couldn't I have chosen an NRA member to date? At least they always slept with a pistol in their nightstand. Or at least the ones I'd dated did, right alongside their box of magnum condoms.

With no firearms handy, it occurred to me to settle for the next best thing. A knife. The bigger, the better. Knees knocking or not, I wouldn't let anything try to devour me without a fight.

Sweaty palm clutching the stair railing, I inched downstairs, silently blessing Pete who'd turned on all the lights in his path out of the house. A lack of knick-knacks meant no shadows or places for scary monsters to hide. I hit the main floor and headed in the direction of the kitchen, or so I hoped. I'd never finished my house tour.

The hall took me to a big archway, and I entered a country-style kitchen, the single glowing light over the sink illuminating wood cabinets and a green laminate countertop. Catching movement, I recoiled, only to realize I'd been fooled by my reflection in the window above the sink.

Talk about giving a girl a fright. With my wide eyes, tangled hair, and pale complexion, I could have passed for the undead instead of just a frightened lawyer dealing with things best left in the movies. A panel of switches to my right drew my attention, and I flicked them, illuminating the space, probably highlighting my location, but with fear my newest close companion, I preferred the light to the hidden terrors of the dark.

Spotting a wooden block with handles jutting from it, I scurried, yanking forth a wide blade. Ha. I was armed. Whether or not I could actually stab anything remained to be seen, but I liked to think if something started chewing on me that I'd get over my aversion to blood and do what had to be done.

If I ended up traumatized, oh well. That's what shrinks were for.

A scratching sound had me jumping several inches off the floor. I landed in a semi-crouch, knife pointed, eyes darting anxiously. No slavering monster from the depths of Hell confronted me. But I did hear a chirp.

Somehow, I'd missed noting the rather large gilded cage on the other side of the table. Another tweet and scratch emerged from within the bars, and chiding myself for my overreaction, I sidled over to take a peek at the birds my boyfriend kept. They kind of resembled mini parrots with their hooked beaks and general shape. Green feathers adorned their bottom half then switched to yellow while their heads and faces were almost pink in color. Inquisitive eyes watched me, and one cocked its head as if to ask, "Who are you?"

"So you're Rocky and Periwinkle." My reciting aloud their names earned me a squawk. "Shh." I held my finger up. "No noise, you two. I don't want to miss the demon if he decides to try and sneak up on me."

Bobbing their heads, the cuddling duo kept their peeps to themselves.

With silence reigning, I strained to hear something, anything. Pete had exited the house several minutes ago. I didn't know if the lack of noise was a good thing or not. On the one hand, it could indicate he'd found nothing. Then again, it could also mean he was dead.

Not a possibility I preferred to dwell on.

Assuming the lack of screams meant he still looked, I wandered the main floor, staying far away from windows—because we all knew from horror movies that the boogey man loved it when the idiot heroine stuck her face against one peering out, so he could yank her through. I discovered new things about my boyfriend. Such as his penchant for action movies, evident from the DVD collection housed in the tower beside his man-sized TV. A partial smile curved my lips at the knitted afghan, hung over one of the chairs, done in tones of blue. An obviously well-loved item judging by the pearled fabric that bespoke many washings and the holes where the yarn had stretched.

From the bay window—and a safe distance—I stared out across his front lawn, the streetlight on the sidewalk illuminating his boring attempt at landscaping, if you could call the low-cut grass and ring of rocks around some sad-looking hostas landscaping.

The horticulturist in me longed to pull on some gloves, dig a few holes, and fill them with something bright and bushy. It seemed I was more attracted to the domesticated life than I'd previously assumed, given my condo greenery didn't extend past what the produce drawer in my fridge could hold.

Nothing moved, and given the expansive, unobstructed view, I moved closer and closer until I stood a bare foot away from the plate glass. Still nothing.

"Where are you, Pete?" I muttered.

A cacophony of shrieks and squawks erupted as Rocky and Periwinkle lost their bird-brained minds in the kitchen, and without thinking, I ran back and skidded to a stop in the doorway, only belatedly realizing that running toward possible danger wasn't a healthy choice.

Lucky for me, I didn't slam into any demonic beings. As a matter of fact, the kitchen appeared free of anything except the caterwauling birdies who flew around their cage in a frenzy, smacking into the bars.

"Calm down," I ordered.

Didn't work.

"Stupid noisy creatures."

Knife still in hand, I stalked over to them, snagging a tea towel on my way because I vaguely recalled reading somewhere that covering a bird's cage made them think it was night and put them to sleep.

If that failed, I could always burn some toast. It's how my great aunt Meredith silenced hers when they got on her nerves. Thankfully, the home that mother put her in didn't allow her to keep pets.

About to fling my small towel over their cage,

I noted a green glint in the window. I jumped back and adopted my best Buffy pose. Of course, hers probably appeared a lot sexier, given my heart raced, my skin grew clammy, and I crouched as if about to pee in the woods.

A chuckle escaped me as I caught sight of the reason for the bird's agitation. In the window sat a big black cat. Its glowing green orbs fixated on the freaking love birds.

"I see animal control forgot to come pick you up." It surprised me to note I felt sorry for it.

Poor thing. It was probably so confused. With its owner dead, the cat didn't have anywhere else to go. No one to feed it. Or protect it from roaming demons.

Unless I came to its rescue. While a little voice in my head screamed, "Bad idea," another voice chanted, "Save the kitty, save the world." Okay, so I had more of a hero complex than I expected.

I glanced outside the patio door, the flagstone lit up by a porch light. Nothing moved in the yard. I could do this. I could rescue the cat.

Sliding open the door, but staying within the confines of the house, I crooned to it. "Here kitty-kitty. Come on over here. I won't hurt you."

It didn't budge from its spot in the window. And the birds continued to freak.

I didn't know how Pete stood the noise. Forget peeing on his neighbor's flowers. He should have invited the cat in and let it take care of the noisy buggers. Wasn't that the Darwin method?

Another quick glance to reassure myself the yard remained empty and I stuck my head out the door. "Come on, you stupid cat. Get your furry ass in here before the demon—" *or my boyfriend* "—turns you into dinner."

The head of the feline rotated. And rotated some more. Um, somehow, I didn't think it was normal cat behavior for it to be able to stare at me exorcist-style.

"Uh-oh." I slammed the door shut. But the damage was done.

Chapter Seventeen

Ever have a moment in your life where you wish you could rewind, slap yourself, and do things differently? I did.

Nothing like seeing a regular house cat stalk toward you, each step resulting in a growth in its size, a ripple in its frame, to make a girl wish she'd listened to her boyfriend and done the cowardly thing.

I should have left the door closed. "It can't come in. It can't come in. The spells will stop it." I repeated this over and over as the feline morphed from cute kitty into beast from hell. It more than quadrupled in size, knobs erupting from its spine, claws and teeth elongating while its eyes shifted from green to fiery red.

Gulp. By the time it stood, breathing hotly against the sliding glass door, steaming the surface, it was the size of a hippo, and it seemed intent on getting to know me better.

Not interested in furthering our acquaintance, I kept muttering, "It can't come in."

As if understanding my words, I swear the damned thing grinned, or at least did something that showed a heck of a lot of teeth.

It lifted a paw and placed it on the glass just as I recalled something one of my boys had said, something important about the magic guarding the house.

I am safe within the wards so long as I don't invite it in.

Fuck.

I turned on my heel and began to run just as the glass behind me broke in a tinkling shower. I screamed. Holy fuck did I ever, and I continued to shriek as I pounded to the front door, not making the mistake of heading upstairs and locking myself in a room. I retained enough wits to know a flimsy bedroom door wouldn't hold the demon at bay. But maybe Pete and his mounds of muscles could.

Thankfully, he didn't believe in an army of locks, only a single deadbolt required turning, and then I was out the front door sprinting down his walkway, still yodeling at the top of my lungs. Nothing wrong with the shape of my vocal cords.

For some insane reason, the song "I Need a Hero" by Bonnie Tyler started running through my head, a soundtrack to my folly. A pity I wouldn't live to write the story and sell it to Hollywood.

Seriously. Things didn't look good for me. I cursed the fact that Pete lived across from some fucking conservation area. No neighbors to flip on a porch light and invite me in to safety. No grannies with a shotgun on the porch taking potshots at the beast on my tail.

Why couldn't I have a boyfriend who lived in the city? Surely, someone there would have had a gun to help a poor woman out.

Nope. My guy lived out in the boonies. Nothing but trees, pavement, and a stupid girl running for her life in pink bunny socks.

I didn't dare peek behind me. Why bother when I heard the click and thump of paws hitting the ground as the demon came after me?

After crossing Pete's stupidly long front yard, when I reached the road, I didn't pause. I sprinted up the middle of it, panting too hard to yell anymore, saving my oxygen to fuel my longs legs, which had never run so fast.

If I survived this, I made a mental vow to take up jogging. It seemed the ability to race might be a handy skill to have for those unexpected moments when killer demons were after you.

If I lived.

A ferocious snarl broke my concentration, and I stumbled. I didn't completely fall, but given I still clutched the knife, it scared me enough to stop my headlong flight lest I trip onto my weapon and impale myself. Besides, it seemed rescue had arrived. Or so I judged by the vicious, guttural sounds coming from behind me.

Hands on my thighs, hunched over and breathing hard, I didn't want to turn around and look. I really didn't want to see.

But I owed it to Pete. He fought to save my stupid ass, the least I could do was watch as he fought. Prepare myself in case he failed. Or—and this would require courage on my part—dart in at an opportune moment and help.

Slowly, I pivoted. Good thing I still couldn't pull in a lungful of air because I probably would have wasted it on another useless shriek.

Ever watch a documentary about animals in the wild? Sure, you have. The one with the cute little cubs that started out as tumbling furballs and grew up to be giant furballs.

Remember how they always had that one scene, the one where they showed in glaring detail how those cuddly animals got their dinner? The violence, the bloodshed, the savagery? Apparently, they really edited the fuck out of it, because the fight I got to view was way scarier and gorier.

A hulking wolfman—think bodybuilder covered in hair with canine features, claws, and wild yellow eyes—attacked the demon, who'd lost all of its feline characteristics. Together they grappled, ripping and tearing at each other, scoring gashes along their bodies, sending droplets of blood and whatnot flying.

Forget darting in to land a stab that would end it all. With the way they rolled this way and that, I was more likely to get crushed. But, at the same time, I could tell Pete wouldn't win this battle alone. Not for lack of trying. My man gave it his all, but the demon was just that much bigger and more powerful.

Where was a superhero when you needed one?

Apparently, timing his moment for the most dramatic effect, because between one blink and the next, Anthony appeared. Clad only in his trousers, white chest gleaming in the streetlight, he joined the fray, and I wondered how he thought he could help, considering he'd arrived weaponless. Shouldn't he have brought a sword? A gun? Something with a sharp edge?

I didn't give him enough credit or had conveniently forgotten Anthony wasn't human no matter his outward appearance. It seemed my vampire lover had hidden his more violent talents.

Fists clenched, he rained blow upon blow on the demon, but where a human would have probably broken his hand trying to hit the monster, Anthony's hands dented the damned thing. And, yes, that was as disturbing as it sounded. Every blow he landed left a fist-sized dimple in the demon, pockmarking its body. But it didn't stop the monster. It did make it madder, though.

With a roar to give me goose bumps, and nightmares, the demon found an inner reserve of strength and wouldn't relent. Neither did my lovers.

Over and over, they pummeled the demon, putting it on the defensive, forcing it to retreat. They followed, not letting up their punishment. I found myself pacing them, eyes trained on the action. A part of me wondered if I should take this moment of grace to run, hide, call for help, maybe arrange a nuke, but I couldn't, not when I was too afraid to look away for just a moment.

I began to think victory could be ours. *We might win against this thing.* Then, the unthinkable...

The demon's tail lashed out of nowhere, the barbed tip catching Anthony across the back and tearing open a huge gash. But it wasn't the wound that distracted him.

I did.

A cry left me, breaking his concentration for just a moment.

A millisecond too long.

The demon pounced, taking my vampire lover to the ground. Horrified, I slapped my free hand over my mouth. Pete jumped onto the demon's back, but tired and injured, he could only yank on the demon's head, trying to keep the jagged teeth from tearing out Anthony's throat. A stalemate that wouldn't end well once his stamina gave up.

I didn't even realize I'd run toward them until I was there, standing before the monster who terrified me, smelling the stench of Hell, feeling the malevolence roiling off it, coating me in an invisible miasma.

Gross. But not as gross as the fluid that sprayed me when I plunged my kitchen knife as far as it would go into its glaring red orb. I'd like to say I did this intentionally. That I took careful aim and found my bravery.

Nope.

Wheezing and caterwauling, shaking— grateful for the Kegel clenches I practiced daily—I blindly stabbed at the thing and got lucky.

Horrified on so many levels, I released my grip on the slippery kitchen implement and staggered back.

But I'd done enough.

With the injury I inflicted, the demon lost its will to fight.

Not my men. Pete, barely recognizable in his other shape, and Anthony, feral-eyed and equally wild, attacked the mortally wounded creature. One raked claws over the other eye, plucking it from its skull and crushing it in a hairy fist, while the other used his teeth to tear chunks from the demon's neck, his throat moving in a convulsive gesture that said he swallowed.

I am not ashamed to admit I turned from the carnage at this point and threw up on the street.

Stumbling away from the tussle, I fell to the

soft and fragrant grass, inhaling only for a moment the vivid liveliness of it before the stench covering me tainted it.

There, kneeling on Pete's front lawn, I shook and sobbed. I couldn't have said why. Was it the near-death experience? The fact I'd helped kill something, even something so evil? Was it seeing my lovers for what they really were? Monsters of their own.

Whatever the reason, when a gentle hand came to rest upon my shoulder, I shrieked and scrambled away on hands and knees. "Don't touch me!"

"Shh, baby. It's okay now. It's just me." Just Pete. Just Pete, the werewolf covered in a layer of gore.

I pressed the heels of my hands against my eyes and rocked. When Anthony touched me next, I flinched.

"It's all right, Chloe, we won."

Won the battle, but at what cost? I'd lost my innocence. I could no longer wear blinders or pretend. I was a human dating monsters. I was just a woman, out of her element. *And I'm so fucking scared.*

If my big moment ever came, I'd always hoped I could handle it with the cool, composed grace seen so often on screen. Instead, I blubbered, and my nose ran. I stank of demon guts and was covered in blood and fluids best not mentioned. Some heroine I'd turned out to be.

I only panicked and thrashed a little when Pete scooped me up and brought me into the house. I didn't have the strength or skill to actually escape. The hot spray of the shower proved a welcome balm to my wounded psyche. As the evidence of my ordeal washed away, so did some of my terror. I took heaving breaths, trying to calm my pounding heart, vaguely aware that one set of arms was replaced by another. But still, I wouldn't respond. Couldn't. With my jaw shaking, I'd have probably bitten my tongue off if I'd tried.

I'd interviewed enough victims in shock to know what I experienced. I just never expected it would ever happen to me. I now had more sympathy for what some of them had endured.

When my teeth finally stopped chattering, I opened my eyes and found Anthony's concerned gaze trained on me.

Of the savage vampire, not a sign remained. His eyes were back to their usual electric blue, concern creasing them at the corners. I couldn't hold his gaze and dropped my eyes to stare at his lips.

Gone were the fangs he'd used to tear at the demon's flesh. Yet I couldn't forget them. Couldn't forget that the same lips I'd kissed, the mouth that caressed my skin, had suckled at the demon, feeding from it. My stomach roiled as I wondered how I could ever kiss those lips again. I couldn't hide my reaction.

"You just started shaking again. What's wrong?"

What to say? What but the truth, or at least a partial version of? "Just wondering if you flossed and brushed your teeth?" And, yes, it sounded stupid, but in that moment, I just had to know.

Did he have demon bits stuck between his chompers? Blood breath? If he attempted to embrace me, I didn't want to puke.

"Yes. I also used mouthwash."

For some reason, this eased some of my tension, and I leaned into him, noting in that moment that while I was naked, he still wore his slacks. "You know, most people find a shower works better without clothing."

"I didn't want to waste more time than needed. One of us needed to go out and answer some questions."

Ah, yes, the handoff. I vaguely recalled it happening. One set of arms exchanged for another. "Is that where Pete is?"

"Yes. The other agents arrived just as we finished off the demon."

"Shouldn't you be down there giving your own statement?"

"They can wait. You're more important. And before you ask, or jump to the wrong conclusion, Pete would have stayed too, but we figured it best if one of us kept an eye on the situation. He lost the coin toss."

It did make me feel better to know they'd both wanted to soothe me. "And did he also brush his teeth?"

Anthony chuckled. "Yes. Yes, he did. He also got a quick rinse off while I took care of my teeth. So if you're worried about running into him still wearing a layer of gore, then don't. We might not be human, but we're not monsters."

Funny how he used that word. "Aren't you?" I couldn't help the query from slipping from my lips.

I didn't miss the way his whole body stilled. I knew I'd wounded him. Knew, but as someone who admired the truth, I had to say it. I owed it to them because I'd seen their other sides. Their non-human side. I couldn't hide from the reality anymore.

"Is that what you think? That we're monsters?"

A heavy sigh left me. "I don't know what to think. I mean, you told me what you were. I understood it on some level, but…"

"But knowing it and seeing it are two different things."

I nodded.

His turn to sigh. "I'm sorry, Chloe. I wish we could have somehow spared you the ugliness that sometimes comes with our job."

"You mean this happens on a regular basis?" Did being involved with them mean I'd have to expect them coming home every other day covered in blood and guts?

"Not to this extent, no, but if you're asking if I've had to fight for my life before, to revert to my primitive urges and instinct for survival, then yes. As has Pete, I'm sure. Someone needs to stand up to darkness."

He made it sound so noble. It made me feel petty. However, unlike some, I'd never aspired to heroic greatness. "But do you and Pete have to be the flashlight?" My poor attempt at humor fell flat.

"Let me ask you a question. Why did you come to our rescue?"

"Because you would have died otherwise."

"Did you enjoy it?"

Um, did he not notice the puking and shaking of my body parts? "No. I hated it." Would probably require years of therapy because of it.

"Well, while I won't claim to hate it, I can

admit that I'm not fond of it. However, the alternative is worse."

"The alternative being?"

"Sitting back and doing nothing while innocents suffer."

Just my luck. Altruistic boyfriends. "So is this your way of saying 'suck it up, buttercup'? In other words, if I'm going to be with you, I'd better invest in some bleach to get out the bloodstains?"

"No bleach needed. Cold water usually does the trick."

My narrowed-eyed glare conveyed my opinion adequately, I thought. He still laughed.

"I'm not demanding you come along with us wielding a mighty kitchen knife or that you like it when we choose to fight the forces of evil."

"You're laying it on pretty thick there, vampire."

He ignored my attempt at sarcastic levity. "But I do hope you can learn to accept me, and the wolf, for who we are."

Accept the fact they were more than human? More than pretty faces and excellent lovers? More than just fuck friends but men I'd come to care for? Oh, for the days of yesterday when my life didn't have such complications. "How about we take it one day, and one demon, at a time?" was my compromise.

"Good enough for now."

But for how long?

Wrapped in a towel, Anthony carried me from the bathroom straight to Pete's bedroom. He deposited me on the bed and stripped out of his sopping, destroyed trousers, revealing his lean hips, and his cock, currently dormant amidst the dark curls at his groin. Good to know he didn't find all the violence a turn-on. I might have freaked some more.

Pulling on a pair of dry athletic pants hanging over a chair—Adidas in a perfect size, leading me to believe his invisible servant had struck again—he left his chest bare to come to me and yank me on his lap. He towel dried me, hair first, fluffing my wet strands until they were damp and no longer dripping. Then he attacked my body, the friction of fabric on my skin not just soaking up the moisture but warming my frigid skin. Then, from another magical pile, he pulled out a pair of woman's cottony PJs with happy faces on them.

At my arched brow, he laughed. "I had my man pick you up some things."

And instead of going for something *he* would have enjoyed, he'd opted for something I would. Little things like that were why I couldn't walk away. Anthony and Pete couldn't help who they were. Nothing about them had changed.

Yet I had.

Tucked into bed, I thought sleep would elude me. However, adrenaline and the emotional upheaval left behind had drained me more than I thought. I drifted into a deep sleep.

And then my subconscious attacked me.

Chapter Eighteen

The monsters are lunging at the bloody heap on the ground. The slurping sounds as they rip and suckle at the flesh echo in the still night. I dare not breathe. I dare not move. I want to do nothing to bring their attention upon me.

But I can't watch. I can't watch and hope to keep my sanity.

I take a step back. Then another. A pebble rolls, the tiniest of sounds, and yet they hear it. A pair of heads lift from the feast. Golden eyes fix on me, and the hairy wolf takes a step. I whimper, especially when I see the dark gaze of the other also eyeing me. I see no humanity in the bottomless depths.

Oh, no. I'm next.

I whirl and run. But I am too slow. Too human. They catch me. Shaking me in their grasp. Growling and snarling and…

"Chloe! Wake up, baby. It's just a dream."

"More like a nightmare, you idiot."

Call it what they wanted, I was just glad it wasn't real. I opened my eyes to see the very normal gazes of my lovers peering down at me with concern.

Pete, while scruffy and in need of a shave, didn't sport great big canines. Anthony's eyes blazed, but with a blue light, no sign of pointed incisors.

I wasn't in bed with monsters. And the sooner I realized that, the faster I'd hopefully heal. Or so the psychiatrist I later saw twice a week claimed.

The rough pads of Pete's fingers gently stroked the flesh of my arm. "Are you okay, baby?"

No. But I wanted to be. I didn't reply to his query. I drew him down instead for a kiss. A stiff one initially, as the fear tried to keep its wily claws dug in. However, as the familiar feel of his mouth slanting over mine awakened my body, it also dissipated my trepidation.

I knew this man. He would never hurt me. I opened my mouth and let his tongue in.

On the other side, Anthony pressed his lips to my ear lobe, tickling it and sending shivers to course through my body. I only tensed a little when he moved his mouth to the soft skin of my neck. Thankfully, he didn't suck at my skin as he usually did, probably a good thing in my still fragile state.

Softly, sensually, with a gentle passion we'd not often indulged in, they made love to me. I could even call it worshipped. I lay between them, an altar of flesh, and using their hands, mouths, tongues, they payed homage to me. Showed me they were capable of great tenderness. I needed that.

I needed them.

Selfish or not, I let them have their way. My participation limited to breathy gasps, the occasional arch of my body, the moisture pooling between my legs. When they both chose to lavish attention on a nipple, I threaded my fingers through the soft strands of their hair, noting the differences in texture as I stroked.

When hands pried my thighs apart, I didn't peek to see whose cock stood poised to enter me first; however, I guessed it the moment the head speared me. Anthony kept his thrusts smooth and slow, pushing into me deep then withdrawing, while Pete continued to play with my breasts, the rough beard on his jaw abrading my skin, tenderizing it.

When Anthony came, I came with him, my body milking his cock with long, shuddering waves.

And then it was Pete's turn. His thick endowment stretched the trembling walls of my channel, and I gasped, my hips arching. Wet, so very wet. I ached for more and he penetrated me with ease. Took up a cadence that pleasured me.

They wanted more from me, though. To my shock, I felt a tongue against my clit. I opened my eyes to see Anthony leaning forward, lavishing my nub with attention.

Dear gawd. How incredible. Sated once already, I couldn't resist the erotic pleasure of having my pussy fucked while my clit got sucked. A second orgasm coiled within me. My breathing quickened, shortened until I fairly heaved to take in air. I couldn't help but watch the erotic tableaux, both my lovers intent on my body. One thrusting, the muscles in his body rigid and slick with sweat, while the other, his slender fingers holding me decadently parted, let his tongue dance upon my most sensitive part.

I don't know what I yelled when I came, but I'm sure it left their ears ringing.

When I regained enough of my wits to notice my surroundings, I found myself in a manwich, Pete to the left of me, Anthony to the right, and there I was, stuck in the middle of the two.

It made me think of a slogan I'd seen on a T-shirt when the government first began to tout the benefits of polygamy.

Two's a couple, three's the law.

Ready or not, and despite what I'd once thought, I had two men in my life. Men I loved. Men I trusted, yet didn't. A life that frightened, and yet left me feeling alive. Did I know what the future would bring? No. Did I fear it? Damned right. But I couldn't hide from it. I, Chloe, defender of the innocent—until proven guilty—would embrace my new life. Even if it killed me. And to those who wondered, I'd finally begun an infamous bucket list.

Item number one: Live each day like it might be your last.

Morbid, which is why number two was: Never skip dessert. Bring on the cheesecake.

Epilogue

With the demon cat vanquished, life returned to some semblance of normalcy. After enjoying the remainder of my two weeks unpaid holiday to recover from my trauma—spent mostly in bed while my lovers lavished me with attention and baked goods—I returned to my desk job.

A few things did change, though. One, I was seeing a headshrink who specialized in traumatized victims of paranormal origin. Pompous little fellow who looked a lot like a leprechaun, but, given the daily nightmares, I needed to do something. Talking to someone who didn't book me a room at the nearest insane asylum helped, as did the prescription sleeping pills, when I didn't forget to take them.

Nightmares plagued me. Lingering fear of the demon attack.

The one thing I didn't have a problem with was the reality of my lovers. I'd seen their true inner beasts. Seen what the world called monsters.

I loved them. I didn't care if Anthony liked to give me hickeys, or that Pete had this thing about fetching my slippers. They loved me.

Everything else, was just everything else.

Unable to return to the scene of devastation, the memory of my precious shoes ruined beyond hope of repair, I leased my condo to Brenda, who was dying to move out of her parents' place. Did I mention she'd developed a certain attraction to the guards who'd spirited her from the scene of the crime? After a massive painting and recarpeting job, she moved in and proceeded to stalk Pete's friends. Or did they stalk her? It really depended on who you spoke to.

I ended up alternating between Pete's house and Anthony's—which did have a maid, a butler, and a cook I would have married if she didn't wield such a wicked wooden spoon.

While I always had a man underfoot, given their different schedules, we rarely spent time with all three of us together. Probably a good thing, given the fact they still hadn't quite adjusted to the whole sharing thing.

Sure, I missed those two glorious occasions when limbs got tangled, bodies sweaty, and everyone came in an erotic, toe-curling orgasm. Maybe they were saving the next one for a special occasion like my birthday. But while we didn't have a wild orgy every night, I couldn't complain about the time I spent one-on-one with them where the climaxes were out of this fucking world.

The night I finally said I love you? Let's just say I might have broken glass.

Amazing what letting go of fear could do.

Speaking of fear, though, given I now knew the boogey man existed, I decided it was high time I learned how to defend myself. I enrolled in some self-defense classes. Pete made fun of them. Anthony offered to teach me himself. I, however, wanted to do this on my own.

Fear was an awful emotion. I knew that from personal experience. I hated those moments I woke up in the grips of it, reliving the moment I'd confronted the demon.

Next time, I would be ready.

Yes, I said next time.

Forgetting the underworld that lay hidden under the human one I'd believed in for so long was not an option.

Once my relationship with Pete and Anthony went public, at least in their circles, my caseloads went from occasional weird shit to full time. I was now the number one public defender of beings who were thought not to exist.

Take, for example, my latest case with Mr. Peabody, accused of trying to set his house on fire while his family slept in it. I eyed the gangly fellow with the comb-over comprised of a few sandy strands and tried not to sigh.

"Let me get this straight. You claim the house is alive and that it's somehow possessing your family."

He bobbed his head. "Oh, it's quite evil."

"So why not call in a priest to exorcise it?"

"I tried that."

"And?"

"The house somehow ate him."

So, Mr. Peabody had tried to burn it down with his possessed family inside. This Amityville claim sounded like a job for the TDCM because, for some reason, I believed the strange little nervous man.

When we did finally convince someone to look into his allegation, what an adventure that turned out to be. But like Brenda and her stalking werewolves, that was a story for another day.

The End but find out what happens to Brenda in Mr. Peabody's House.

For updates or to get to know me, follow me on Facebook or visit my website, EveLanglais.com

CPSIA information can be obtained
at www.ICGtesting.com
Printed in the USA
BVOW03s0949100417
480817BV00001B/76/P